When Mountains Crumble

by

Claudine DiScala

Cover Art by *Teddi Black*

The Wild Rose Press, Inc.
PO Box 708
Adams Basin, NY 14410-0708
Visit us at www.thewildrosepress.com

Publishing History
First Edition, 2025
Trade Paperback Print ISBN 978-1-5092-6326-4
Digital ISBN 978-1-5092-6327-1

Published in the United States of America

Dedication

To the reader willing to follow the thread, even when it tangles.

Warning: This book contains descriptions of suicide and grieving which may be distressing for some readers.

There are some people who live in a dreamworld,
and there are some who face reality;
and then are those who turn one into the other.
~ Desiderius Erasmus

Chapter One

Beautiful and terrifying all at once
Faith 2026

Sometimes my mind plays hide-and-seek with important things. Like today, I nearly overlooked my weekly lunch at the Great Eats Café on Long Island with my closest friend. This tradition has carried on for over a decade, not something easily forgotten. How do thoughts slip away and find their way back to us?

The solution may lie within Leanne's realm of expertise, the brain, where answers to mysteries like to hibernate.

"Faith, there you are! I was getting worried I had the wrong day." Leanne beams across the café as I step inside. Her mastery in psychology shines, positioning her as a top professional in the field.

We've known each other since sixth grade. Getting together is one of my most cherished comforts, like slipping into those cozy old sweatpants I can't live without.

"Sorry, my fault." I pull out a chair and sit. "Got caught up with Jeremy again and lost track of time."

"At Pinelawn?" Leanne runs her fingers through the top of her auburn hair. It falls right back into place like it knows exactly where to go. "You know, I could go and sit with you next time." She passes the coffee carafe.

"Maybe." The coffee steams and flows into the ceramic cup. Pinelawn is not a town in the traditional sense. There's a street running through it, appropriately named Pinelawn Road, a railroad station and a park, but all its inhabitants abide underground. Pinelawn Memorial Park and Arboretum is the largest cemetery on Long Island, "providing families with peace and tranquility since 1902." Hundreds of acres of vibrant flowers, flowing fountains, towering trees, and sculpted gardens. Not a bad place to sit if one must.

"Have the police finished their investigation?" Leanne eyes the waiter.

"No, but they don't believe there were any other cars involved. They think Jeremy just lost control on the hill down around that curve." The sweet, nutty aroma seeps into my nose. "The odd thing is Jeremy brought his car into the shop the week before because the engine light was on. They said it was nothing. The police say he must have been driving too fast. One detective estimated eighty miles per hour, Leanne! I've gone over it in my head a gazillion times. Something *had* to have happened. It doesn't make sense."

"It was such a fluke early spring blizzard." Leanne's eyes hug me from across the table. "Don't do this to yourself, Faith. Your tenacity is what makes you a great private investigator, but Jeremy's gone."

My head involuntarily shakes off the words. "He's been down that mountain in the snow and ice a million times, always cautious. You know him…knew him."

"I hate to see you suffering like this, running and rerunning over the circumstances surrounding your husband's death. You did the same thing before, Faith, to no avail then either. Remember?"

Yeah, I do remember.

The waiter, with dark hair and striking blue eyes, appears in front of us. "What'da you like?"

If I know Leanne the way I'm sure I do, she likes you.

"Egg, bacon, and cheese on a roll." Leanne tries not to make eye contact, a definitive sign I'm right.

"For lunch?" I tilt my head. "Did you skip breakfast again?"

Leanne shrugs. The waiter looks at me.

"A slice of cherry cheesecake, please." I push the untouched menus toward him.

"And now *you're* skipping a real lunch." Leanne nods at the waiter. He leaves our table and she continues what she started. "Faith, grief does things to the brain. There's memory loss, confusion, disorientation, lack of focus, or even the opposite— hyper focus—on the event. It's understandable because everything's changed. It's not a normal time. Grief and trauma can rewire the brain, locking it into a permanent stress response."

"I love having an award-winning therapist and *New York Times* best-selling author as my best friend. Well—" My right eyebrow rises. "—most of the time."

"You love it, and you hate it because you're always going to get the truth from me."

"Truth is—" The hot coffee singes my lips. "—it all feels jumbled, like I'm losing my mind *and* have valid reasons for believing something's amiss."

"It's normal, Faith. But no one knows you better than me. You'll drive yourself crazy thinking through every angle until it all fits. Sometimes we're not able to get all our questions answered."

"Can't help it. Unfinished business irks me." And I change the subject to the hot waiter who seems to be a perfect match for my newly divorced friend.

****

Two slices of cherry cheesecake later, I drive up the mountain to my home, careful to take a different route from the one Jeremy drove. Passing the death scene and thinking about it all over again does no good. Leanne's right, the potential for crazy exists.

No matter which route one chooses, the asphalt winds up and around Stone Mountain, hugging the slick black rock on one side while ready to drop you off on the other. There's nothing between me and the bottom of the green valley but a dented, flimsy-looking metal guardrail. It's beautiful and terrifying all at once, and there's nothing like it. Yet, somehow, the scenic drive calms me every time.

The perfect spring day Jeremy and I moved up here sits in stark contrast to now. Stone Mountain is an hour and a quarter's drive north of Long Island. The meandering roads create a tree-lined tunnel to our home, set into the side of the mountain surrounded by still higher peaks delivering breathtaking views year-round. A modern A-frame log and timber dwelling, its sloping black roofs are supported by towering caramel-colored wood resting on a base of gray and black stacked stone. It was designed by both of us ten years earlier, with oversized floor-to-ceiling windows and glass sliding doors in every direction, giving it an open feel to the outside so we could make the most of the scenery. It was the property we paid for, not the house.

As usual, I stop my car at the end of the driveway

to grab the mail out of the box. Being too petite to stick my arm out and retrieve it like any other normal human, I'm forced to get out. A figure catches the corner of my eye, and my head involuntarily turns toward it, squinting to see. Wait, is that...?

No. Just my imagination. Maybe *I am* losing it. Work has been stressful lately, and it's been happening again since the accident—I see him. Not Jeremy. The other one. The one I dated *in between* Jeremy way back in time when we briefly broke up.

Sometimes he just appears, tall and handsome and smiling, almost watching over me. It always happens too fast though. I try to get a better look, but then he's gone. This time, it's a jogger looking like him running on the road as it curves away, and now, he's out of sight. It's ridiculous, but why does it have to hurt so much? A dream, a wish, I suppose. Or maybe he *is* watching from somewhere else, some *time* else. Maybe he's been watching me all along. The thought soothes my heart and fractures it at the same time.

Or maybe there's a pill I should take for this.

Plopping myself back into the driver's seat, I pull into the attached two-car. The creaking garage door leisurely closes behind me as I struggle to gather my bag and loose mail.

Walking through the door to the kitchen, I drop my keys with a clink into the white ceramic candy dish. Jeremy's keys have been painfully absent since the accident, still with the car at the police impound yard. I should put them back in the dish when they release the car. They *belong* there.

There's a few mini peanut butter cups left in the bowl from the last time Jeremy filled it, knowing I like to exchange my keys for a chocolate upon arrival. Not today. The whole house feels like it's waiting…and exhausted…and so do I. It's only 5:20 in the afternoon. Turning off my phone and going to bed sounds delightful. But I don't.

Finn greets me, nails clicking on the wood floor as his long orange tail slaps against my leg at warp speed. He receives a good rubdown as I walk into the kitchen and when he's had enough, lets himself out through the doggie door. The mail gets tossed onto the counter for later, and I start the coffeemaker while jotting down notes on this morning's surveillance case that'll end up on the desk of my assistant. She'll magically transform them into a coherent report at some point in the future.

The coffee pot spits and burps way sooner than expected. That's my cue. I walk to the counter and pour some, tired eyes running over pieces of scattered mail. One's handwritten, addressed only to me.

Who doesn't love getting a handwritten envelope? Technology being what it is, it's so rare these days for anyone to take the time to make something so personal by handwriting it, much less dropping it in the snail mail. It's a treat and piques my interest enough to reach for it now instead of later.

The blue-penned lettering stands out on the crisp white envelope with neat hand-printed writing, nothing special, just nice. To my surprise, there's no return address on the back. The postmark is dated today, and it came from Devenport, our hometown on Long Island. Maybe this is another condolence card, but it seems too small to be one of those. It's a simple three-by-five envelope, unlike the larger envelopes cards come in. Whatever's inside is thin and small.

Maybe it was sent by a friend from our childhood wanting to share more memories. How sweet that would be. But at this moment, Finn's wild barking in the backyard is a distraction.

I am ever aware that what I do for a living has a tendency to piss people off, so I, like my counterparts, have taken precautions to be as unidentifiable and hidden as possible, but there are no guarantees. Finn's bark seems urgent. Rushing outside to the back deck, gun still holstered at my side, Finn is in the back corner of the yard looking up the mountain, intent on something.

Beyond the pale blue waters of our pool, an emerald-green lawn sprawls out meeting rich soil that leads up the mountain. Dotted with bright wildflowers, shrubs, and trees, it's a steep incline. At some point, it levels out to terrain you can hike, but it's impassable from our property, too vertical and dense, which is why we never bothered to fence ourselves in. About a quarter mile away, there's access to that mountaintop via any one of the many trailheads. It's not unusual to see people up there. From my vantage point, they're the size of toy soldiers.

Finn continues his rant. He has such a laid-back disposition, this is odd, and it makes me uneasy.

"Finn!" I yell over his bark.

He wavers but comes with a frustrated whimper. Squinting to find what has interested him among the trees and brush doesn't help. There's nothing, not so much as a leaf quivering up there. I bend to Finn's eye level and rub his head. "What'd ya see, boy? A squirrel?"

Returning inside, my eyes meet the little

handwritten letter. Might as well read it now.

I take my steaming mug and the letter through the expansive kitchen/living room to my favorite corner of the oversized cream-colored couch. The delightful little envelope is examined and turned over in my hands. Who might have missed the funeral and felt the need to write? It could be anyone really.

My finger slips under the corner where the fold meets the crease, carefully prying it open. The white piece of paper inside matches the envelope. It has a heavy texture and pattern to it. This is from someone who took the time to purchase a note-writing set, someone who likes to write letters. A new clue, but still, no names come to mind.

I gently pull out the letter. It is perfectly folded in half with no writing on the outside. I unfold it. My eyes first focus on the whole sheet instead of the individual words. It's almost a full page of writing in the same blue-penned neat writing that matches the envelope. My eyes drop to the salutation:

Dear Faith,

I hope this letter finds you well, as well as can be expected after your loss. I didn't make it to the funeral and feel entirely regretful about not being there for you during such a terrible time, so I'm reaching out to you now. You and Jeremy had something very special. I always thought the two of you might end up together. Losing him must have been one of the hardest moments in your life. I think of you often, and my wish is that your suffering does not linger too long. You're a wonderful person and deserve all the happiness life has to offer.

You may have noticed there's no return address on

this letter. I apologize for the mysteriousness of it, but I'm concerned that receiving this letter from me may constitute something inappropriate for you at this time. You see, I'm someone who knew you well in the past, and whether you realized it or not, I was quite smitten with you. This may not be the appropriate time for telling you, but I do want you to know that there's someone out here for you, concerned about you and thinking of you, should a time come when you're ready for it. You may think it cowardly of me not to reveal myself now, and for that, you're probably right, but I'll leave it there for the present moment.

You'll most likely receive more correspondence from me, and I hope you accept them. I expect nothing in return except the possibility that they make you smile and ease your grief even if it's only for the few moments you're reading them.

Sincerely

It's not signed? I flip it over.

It's not signed!

Is this someone from high school or college? Someone Jeremy and I both know or only me? A co-worker from a previous place of employment maybe? Someone I dated? That list was long. Or could this be someone who liked me but never said? My mind browses through the boys and men of the past, thumbing through them as one would standing over the long open drawer of a card catalog.

It's so beautifully written. The style and rhythm are not immediately recognizable. Maybe that's intentional, to keep me from guessing this person's identity for the time being. Probably best for now. I'm starting to feel guilty for being so intrigued. It's too soon for this.

Or is it?

Chapter Two

And then it happened
Faith 2012

I'm not sure who I am anymore. Then again, who is?

That's me in the mirror. Faith Ansley, a seventeen-year-old senior at Devenport High School with a left-sided cowlick she straight-irons down every day, who is also one swipe of lipstick away from going out for the evening. But is this the same Faith who stared back at me yesterday? Or last month? Things are changing so fast, the person I was, or is, or am becoming continues to elude me.

I tug at the cowlick again, and the photos stuffed into the sides of my mirror come to life. There's one of my dad teaching me to cast a line at the marina when I was six and another of me holding Buddy the day we brought him home from the shelter. My mother is in the background of another photo, busy tanning and ignoring my dad and me as we built the most epic sandcastle and moat ever. That was a great day.

My eyes drift to the empty space where one photo used to be, but quickly move to the one below it—a dance competition when I was twelve, dressed in sparkly blue and silver with the winner's medal around my neck. A more recent addition to the mirror is my induction into the National Honor Society, a reminder to stay on track and graduate in at least the top five percent of my grade. Top one percent is the real goal.

Each point in time has made me who I am, every experience baked into the recipe of Faith. Delete or substitute any of the ingredients, and I would be a different person. Add more in, and another Faith will take shape in the future. How can anyone know and rely on who they are at any given moment?

One of my favorite photos—well, they're all my favorites; that's why they're up there—is of Leanne and me the day we met in seventh grade, learning how to prepare balanced meals in home economics class. We instantly became best friends, never laughed so hard, so much, and for so long with anyone as we did with each other. We passed intricately folded notes in class written in shorthand, a cryptic language using symbols we looked up online and taught ourselves. Walking through the halls, we'd pretend to be special agents, spying, collecting top secret intel on everyone and analyzing the data. It wouldn't be a stretch to say I never really outgrew this.

In ninth grade, we had our first boyfriends, first loves, first everythings. Hit first, second, and third base, had arguments, cried to each other, broke up, and got back together. We lost our virginity in the most sweet and innocent of ways and were sure we'd marry those boys. It was that time in life when everything was great, even when it wasn't. We believed it would always stay this way—how could it not?

Well, not. The relationships started to crack. Leanne and Evan broke up first, followed by me and Jeremy. Then Leanne and Evan got back together but fought so much she eventually cut him loose again. Leanne was so devastated, she read everything she could find about relationships, between the crying, that is.

It started with light reads like *Cosmopolitan* and *Seventeen*, but those articles didn't go nearly deep enough for Leanne. She moved on to *Psychology Today*, and that's when her hobby with the mind and behavior turned into an obsession. She became something of a child prodigy, a walking "psychlopedia." To this day I find her both helpful and annoying.

"This breakup with Jeremy is all my fault," I whined at the football game one night. Whining was so not like me.

"Well, of course you feel that way. You were raised by a narcissist," Leanne blurted without hesitation. "They have an uncanny ability to blame-shift and make others feel responsible for things that are *not* their fault while avoiding personal accountability."

"I was fine at first. I really was, Leanne. Happy to be rid of him actually."

"Obvi—you're juggling how many boys now?"

"But then in bio, Mr. Riggs used the word *innards*."

"The word you two couldn't stop laughing at on game night?" Her eyes widened.

"Yep. Jeremy and I looked at each other and busted out laughing as silently as we could. It hit me all at once. What the hell happened to us? If this can end, *anything* can. And why haven't I been more bothered by this breakup until now?"

"Because you didn't have secure attachments

growing up, Faith. Again, raised by a narcissist, you've been forced to detach from your emotions and deny they exist. Instead of *feeling*, you throw yourself into *achieving*. You're at the top of the class, head of the debate club, and captain of the dance team. Your relentless focus on perfection is only adding new layers of dysfunction on top of the old ones. In some ways we all are. Behavior is simply adaptation—protection to keep us safe from pain."

I held back a laugh knowing how seriously Leanne takes this stuff. "What do you do when we're not together? Memorize all this shit?"

I continued to see Jeremy and several other boys at once. Jeremy was dating too. But during Christmas break, we slept together. When he had a new girlfriend, we slept together. When he broke up with her, we slept together. And the boys I was dating may have thought I was being faithful too, but it wasn't all just sex. Jeremy and I were still emotionally tied, and there seemed to be no end in sight. It went on and on. I wanted him back, and I wanted nothing to do with him. And then it happened. Senior year, first semester, gym class, fourth period.

"He's in love with you!" Leanne was giddy with matchmaker excitement.

The badminton birdie came soaring over the net. Without missing a beat, I swung a strong backhand, smashing it back over.

"Oh, come on, he doesn't even know me." I smirked.

"No, he really is," Leanne continued, forever the romantic. "He's been asking me about you for weeks."

I clicked my tongue and snorted. "Ridiculous!"

Racing forward, my sneakers squeaked on the glossy floor, echoing throughout the gym like high-pitched screams as I slammed the birdie over the net for the game point.

"He" was standing in the doorway of the high school gym. The double doors were open as usual for anyone to drift by and glance inside. Or, as it was with this boy, to casually lean one shoulder against the doorway, rest one foot on its toe over the other, place one hand halfway into the front pocket of his jeans and have the nerve to stare directly at me, smiling no less. The only thing rehabilitating this moment from creepy to flattering was the fact that he was smoking hot. His face was a perfect ten. Hair dark, eyes penetrating, he was not my usual type. I preferred fairer features, but at this moment it didn't seem to matter. Through his clothes, it was clear he had an athletic frame and that was, in fact, my type. What was the point of dating any other?

Not to be outdone, I stared right back. He looked down but not for long. His head remained low, but his eyes lifted and met mine, the corner of his lip curling into a half smile.

Hmm. Nice. I tore myself away from his dreamy eyes and turned in the opposite direction toward Leanne, who was waiting for me to start our usual new boy analysis.

"Name?" I barked.

"Cole."

"Sports?"

"Football and lacrosse."

"Year?"

"One class under us," Jen, who we call our

imaginary friend because she rarely rips herself away from her boyfriend, chimed in.

I shook my head in derision. We were seniors, for God's sake. "What else should I know about him?"

"Plenty, Faith. He grew up in Seaside, parents are divorced. His aunt and uncle live next door to me. He used to stay with them for the summers, but now he's living with them. I've known him for years. We practically grew up together. He's super sweet."

"Why isn't he living with one of his parents? What kind of worms are lurking inside that can?" I put up a hand. "Don't think I want to know. And why haven't you ever mentioned him before?"

"If you're not interested, what does it matter?" Leanne shrugged, seeing right through the way I was headed toward a casual dismissal of him. "I know your plate's full, but I really think you should give this one a shot. Trust me."

After everything with Jeremy and now this, in gym class, playing badminton. What was Leanne thinking bringing another boy to my attention?

"I'm telling you, Faith, I know him. He's different, and he could be good for you."

I didn't want to hear it. And yet, there he was, standing in the doorway looking like that, an invisible lasso of energy connecting us, drawing me in while I did my best to act like it wasn't happening.

He was singing to himself, "You're just too good to be true…can't take my eyes off of you…"

Cute. But no way.

That was last week. Maybe staring, singing gym boy can have the empty space on the mirror where Jeremy's photo used to be. Anything's possible because who knows which Faith I might be in a week compared to the one still looking in the mirror, trying to be happy with the cowlick that refuses to relax. I puff out a dissatisfied breath, grab my car keys and bag, and head out.

After picking up some goodies, I walk into Leanne's house without knocking because that's how it's done on game night. Large whiteboards, colored markers, friends, food, and laughter are what make game night one of my favorite rituals. Everyone looks forward to it. I didn't bother to ask Leanne who's coming. Doesn't matter, it's always fun.

The usual gang is here, minus Jeremy, of course. Making my way around the room and hugging everyone hello, I don't know how I missed him—Cole, standing there smiling to greet me like everyone else. My back stiffens for a quick second, but I'm nothing if not adaptable, so I hug him too. The charge of energy between us the moment we make contact is like nothing else. He's warm and solid, and we fit together perfectly, like puzzle pieces. Makes me not want to let go.

"Let me bring this into the kitchen for Leanne," I say, pulling back from him, almost dropping the box of pastries.

"Sure." His cheery voice catches me off guard.

"Leanne!" I whisper-yell once inside the kitchen. "You didn't say *he* was gonna be here!"

"I know." She grins at me with the same look from the gym last week. "You didn't ask."

I'm not sure if I want to laugh with her or grab the cake knife from the counter and plunge it into her. She loves using game night for her own personal psychosocial experiments.

"Don't worry." She places the knife on the tray alongside a pie. "I warned him about your current commitment issues."

"And?"

"He didn't care." Leanne cocks her head at me. "Told you."

We leave the kitchen and return to the dining room where everyone's already pairing up for a drawing game, debating the rules. Since Cole's new to game night and I used to play with Jeremy, neither of us has a partner. Very clever, Leanne.

Cole seems to notice at the same time and is staring at me, smiling. Again. We're about to get to know each other much better whether I like it or not.

After a few rounds, Cole and I realize we're able to guess each other's drawings no matter how bad they are. This makes us unbeatable. Everyone accuses us of cheating and that makes everything funnier. It's us against the entire room making our newfound bond stronger as we fight off the rest of the room. We're getting a microcosmic preview of what a future relationship might be like. Right now, with him as my partner, I feel invincible. We're in sync; he *gets* me. And I get him.

After wiping the floor with everyone for almost two hours, we bow out, partially to make it more fair for the others, but also for some alone time. We take our drinks and relocate to the couch where Cole moves pillows out of the way so I can sit.

"Can I get you something to drink besides water, Faith?"

"No, thanks. I'm good." I place the glass on the table. "How do you like Devenport?"

"It's nice enough. I hear you're in the debate club and the captain of the dance team. Aren't those practices going on at the same time? How do you manage it?"

How does he know *that*? "Some days they are. The rooms are next to each other, so I jump back and forth. Most of dance is sitting around between rehearsals gossiping anyway."

He's still smiling in the most adorable way. I wish he would stop.

"And you play football and lacrosse? How do you have any free time?" Hope it didn't sound like an invitation.

He's answering, but I'm not exactly listening. Can't stop staring at his lips. They're perfectly shaped and undoubtedly soft. *Stop looking, don't make it weird, Faith.* To distract myself I switch to his nose, that should be safe, but there's an underlying current of electricity flowing between us. What is this, and does he notice it?

He's sweet. There's a kindness about him. He looks directly into my eyes when he speaks as if there's not an extremely animated to-the-death board game going on feet from us. But he's younger. I'm seeing older boys, some in college. In fact, I came here from Jeremy's an hour earlier, naked and tangled up with him. Right now, Cole's somehow making that feel *wrong*.

"...the coaches here are different from what I'm used to..."

I'm mesmerized by the features of his face, mostly his eyes, soulful and innocent. The kind of eyes that are unable to hide anything. An image pops into my mind, the two of us at dinner months into a relationship sitting on the same side of the table as couples sometimes do, with his hand on my inner thigh, slowly moving up…

Snapping myself back to the present, I ask, "How old are you again?"

"Older than you in dog years."

Cute, but not factually correct.

"What do you want to be when you grow up, Cole?" Does he realize this little one-on-one is actually an interview?

"A pirate," he answers, completely straight-faced.

I cock my head at him.

He breathes a laugh through his nose. "Haven't given it much thought."

Wrong answer. Noted. Moving on. "That was an impressive performance tonight, Cole. Have you ever played before?"

"Only once." He sips a soda. "I'm not much of an artist. It was really all you."

"I'm even worse. Did you see my stick figures? I think you were reading my mind."

"I was." He raises an eyebrow.

"It's like we're one person tonight." Oops. Did I say that out loud?

"Maybe we are. Maybe you're my twin. Do you know my mom?" he jokes, quite poorly.

"That would explain it." I indulge him.

"Do you ever think about that?" He turns his torso toward me. "I mean, not that we're twins, but about meeting someone you somehow already knew?"

"Not sure I'm following." I'm still sitting at the imaginary dinner table with him and should probably stop that.

Cole leans in, as if he's about to tell me a secret. I mirror him and wait.

"Do you ever get the feeling you've met certain people in another time and place?" he asks. "Like you're so close and you get along so well, maybe you've already been friends in another life and now you're continuing what you already started?"

"That's deep." I look directly into his cautious eyes and nod. "Is there anyone you think you've met in another life?"

"My uncle. We think the same exact thoughts. We even finish each other's sentences, and whenever I'm thinking about calling him, he calls me first. We have this invisible connection. Feels like I've always known him." He pauses. "And you."

"Me?" I hinge forward, taking my water from the table. "No, I'd have to give it some thought."

"It wasn't a question, Faith." He gently places his hand on my forearm. "It was a statement—and you. I feel like I've known you before. Like we've already shared a life together."

I take a long sip to buy myself some time. I mean, how does one answer such a question? His eyes are the warmest shade of brown I've ever seen, and I'm locked into them, into him. My heart burns, and tiny flutters tickle the lining of my stomach. This means trouble. No words are forming or coming out, and I'm feeling swept away.

Cole notices. "Sorry, didn't mean to make you uncomfortable," he assures me. "I feel a connection to you. You're easy to talk to. I meant it as a compliment."

"No, sorry. I blanked, but you might be right. I could talk with you for hours." Did that really just come out of my mouth? *Shit.* The longer we sit together, the more drawn to him I feel, like magnets whose electrons have been aligned to each other. What is it about him?

"There you two are, the cheaters." Bryce Henderson has gotten up from the game table and come over. He's friends with Cole, in his class and lives down the block. "Plotting your next caper?"

"Yeah, Bryce." Cole looks at me. "We've been sitting here honing our ESP skills."

"I knew it!" Bryce covers his mouth with a hand, feigning surprise.

"It's getting late. I should get going," I say.

"Can I walk you out?" Cole offers.

I hear "no" in my head but "sure, thanks," is what comes out. Is he gonna ask me out? A list of gentle ways to turn him down runs through my head because no. Well, yes, but no. There it is again. The erratic, inconsistent version of me I can barely recognize, or manage. Who would want any part of this?

Cole retrieves my jacket and holds it open while I slip my arms inside. There's a mark on his right hand I noticed earlier but couldn't get a good look at.

"Did something happen to your hand?" I ask.

"Oh, you mean this?" A shade of red spreads across his neck as he twists his wrist and hand around for me to see. There's a large raised brown blotch on the web of skin between his thumb and forefinger.

"What is that?" Genuinely curious but also picking up on how self-conscious this has made him, I say, "Sorry, I shouldn't have pointed it out. Thought you might have scraped it on my zipper."

"Na. It's a birthmark. It lets everyone know I'm the chosen one, the highly defective chosen one."

"Well, I think it makes you unique. One of a kind even."

The side of his lip curls, the same way it did at the gym doorway.

We say our goodbyes and walk into the cool night air. Lightning flickers, followed by low rumbling thunder, as if the sky's clearing its throat to speak. We approach my driver's door. I feel him wanting to say something.

"I'd like to see you again, Faith."

"I'm sure you will." Intentional evasiveness is my superpower.

"Just the two of us."

Even though this is no surprise, I'm still unprepared. Doesn't he realize what he's getting himself into? Didn't Leanne talk to him?

"Cole, I'm sorry, but…"

A veil of disappointment clouds his eyes at the same time a desire to take it away runs through me. Without thinking, I continue, "…but I'm not free until next week."

His clear, happy eyes return. "Okay. I can wait."

"You live right here?" My head motions to the ranch-style home next to Leanne's.

"Yep."

At this exact moment, the booming angry sky lets a downpour loose on us. It doesn't seem like the right time to end our conversation, so I yell, "Get in!"

Cole runs around my car ducking giant raindrops like he's behind enemy lines in a firefight. The rain rushes down so fast and hard, we're quickly drenched. We throw ourselves into the car seats, hair dripping, and slam the doors shut. Out of breath and still shocked by the icy wetness, we get a look at each other and laugh in disbelief at the sudden deluge.

"God, we're soaked!" I say in a huff, twisting myself to search the back seat. "I usually keep a towel back here."

"It's all right." His voice is deep and reassuring. I turn toward him and his right hand gently comes to rest on my cheek. "We don't need a towel."

We're face-to-face in this small, quiet space, and again, I'm transfixed by his eyes. His hand is somehow warm and calming on my skin. Everything slows down as he strokes away the rain dripping down my face. My heart beats hard in my chest as if it just started. The scent of him is intoxicating, rain and berries, fresh and sweet at the same time. Is that cologne, or him? Studying my face, his longing wraps around me like a heated blanket.

Cole lightly tugs me to him. Our foreheads meet as he exhales a long warm breath onto me, lips so close our breath has become one. I know what's coming and have no desire to stop it, melting into him, losing myself, waiting for him to do whatever he wants.

This is new, the feeling of not being in control, but I don't care. I want this. I want him. The waiting is almost too much as he tilts my head that last bit and pauses again.

Breathe, Faith…

His mouth moves onto mine in the gentlest of ways, as if knowing he's introducing our bodies for the first time in what will become a lifetime. Heat instantly ignites a path through me, spreading from my face to the top of my head and down my back. The softness of his lips and the warmth of his hands on my face consume me. The pounding of the rain hitting the roof disappears as his tongue moves into my mouth and the pressure of his lips on mine intensifies. My body's already responding to him in the most intimate of ways. I want his hands all over me, but he remains a gentleman.

The rain diminishes, and we seem to be in sync with it, slowing to a stop. I'm completely dazed by this turn of events. Moments earlier, I tried to turn down his attempt to bring us closer, and now, well, I can't even think straight. We hold each other's stare. Neither of us says a word, but there certainly isn't silence.

"I'll call you?" he asks, breathless.

"Yes," I say, *finally* with some definiteness in my voice.

"Maybe you'd like to see a movie?"

"Yes." I'd agree to anything right now.

"Okay. Good. Great. This is good. See you in school?"

"Yes."

He gets out of my car, looking back with a wave, pulling all the energy out with him like a tailwind. The door slams shut.

I'm able to breathe again. *Shit.*

Chapter Three

The lingering scent of flowers
Cole 2012

It finally happened. I, Cole Anderson, a junior at Devenport High School and new to the school, kissed Faith Ansley.

The red digits on the nightstand clock glow one thirty a.m. as I lie in bed, still riding the high I felt since getting out of her car. I'm amped and jittery and suddenly confident and…about a billion other new and previously alien emotions are coursing through my veins since the second our lips touched.

Little does Faith know I've been working to get to this exact moment for months. Holding her wet face in my hands, bringing my lips to hers, and watching her eyes close was…I know I'm supposed to close mine too, but I didn't. Couldn't take my eyes off her, needed to study her face. The same way I've been studying her for months. Last week, she saw me outside her gym class, but not the other days.

The first time was in the principal's office at the start of the school year. I was called down to hand in the new student paperwork. The long desk seemed higher than it needed to be, but I put my papers down on it, waiting to be noticed. The principal's door flew open with a sweeping wind that caught my attention.

"I absolutely will, Principal Kelly!"

She was gorgeous. Petite with thick light-brown hair, dark eyes, a face that lit up the room, and a body that could have been carved by Michelangelo himself.

"I better not see you in here again, Faith." Principal Kelly was pointing a finger but clearly charmed by her. "We talked about your tardiness last year. Now you go and have a great first day, but remember what I said."

She glided right past me and out the door, skirt swooshing up just far enough for me to see the muscles in her thighs, leaving the lingering scent of flowers behind.

"Are you dropping those off?" the secretary asked.

Who is this girl? Faith, that's her name. I have to know more. Immediately. Maybe Leanne will know.

"Are you dropping those off?" the secretary repeated, louder this time, as I watched Faith walk into the hall.

"Yes, sorry." I handed them over.

She looked at me sideways, took the papers, and scanned them through glasses on the tip of her nose. "Looks like it's in order." She leaned in and whispered, "Faith Ansley, she's a senior. And she just broke up with her boyfriend."

"Do you think I have a shot?" I asked, embarrassed at how obvious I'd been, yet suddenly feeling very comfortable in this school.

"Maybe…" She leaned back and continued her work with a discerning half grin.

After that, I learned Faith's schedule. I'd get the hall pass and stroll over to her third and sixth period classes on some days, second and fifth period classes on others. Is that fucked up? Am I some kind of psycho? I don't think so, only wandered by to get a look at her. The way her jeans perfectly hugged her ass. The way she scrunched her face to see the board and tilted her head downward to take notes. And how she'd get angry at herself when she made a mistake, slamming the eraser side of the pencil down, squishing it back and forth in a huff. I've watched her interrupt the teacher with questions, pass notes not caring who sees, and laugh out loud when no one else does. I liked her confidence and wished I had some of it. I've also caught her staring out the window with such immense heartache, I could feel it too, feel *her.*

I've only wanted to see her up close, so I can *be* close. Is that creepy? Fell hard and fast for her months ago. She's free-spirited, fun, moody, and popular with the face of an angel, and I want all of her, all the time. But one day I saw her in the hall with her ex, Jeremy. He's so, so…overblown, a typical jock but worse because he's smart. I may be a jock too, but not like *that ass.*

"Hi, Cole, happy Monday!" Faith said, as I rounded the corner to math class. She was walking into the school late, with *him.*

"You too," I said, making eye contact with both of them. A piece of my heart chipped off envisioning the two of them spending the night together, coming to school late because they *had* to have sex one more time. I was sick to my stomach. I wished it were me.

First period turned into a disaster. I couldn't understand a word Ms. Lynn said about the slope of a line being the change in x over the change in y because all I could think about was Faith's ex and why was she still with him?

Was she still with him?

The situation got more desperate. If those two were still together, how would I ever get her away from him? Jeremy's captain of the hockey team, and they're county champs. He's a beast in the gym, at the top of his class and me, a lowly junior with nothing more than a boyish crush from her perspective. Fuck.

I had to step it up. When the bell rang, I was first out of the classroom. Instead of heading to my next class, I made my way to Leanne's locker and poured my shell-shocked heart out to her about what I saw.

"I'll take care of it, don't worry." Leanne hates seeing me unhappy, plus she loves this shit. "Give me some time. I'll come up with something."

Turned out, Leanne invited the exact right amount of people that would force Faith and me to pair up and it worked. I pulled off game night flawlessly. And our kiss sealed the deal. I'm in Faith's head now, I can feel it.

This is all so new and foreign to me, like I've been wandering through a desert for seventeen years and Faith is the first glass of water I've had. What is it about her that makes everything else not matter? This has gone way beyond a crush. Call it lust or infatuation or whatever, but I'm in deep. The high I get from being close to her is as real as any drug.

The house phone chimes a half ring and goes dead. That's the signal—it's Leanne. This is how we avoid waking our parents. She'll want to know everything that happened outside when Faith and I left her house. I call her right back. She picks up before it even rings.

"Well?" she asks.

"Well, what?" I tease.

"I knew it! I can practically hear you smiling through the phone!"

Chapter Four

The watered-down version
Faith 2026

I'm hovering without a body, suspended, looking down at the lawn as larger-than-normal raindrops whiz by me. I watch myself fall to my knees, strands of wet hair plastered to the side of my face, blood intermingling with rain dripping down my neck. Cole looks devilish and sad all at once. I know what I must do. With steely nerves, I stab myself over and over with the eight-inch knife he has handed me—stomach, ribs, legs, neck—so much blood. He claps, slow and methodical because this was a long time coming. The sound pierces my ears and head, morphing into a high-pitched squeal...

I wake, hyperventilating, grabbing and clutching everywhere the knife entered, trying to stop the bleeding.

There is none.

The high-pitched squeal is the house phone. We still have one by the bed and in the kitchen. I stretch across Jeremy's empty side to answer it, expecting to see blood-soaked sheets.

"Sorry to call you at home, Faith, but I couldn't reach your partner, Brooke."

The words start out echoey, then stabilize as the

dream fades into the background. The Cole nightmares started again after Jeremy's accident. Leanne would have a field day with this.

"I've been sitting on Mrs. Miller all night. Got her with her latest boytoy who came and went, literally, ha! There's three hours left on the clock. Want me to sit tight or save the billable hours for another time?"

Andy is one of my newer field operatives. Young, hungry, and slightly twisted, the last of which is a prerequisite for this job.

"You can go, good call." I'm still inspecting myself for wounds, grateful there are none. "Did you get video?"

"Yep, the X-rated kind." He laughs.

"Perfect. Do me a favor. On your way home, swing by the Skyline job site and see if our friend is working today. You know what to do if he is. Shouldn't take more than a half hour. You had a long night. You up for it?"

"Absolutely, boss!"

Gotta love the newbies. They're eager and willing to do anything. I, on the other hand, am not. Coffee first. In the kitchen, waiting impatiently and sifting through the mail still on the counter, I find that intriguing little letter on its crisp white note paper. My eyes fall to the nameless closing. "Sincerely…" Kinda cute.

Kinda laughable too. Doesn't he realize I'm an investigator now, in an age where almost nothing is unknowable? Have access to a vast network of people and databases making it virtually impossible to hide? I might want to dig into this if for no other reason than the fact that I can. There'll be plenty of time to do that a little later today.

After a few warm sips of liquid gold, I carry my mug through the master bedroom, stand in the closet doorway, and lean against the frame in my jammies. My eyes move slowly from Jeremy's work-out clothes to his suits and ties, wandering over to his jeans.

It's cold in here, tomblike. I enter and run my hand along his clothes, feeling the mix of soft and rough fabrics against my skin, inhaling eucalyptus and mint, the smell of him, lingering behind. My heart aches. His old varsity hockey sweatshirt stands out among the rest, the one he'd wear from time to time, knowing how I loved to be reminded of our history together—high school sweethearts, first loves, who didn't make it to prom but found each other again after college nonetheless.

We'd gone our separate ways after graduation. I would hear about him and eventually he told me he'd hear about me too, but it wasn't until years later that we ran into each other again. Jeremy's dream job offer brought him back to Devenport. Seeing each other after all those years made us both smile the same smile, like a secret handshake only we knew. We sat together for hours that day at the café, filling each other in on our new lives, sharing glances, and reminding ourselves of old memories. We noticed we were both different but the same and realized even after all this time, there was still something there.

Of all the things we talked about, we left one item out. He was being a gentleman, waiting for me to bring it up, but I didn't and neither did he, on that first day together. We saw each other again and again in the following days and fell into our old familiar pattern of loving each other. The drama of the years we'd spent apart had washed away some of my resilience. I was more guarded now, less trusting, and he knew it. Being the big, strong protector type, he wanted nothing more than to fill the niche. I needed that. We were just as compatible in bed as we'd always been, and we grew closer. But there was still that one item to deal with, always hovering in the room with us.

"Faith, you know you can talk to me about it, really think we should. I don't want to push, but I'm here for you."

"I know, but…I wouldn't even know how without hurting you."

"You won't be hurting me. But *that day*…we need to talk about it, Faith."

"No, we don't." *That day* is something I'll never talk to you about, Jeremy.

"All right, I'll leave it alone, but we were leading separate lives. He was there with you. I wasn't. Whatever went on between you two, it changed you. I can see it in your eyes, feel it in your heart. But for me, nothing's changed. I loved you then, and I love you now. I hope you let me in on that part of your life, but if you don't, I understand."

So I did, but gave him the watered-down version of it. The one that didn't describe a love so pure and perfect, nothing could ever compare. The version without the details of the all-consuming flame of passion between myself and Cole that burned up everything in its path. The one that didn't include the years I spent trying to rebuild myself into something resembling a living, breathing being with a heart. Nope, didn't tell him any of that. But I did give him just enough to fill in the blanks between what people told him and the newspaper reports. It would have to suffice.

And it did. We built a beautiful life together, while it lasted. But after ten years our marriage was not what it once was. After that much time, is anyone's? Time has a way of wearing the shine off the surface of everything new, changing its appearance. You start to wonder if it was ever really what you thought it was in the first place. People change, circumstances find a way to take care of that all on their own. You grow together, you grow apart. The tide of love and passion ebbs and flows, wearing at the shoreline of your relationship, creating new patterns and landscapes.

We weren't perfect. No relationship is, is what I would always tell myself. We'd disagree, fight, hold resentments toward each other. Sometimes I hated Jeremy from a place so deep, I wasn't even sure where it was coming from. It wasn't fair to him. He may have sensed it too, but he wasn't the type to leave. Loyal and faithful, he was going nowhere. We still respected and cared for each other, but by the time of Jeremy's death, we were more like roommates than lovers. And I'm certain he'd want me to be happy again, if not immediately, then sometime in the future.

But today's the day. It's been one month. Time to divide items into "keep" and "donate" piles, box some up to save, and fill others for charity. By conventional standards, others may think this is too fast, but I know myself. I will only dwell on it, ruminate and prolong the healing. Already done it once before. Letting go always seems harder for me than it does for others. Maybe they are able to hide it better. Plus, something's nudging me to clear Jeremy's stuff out now, even though I can't quite make sense of it.

Within two hours, I'm driving along tree-lined streets with those boxes in the trunk, heading to the local charity. The white and pink buds of the dogwoods are announcing spring in New York, and the yellow brilliance of the forsythia has made its appearance. Cars are covered in the annual green pollen blanket.

I arrive, take care of business, and before I know it, find myself walking out of the charity with a receipt in my hand *to be used for my taxes*, according to the lady behind the counter. If she only knew she just relegated another woman's dead husband as a tax write-off, she probably wouldn't have said it.

Returning to the driver's seat, I start the car. The music blares because I like it loud and never remember to turn it down, startling myself, but it's a good oldie. It's been scientifically proven that music is a medium of memory, triggering parts of the brain, evoking emotions and past events. And true to form, an avalanche of emotions are blanketing me under the weight of Jeremy and the other one. The one whose name I avoid. The boy who so fully consumed me, there was nowhere to go from there.

I couldn't forget him or accept our ending or conjure up any kind of toxically positive silver lining. There was no closure. Nothing to slow the spinning gears of regret. But I *could* compartmentalize, *could* box up what happened back then and put it on a high shelf tucked safely behind the other metaphorical boxes of nostalgia and personal life experience. I *could* keep the memories at arm's length and dormant. For a time.

And now it seems that time has ended, and another

has begun.

As the song plays, the past lurks in the recesses of my mind and bursts out, casting images in front of me as real as any others. Like a ventriloquist throwing its voice onto inanimate objects, breathing life into them, it's coming. The flashbacks. The memories. Of *him*. Starting up again with all their joy and darkness and mind-bending abilities, bringing the past to life. Might Jeremy's death have knocked the past loose? Leanne would probably say so.

It's quite remarkable, almost a superpower, how we're able to function on autopilot, one side of our brain walking around doing things, thinking and talking, while the other side can be somewhere else with totally different people. Is this any different from the multitasking we're all capable of? Or have all those hours of surveillance and undercover work trained my brain to split in two?

Or is it the trauma?

Or both.

Chapter Five

Famous last words
Faith 2012

"I don't want a boyfriend." I plop myself onto the couch next to Leanne. She came over to watch *American Idol*. We're both rooting for Phillip Phillips.

"Well, of course you don't. Not after Jeremy." She passes the bowl of popcorn. "Plus, you usually operate in a state of emotional avoidance."

"Wrong." I roll my eyes. "I tried with Jeremy. Look what happened. It only proves my point. Him, my parents, you can't trust anyone, can't get too close. Suffering will follow. I need to take care of myself."

"You're going to base the rest of your life on two experiences?"

"Well, yes. And I need to stay focused on the target, which is getting out of my house, getting into my dream college, and the career that will follow if it all falls into place the way I've planned it. And I want to be single and have some fun. What's wrong with that?"

"Absolutely nothing." Leanne crunches popcorn. "You shouldn't be tied down to anyone right now."

"But Cole's adorable." I grab a handful.

"Yep, and he really likes you."

"And that kiss…"

"A great first kiss is everything," she agrees.

"He's a virgin, isn't he?" I pick out a few butter-loaded kernels.

"Yep. And he can be a tad obsessive."

"I'll go out with him a few times. What could it hurt?"

"Famous last words…"

"I was caught off guard when he called. I didn't want to hurt his feelings."

Leanne pauses the show. "*You* didn't want to hurt his feelings? *You*? Who's been ruthlessly single and mercilessly independent since the split with Jeremy? You are a walking contradiction, my friend."

"It's one date." Not sure if I'm justifying it to Leanne or myself.

****

Cole has been a perfect gentleman the entire evening, ordering dinner for me, making sure I have enough to drink, purchasing the movie tickets, and putting his arm around the back of my seat, letting it lightly drape over my shoulder in the appropriate way. He looks hot in the black tee he's wearing. The width of his biceps make his sleeves look too tight.

After the movie, we walk five blocks to my house, talking and laughing the whole way. We were supposed to see the new Harry Potter, but it was sold out, as was almost everything else. We ended up seeing *Key Largo*, some vintage oldie my parents would've liked. We totally bonded over how bad it was and why it didn't win any plot awards. It was slow and overly dramatic with an excessive amount of bad acting.

Cole's amusing and funny, which is all I want from the current boys in my life—entertainment. But there's more here. A connection, a synergy. The conversation is so easy with him, never forced, and he doesn't let a pause go on for too long before having another topic ready to go. It all flows. *We* flow.

Reaching my house, Cole opens the screen door and holds it for me as I unlock the door.

His hand rests gently on my lower back, igniting a flash through me like a Roman candle on the Fourth of July. I lead him through the door and walk across the kitchen to the cabinet holding the glasses.

"Would you like something to drink?" I ask.

Backing himself into the cabinets while resting both hands on the counter to either side of him, his smoldering innocence has me burning to be the first one to take advantage of it…and oddly, protect it.

"Sure, whatever you're having. Your parents around?"

"They won't be home anytime soon." I reach into the cabinet.

I've already decided we'll see each other naked tonight, so everything's foreplay from here on out, yet my breath feels strained under the weight of what is about to transpire. My focus is on consciously inhaling or I might not breathe at all. I'm sensing the same for him.

"Wanna stay a while?" I'm taking the lead.

He seems relieved. "Yeah, that'd be nice."

I pour some iced tea and hand it to him, standing closer than necessary, intentionally letting my hand brush against his. He seemed calm until right now, when I notice a slight tremor in that hand, the one with the raised birthmark, and I'm reminded of what I'm dealing with. He's younger and alone in a house with a girl whose parents are nowhere in sight. There's an urge to throw my arms around him and tell him not to worry. I don't. He's less experienced, but what he does have is a combination of raw vulnerability and seductiveness that's bubbling under the surface like a panicked scuba diver. It's hard to slow down and not be the hunter stalking her prey.

We move to the living room. He sits on the couch, and I hand him a few of the CDs we were talking about on the walk over.

"Which one do you want to hear?" I ask, standing over him.

"This one." He removes the CD from the sleeve, handing it up to me. The player sucks it in. We sit together as he flips through the rest of them telling me about the stories behind the lyrics. A love for the meaning behind the words is something we've learned we have in common. I purposefully hold his gaze as he speaks and stay close enough to make it easy for him to initiate the first move. I want it to come from him so he feels like he's in control, even though he's not.

Mid-sentence, rattling on about the song, Cole takes my hand, stroking it, studying it. With a new confidence, his eyes meet mine while his other hand moves beneath my chin. I say yes by leaning in a hundredth of an inch. His eyes move down to my lips as he places his onto mine ever so gently, like he did in the car.

His hands move to the sides of my face. He stops and pulls back far enough to look into my eyes again, then tilts my head up before diving back in, breathing me in as our mouths connect. Skin flushes and dimples from my face down through my legs.

The feel of his hands on me makes every nerve in

my body come alive. I'm hyper-vigilantly aware of each move he makes as one hand drifts from the nape of my neck, down my back pulling me in even closer. The pressure of his chest on mine warms me, biceps pressing against the sides of my body as he holds me. He's toned and hard and strong, and before I know it, we're lying down on the couch but in an awkward way, like he is afraid to put his full weight on me. His hunger is obvious as his tongue moves deeper into my mouth— like he's searching for something he lost long ago. Connectedness, love, confidence, trust? If I knew what it was, I'd give it to him.

We kiss, pressing against each other, hands everywhere, for what feels like hours. His level of passion mixed with innocence makes me feel both in control of him and yet out of control because of him.

"Do you want to stop?" he breathes.

"Absolutely not. You're driving me crazy," I whisper.

It isn't long before I make the executive decision that we will *not* see each other naked tonight. I can't let this go any further. He isn't ready. I can sense it. If anything too serious happens on this couch, it will get weird in school and he will be calling me every night before bed, thinking we're in a relationship. Maybe I'm the one who's not ready for him. Either way, this sudden feeling of protectiveness over Cole is too strong to let this be *the night.* I will be his first and I want that memory tattooed on his soul. Plus, my parents might come home soon.

"Cole. Is it okay if we stop here?"

"Of course, whatever you want." He's still a gentleman.

We lie there, intertwined in each other. He kisses my forehead, his long, strong arms still around my body.

"You're beautiful," he whispers. "And perfect."

"And you're an amazing kisser." He's happy for the compliment and kisses me again, more intensely. Our bodies start responding again, but I sit up, stopping it from going any further.

"What time is it?" I ask.

"Holy…" His eyes widen on his watch. "It's eleven thirty!"

We've been on the couch for an hour and a half.

"I should go. Don't want to, just so you know. I was supposed to be home half an hour ago."

"Ooh, then you should. My parents'll be home soon too."

I walk him to the door.

"Can I call you tomorrow?"

I nod. He kisses my cheek and off he goes down the driveway toward his house.

Don't want him to leave. I really don't.

Shit. This was not part of the plan.

Chapter Six

The head tends to stay fucked
Cole 2012

I love her. I mean, I loved her before, but now I'm *in* love with her. She's so much more than I imagined. Her perfect lips, those chestnut eyes penetrating straight into my soul, the feel of her sculpted body under my hands. She knew exactly what to do when I didn't. And she knew I was floundering. How? Was it that obvious? Fuck. I don't think she minded. She said I was driving her crazy. *She actually said that*.

I float through my front door as quietly as possible and make my way downstairs to my bedroom, wide awake and high—she's the drug. Leanne's waiting, so I dial her number.

"You did *what* with her?" was the response after she'd been debriefed.

"It was pure magic, Leanne."

"Then I'm happy for you, Cole. Did you make more plans?"

"I'll call her tomorrow. You think she'll see me again? She will, right?"

"Sounds like you two had a great night, so I bet she will. But Cole…"

"I know, I know, she's a free spirit, I need to be careful, might get my heart broken. I love that you're so worried for me, but I don't care. I'll take the broken heart. She's like a book I can't put down—have to know what's gonna happen next. Shit. I should get some sleep. Need to be up at five for football. Will you let me know what she says?"

"Of course. But do you want the whole truth or the filtered version, because if it's not good I can sugarcoat it. I have no idea if this is going to be another conquest for her or if she's really falling for you."

"I want the truth, the whole truth, and nothing but."

Practice at the crack of dawn on Saturdays suck, normally, but this is no normal Saturday. It's a new day, a new chapter. I jog home from practice remembering what the coach said. *Cole, who are you today? Keep this up, and you'll be starting in no time.*

I was awake all night, too amped up, but the lack of sleep didn't affect my performance in the least. Held nothing back on the field. It paid off and got me noticed. The jog home was effortless and put to good use planning my next conversation with Faith.

Living with my aunt and uncle isn't so bad. I've been in worse situations. Way worse. I overheard my aunt and uncle reading the child protective services report from when I was eight. The investigator peered through my mom's Seaside window, saw the gruesome conditions in the living room and straight through to the kitchen, where I was standing in my underwear in front of the open, empty refrigerator eating a stick of butter with the wrapper rolled down like a candy bar. That's what it said. I only remember being hungry a lot. My father visits me here when he's not drunk. Haven't seen my mom since I was removed from her custody and they forced her into rehab, which was a few years ago.

Broken bones and bruises heal. The head tends to stay fucked. So yeah, this ain't too bad.

My aunt has me busy doing yard work, but I keep having flashbacks of Faith's lips on my neck, the feel of her perfectly round breasts in my hands, her tiny body grinding into me and the purring coming from her when I touched her the right way. I have to see her again—as soon as possible. Don't want to seem too needy, so I wait until late afternoon and use my best mannered voice when her mom answers.

"Hi, this is Cole. I'm calling for Faith, please."

"Oh, I'm sorry, Cole. She's out. Can I take a message for her?"

Crushed.

Chapter Seven

Live truthfully in imaginary circumstances
Faith 2026

That's all I remember, being handed the tax form that turned Jeremy into a write-off and sitting in my car while the music and lyrics gently whisked me back in time, suspended me there, and abruptly slingshot me back into the present. My eyes refocus on the relentless pollen on my hood, and I'm *back*. My shoulders slump.

Should I try the medication again? Nah, too busy. It'll only slow me down.

Flipping down the visor, I automatically smooth the cowlick whether it needs it or not. Eyes are still a bit swollen from the closet crying earlier while packing up Jeremy's things. *Nothing's forever*, the little voice in my head whispers.

My next stop is a quick stint of undercover work three towns over. After dropping off pieces of my life somewhere never to be seen again, not sure I'm up for it, but I'm nothing if not resilient. I'll get it done. After that I'll head home. Short day for me. Brooke thought I should take a few days off around the one-month anniversary. This is me taking a few days off.

Thank God the traffic downstate isn't anywhere near as bad as it is on Long Island. The car is my personal think tank on wheels, but my head's spinning, damn it. I don't like that I'm so intrigued by that letter, drawn in even, by this…this…person, who's either being cute, fun, and creative or stealthy, cunning, and underhanded. The PI in me says it's both. Is he baiting me? I feel challenged. I like challenges.

And it's unsigned—coward. What's with all the cloak-and-dagger shit? Maybe he's shy or embarrassed because he's revealed his feelings for me. Or maybe this is not an admirer at all. Maybe it's the subject of one of my prior investigations, angry and playing me, eventually going to set a time and place for us to meet and…

Truth be told, I *have* blown up a lot of people's lives over the years with my work, but it's not my fault there's been something to blow up. My chest is on fire. I'm irritated. No—incensed.

So I'm gonna do what I do. Every investigator worth their salt has a network. It doesn't have to be a large number of contacts, just the right ones, in the right places. There's three sides to the private investigative world—the ethical, the unethical, and the gray. The legal, the illegal, and the questionable. The laws governing what we can and can't do are clear, but sometimes they're…open to interpretation. Sometimes they become…murky. My network can be exactly that.

The obvious and simplest first step in this instance is the postmark—Devenport. These days it's hard to know where a letter with no return address originated. Gone are the days of mail coming through a local post office, where the postmark would tell you when and where it came from. Now, letters are moved through huge, designated mail-processing stations for sorting and distribution. For any normal human, tracking a letter back to its origin means finding out if it was sent certified, returned receipt, or with a request for proof of delivery. My letter writer appears to be too smart for that. But I'm no normal human.

Next step, narrow down the day it was dropped off and at which post office, take a visit over there, and see if I can persuade the manager into letting me see the video footage on the surveillance cameras, and get a look at any nearby businesses' footage as well, if necessary.

This is gonna be fun—challenge accepted.

In the meantime, however, my client, the soon-to-be ex-Mrs. Englehoffer, is sure her husband is hiding his full financial worth by making his once-thriving gift shop business appear to be on the brink of collapse. Besides her attorney hiring a forensic accountant to work the paper end of things, he hired me to work the real-world end, specifically to put boots on the ground and into that shop to find out what's really going on.

Almost there and stopped at a light, my always-on-alert eyes notice the same blue van behind me from three towns over. Female driver, not that it means anything. When the light changes, I swing a U-turn. Yep, she's following me. If a tail has been made and breaks off, it usually means they've been hired to gather info and not be seen doing it. This one's being obvious about it. Doesn't care I know she's there, which means someone told her to stay on me no matter what. Why?

It's not my first rodeo. When I was seventeen, I fled from a cop chasing me for, ironically, speeding. No way was I rolling over for another ticket. It was the first time I learned how to hide a car in plain sight. Now, me and my nondescript SUV should surely be able to outrun a van or at the very least, outsmart her. This woman is pretty good though. She's right on my ass like she wants to ram me off the road. I would love to slam on my brakes and force her into me for the fun of it, but I speed up instead. Adrenaline burns my chest. Is this how people feel when I'm following them? Huh, interesting.

I'm betting I know this area better than she does and lead her toward an isolated part of town where the streets curve and cross over each other multiple times. It's very disorienting if you're not familiar with it. I press the pedal to the floor on the long straight-away that leads there. It takes her a sec but she catches up. Instead of staying behind me, she moves to my left, trying to drive up next to me. Can't let that happen. I jerk the wheel to the left and box her out, letting off the gas a little. She brakes, slides to the right, and tries again on that side, engine roaring. She *is* trying to ram me off the road. And into a ravine.

I check my right sideview. She's gaining on me. The front of her car is level with my rear tire. Shit. I hit it again, pull ahead and make a left turn into the first winding street of many. It takes much more evasive maneuvering than I'm used to, but eventually, I lose her. I can probably chalk this up to an old investigative target who's pissed and wants to scare me. Or maybe not. My hands shake. I head back to the straight-away and past the ravine, unaccompanied by the van. I'm going to file this little side excursion away for later so I can focus on the task at hand.

I pull into the gift shop parking lot, turning off one of the busiest intersections in this area and into something suburban New York is famous for—strip malls. They're all over, and you couldn't own a business in a better location, high traffic and convenient, the locals have to pass it on their way to and from work. You can't fail here, unless of course, you're trying.

"Hey, Alex." I wave at Mr. Englehoffer who's behind the counter with a customer.

"Hi, Sofie! Those Squashables you were looking for came in. They're around back."

"Sofie" is my alias for this undercover job. She has a three-year-old girl at home who loves collecting Squashables, just like him. Coincidently, she's recently moved to town after a nasty divorce. And after some background research on Alex and two weeks of regular visits to this shop, we've realized we have many things in common. Now we're best buds.

I consider the formation and use of pretext in my undercover operations similar to a piece of fine artwork. The use of dissemblance, ruse, psychology, and artful deception to gain confidence and information is a time-tested investigative technique where the skill of the investigator is directly correlated with the results. It's the ability to live truthfully in imaginary circumstances. And it's up close and personal, just the way I like it.

I pick out a multicolored Squash and head to the counter where Alex is finishing up with the customer. Without having to ask, he puts a peanut butter cup on the counter for me with flirty eyes. My eyes flirt back. He *may* be under the impression I like him…and we have a connection…and we'll be going out on a date as soon as things slow down for me.

In the meantime, he wanted me to know this little

gift shop of his is the fin of a much larger shark for his import/export business, and he has limitless access to inventory and funding from around the globe. Boy, I must be really cute. He can get anything I want. And I do want. Not only for me. He *may* be under the impression I have a rather large family with a business in Nassau County who would buy from him, at a discounted rate, of course.

Alex comes over to me in the aisle, leaning in, using a hushed tone.

"We're on for next Wednesday. The shipment should be delivered right to the warehouse. You want to meet me there? You can check out the inventory and pick something you like for yourself. And maybe as a thank you for the business"—he stares into my eyes— "I can take you to dinner."

Alex seems happy with himself.

I bat my eyes while picturing myself walking through his warehouse wired with video and audio to document the full inventory. Then, I'll work backwards. The shipping receipts will help me uncover the name of the shell company he's doing business under. I'll trace it back to not only this particular company he ordered from, but others as well. That'll point me to his method of payment and the banks he's using, account numbers, balances, transactions, and everything else he claims is not happening. You're welcome, Mrs. Englehoffer.

"Oh, but dinner is not necessary," I say.

"I insist." He charms.

Insist away, my friend.

Chapter Eight

Intimate in a routine kind of way
Faith 2012

I wake Saturday morning tangled in my comforter,
blinking myself awake. Sunlight streams through the
blinds, casting mirror images on my wall like hands and
fingers, reminding me of the night before. Tingles rush
through my body. Blurred images of fingertips on me,
lips touching mine, the tremor of his hand holding the
back of my head as he laid me down, the feel of his
body on mine. I close my eyes to summon more of it.
The evening with Cole was so intense I'm able to relive
it lying here. My body arches upward as if he's still on
top of me. Damn it…

I throw off the covers and jump out of bed because
I can't—won't—have this. I'm a senior, for God's sake.
Need to stay focused on my grades, debate, dance, and
every other overachieving checkmark needed for my
transcript. My applications to the top schools for
Criminal Justice are ready to go even though the early
decision deadline isn't until next month. I'm leaving for
college in less than a year. Don't want another broken
heart. Don't want to be attached to him and his
quivering vulnerability making me feel things for
him…making me want to be everything he needs. Sex
is one thing, love is another entirely. And that's what he

wants from me, commitment, devotion, loyalty. I will fight him every step of the way.

An hour later, I find myself at Jeremy's, naked and catching my breath as the orgasm subsides. He called. I went. The release feels good after the events of last night, but my desire for Jeremy is falling off the cliff. The way he kisses me is stiff, his hands move too quickly, and his body's overly rigid. His level of desire doesn't hold a candle to Cole's. I realize now it never had, even when we were newly together, but it sufficed. It was all I knew.

Jeremy moves up my body, letting his lips lead the way back to my neck. I'm bored now, but won't leave him hanging. He enters me and I take a deep breath, inhaling eucalyptus bodywash. It's effortlessly intimate in a routine kind of way. He still feels nice, but I'm imagining how Cole will feel instead. Jeremy climaxes and kisses me sweetly while stroking my hair. I listen to his breath and the clock on the wall tick. He still loves me, I can feel it. But our love has faded, like music that's too loud in a car with its windows open. The sound builds as it approaches, reaches a fever pitch as it nears, then passes and cuts out. Right now I'd say our car of love has stalled down the road a bit.

"Do you think we'll ever get tired of each other?" He adjusts so we're both lying on our backs looking up at the ceiling.

"I don't know, Jeremy." My voice is flat.

"Flash forward ten years—where are we?" He bounces himself onto his side toward me like we're playing a game.

"How should I know?"

"We'll be twenty-eight by then. I see myself as a

successful entrepreneur and you as the world's best mom to our two point five kids and golden Lab."

"Good God, how do you come up with this stuff?"

"Why not? It wouldn't be so bad. You never know how we'll end up, Faith."

"I'm going home." I sit up with blankets pulled over my breasts, looking for my shirt and underwear. Sure, the future is full of potentials, but I'd rather act exasperated with him. "Have to study for Riggs' bio test. You're only gonna need an hour to review your notes, but it's not so easy for me."

"You'll do fine. You always do." Jeremy's always been my biggest cheerleader. "Hey, that new kid on the football team—heard he's got it bad for you."

I zip up my jeans and shrug.

Jeremy clasps his hands behind his head. "He doesn't think he has a chance with you, does he?"

"Your arrogance never ceases to amaze me."

Arriving home, there's a message from Cole. I read it, not feeling the least bit bad about where I've been. That's probably wrong, but what he doesn't know won't hurt him.

Chapter Nine

Pushing against the shore
Cole 2012

"You may be getting too much sun, Faith."

Running a finger along the shoulder strap of her bikini top, I lie on a towel on my side, head propped on my hand. Faith is sprawled out next to me on her back, arms over her head resting on top of her flowing honey colored hair spread like a fan. Stunning. And hot, like the Indian summer we've been having.

A full month has passed since our encounter on the couch. I call her every night before bed. We've been on one other date, see each other in school, and except for a quick make-out session in the empty hallway after both our practices, we've not been alone together like that night since. She might be putting me off, but our chemistry is too strong for that. Or is it? I don't know what's in her head.

"You think I'm getting burnt?" She looks up at me, using her hand as a visor.

"Definitely." I check her again. I'll use any excuse to touch her.

Faith sits up, pulling the bikini bottom away from her skin to see the difference. "You're right. This suit is new. I shouldn't have worn it. I'm getting a sunburn in new spots."

"I think it's perfect for you. I about died when I saw you in it."

"Oh, stop." She smooths down the side of her hair that's always a little bit uneven.

"And if I did, what color roses would you bring to my funeral?"

"Hmmm." She hesitates, probably knowing what I want to hear. "Maybe yellow."

"I'm crushed," I tease. "We should probably get out of the sun. We've been out here for hours, and you didn't have much of a base." The plan was to hang out at the community pool for the afternoon, stay for dinner, and then catch the evening movie on the lawn.

"You're right, my skin feels tight. I'm going to the cabanas to change. Wanna come?"

"Of course."

She's a perfect ten in that bikini, like it was made for her. Coming to the pool has given both of us a chance to get a look at each other half naked. She eyed me over more than once. We spent the day sunbathing, talking, laughing, and playing in the pool touching each other under the water.

The cabanas are wooden shacks painted in alternating bright colors. They're attached to one another in a line of ten across. Situated in three rows, each has its own private locking door. They're unisex. Inside is a small shower stall with a curtain, a sink, a mirror, and a changing area with three hooks across the wall over a bench. Add a bed and hotplate and it's passable for a studio apartment.

We approach the cabanas carrying our towels and bags. Faith unexpectedly takes my hand and leads me around to the second set, hidden from the view of anyone who may be walking by. She picks the stall at the very end and pulls me in.

I need no cue from her. The minute the door closes, I turn her around and kiss her. She wraps her arms around my neck and guides me backward to the bench. Her weight forces me to sit, and she's on top straddling me before I know it. The aggressiveness makes me want her even more. Those few weeks gave me plenty of time to play this moment out in my head.

"I missed you," she whispers in my ear, nibbling on it.

"You have no idea." I lean her back, both hands around her shoulders supporting her as I kiss the overflowing cleavage of her breasts.

Our intensity for each other is much stronger than it had been on the couch. It's at a whole other level, but who knows how far she'll let me go this time. I pull her up and close into me, kissing her neck. The faint scent of coconut sunscreen rises as we embrace, sun soaked and familiar, I find myself sinking into it, into her. She loosens the string on her bikini top exposing her breasts to my skin. Our bodies mash into each other so tightly, it's hard to tell which one of us is pulling the other in harder.

I'm anxious. It's all moving so fast, yet the heat of her lips and tongue intertwined with mine feel as comfortable as sliding into a pool of warm water—once you're submerged there's only the water. She wants me as much as I want her and being with her is effortless, like waves pushing against the shore.

Courage places a hand on her breast, and I'm blindsided by how dizzy I am with lust for her. Her skin is warm and soft, and I'm helpless against her charms. I love her, and the words are practically falling out of my mouth as we stare into each other's eyes, but I can't let that out. Not yet.

"Do you bring all your boyfriends here?" I whisper instead.

"Just you." She rubs her lips across mine. "And who said anything about a boyfriend?" She's teasing, I hope.

"I think it's time you agree to see only me," I say, suddenly worried I've misread everything that just happened. Fuck. Is it too soon? Is she like this with everyone?

"You and nobody else?" she continues, stringing me along.

"Yeah." I'm dying inside. Is she considering this as a serious possibility or is she playing with me? Running her fingers through my hair, she grins. Is this because the thought of us being exclusive is so ridiculous she can't believe I even asked?

"Of course I will." Faith laughs. "How could you think I'd say no after these last few weeks with you, Cole? The last thing I want right now is a serious boyfriend, but I can't stop thinking about you."

I was right! There *is* something real between us. She feels it too and she said it—out loud. I want to pull her into me and smother her body with my mouth. She's perfect. She's beautiful. And I have her. It took months, but she's mine and I'm not gonna let anything come between us—ever.

Chapter Ten

A mangled mess
Faith 2026

"Here are your keys back, Faith," Joe says with a cautious face, sliding them across the counter. Joe's been my and Jeremy's mechanic since we moved up here. "And here's what we did today." He leans over the counter toward me looking down at the work order in his denim button-down and scruffy face.

I focus on his mechanic hands as he points his pen to each line explaining, but I'm not really listening. Not interested. My mind wanders to Jeremy who must have stood in this exact spot talking to Joe as he explained what was wrong with *his* car only one week before the accident. That damn engine light…

"…and Faith, I want you to know, I think about Jeremy often." I fade back into the conversation. "I've gone over it in my head more times than I can stomach, wondering if I missed something. I didn't, I'm sure. The engine light was on, and we diagnosed the car properly. He was low on brake fluid, and we filled it."

There's worry in Joe's eyes, what I must be thinking about him and his shop.

"Jeremy didn't mention anything was wrong when he got home. Was there a leak?"

"No. There was nothing to repair or replace." His

voice has a slight shake. "The fluid was low. It's completely normal and requires refilling from time to time. We got under the hood, pulled out the…"

I'm fading out again. He's either over-explaining for himself or mansplaining for me. I have the patience for neither.

"It's all right, Joe." I cut him off. "I never thought to blame you. Even the police think there was nothing mechanically wrong with his car. We've been coming to you for years, and I intend to continue."

But the truth is, the wheels are set in motion in my head yet again. Something's not right about this accident. I knew Jeremy too well. He wouldn't have been driving down the mountain around that curve at such a high speed in the snow intentionally. There had to be something wrong with those brakes. Or…what?

Another car could have been there. Maybe it slid into Jeremy, pushing him off the road, and the driver left the scene in a panic. But the police said they ruled out this scenario. All the damage to the car seemed to be related to the impact with the tree.

"Have a good day, Joe." He looks at ease.

I walk to the car, start it up, and head to the office. My usual car-ruminating commences, and my brain returns to Jeremy. It was a morning like any other. Until it wasn't. I woke up first. Jeremy liked to sleep in. I started the coffee pot and flipped on the news. It was the day after the Paris terrorist attacks. You'd have to be living under a rock in a very deep cave to not know about it, broadcast on every station nonstop. The world was as mesmerized and heartbroken as it was on 9/11, with the exception of the animals that did it. Unlike the 2015 Paris attacks, this time the entire city was decimated, tens of thousands of lives lost. Major targets like the Eiffel Tower, the Louvre, and the Arc de Triomphe lay in massive towering heaps of smoking ruin. Rescue workers poured into the city from everywhere, all captured on the twenty-four-seven news cycle.

Jeremy woke, and we watched together as rescue workers raised flags from different countries atop the mounds of crumbled rubble in a show of solidarity. But then he got himself dressed in workout clothes and came back to the kitchen. He was going to the gym. He always went to the gym. Why couldn't he have stayed home and watched a movie like I suggested? Why didn't I try harder to convince him to stay? He was the kind of person who'd never miss a workout, not a day in his life if he could help it, and that day was no different. Even in the storm, when it would have been safer to stay in, wrapped tight and cozy in a blanket with me, he went anyway. I don't blame him, only wish he hadn't gone. If anything, I blame myself. I should have trusted my gut. Even Finn, our golden lab, stood in his way at the door.

Driving down the mountain from our home in a snowstorm is treacherous. Jeremy had done it a thousand times without issue, but not on this day. On this day, his car left the road and veered into a tree, killing him instantly. The police said the force of the impact was too great for anyone to bear. I demanded to be taken to the scene and against the officer's better judgment they did. Couldn't have stopped me anyway.

It was a mangled mess of metal, leather, plastic, and blood. There wasn't much left of the car. Most of it was strewn along the road. The right side had exploded into pieces when it hit the tree, spinning down the road before coming to rest. This was the violent death he suffered, but the fact that it was immediate brought a small level of comfort, amid the nausea.

And now, all the what-ifs begin to circle and loop again, like the road that took his life. What if he fell asleep behind the wheel? The car would have gained speed on the descent. What if there was something wrong with the tires? If he ran over an object causing a blowout, that could explain it. Or maybe an animal jumped out in front of him, and he swerved too quickly, losing control.

There *is* another workable hypothesis I've been suppressing for fear of inciting a riot inside my head. What if…it wasn't an accident at all? I mean, I was just followed. Could these events be linked?

Damn it, Faith, really? Is there anything to genuinely question about this accident, or am I simply repeating what I did years earlier with *him*? Cole. He's been on my mind again. It would make sense. Or am I confusing the two? Is this the PTSD rearing its ugly head, making me look for something that's simply not there?

The sound of a text message screeches my brain to a halt. Our biggest client, Mrs. Eleni Makris, is coming into the office, and she's not happy.

Chapter Eleven

The tears that want to fall
Faith 2012

Standing at my back door, I fumble with the house keys in the dark. It's after curfew. Shit. Jamming the key into the lock reminds me of the cabana…and Cole's body…and the way it was smashing up against mine. What have I done?

I lean on the door, the latch clicks, and it flies open faster than expected. Everything in my pool bag tumbles to the floor.

"Let me help you, Faith." Dad's in the kitchen. "Where you comin' from?" He bends down to gather my things, never troubled by my lack of respect for curfew.

"The pool."

"Wow, this late? You and this new boy have fun? He must be something special if you spent all day with him."

"I guess." Once everything's picked up, a nauseating quiet settles in the house, cut only by the low drone of *Star Trek* in the living room. Most nights, Mom's out, which is good because she's the enforcer. He's the one who waits up. The only time my mother notices me is when I've done something wrong. Otherwise, I'm mostly invisible to her, and now I'm back in this house with all its heaviness. Its lies and half-truths strung tight through all the rooms as if, over the years, someone had taken very fine twine and laced it up, crisscrossing from walls to ceilings to floors and back again, creating a giant web of marital and familial bullshit. It's hard to take even one step in here without getting tangled in it.

Their marriage is all but over now, while they go through the motions for appearances. My mother's out, doing whatever she God damn well pleases while he waits, mopes, pines, hopes, wishes she'll come back. And she does. He forgives her over and over because he loves her. She can do no wrong, even when she's doing *wrong*. Claims she won't do it again, until she does. But he adores her, absolves her of each transgression every time she comes home, and cleanses her of all immorality, much the same way the welcome mat at our front door cleans a shoe.

"Has she been home at all tonight, Dad?"

"Haven't seen her," he answers, head low. Then he perks up. "Tell me more about your night?" He's good at hiding his emotions. He opens the drawer and takes out a spoon.

"Uh, nice," I say hesitantly. Not sure how I'm feeling about my night.

"So, what about this new guy?" He knows I want to talk. He always knows. At least one of them's interested in my life.

"Cole? He's sweet, and I think I like him a lot. But…" I don't have the words to convey the feeling of wanting to be with Cole *and* wanting to be with every other guy within a ten-foot radius, to my dad.

"Yes, Cole." Dad scoops vanilla fudge ice cream

into a bowl. "Want some?"

"Nah," I say.

"You know, Faith, sometimes boys his age don't know how to be what you need them to be."

"That sounds more like Jeremy, Dad. Cole's completely different, falling all over himself to be what I need. He shouldn't be trying so hard. I don't trust myself, kinda want to be a free agent for now, but the thought of being without him feels awful."

"Sounds like you found yourself a keeper. But remember, the kind of person who will always put you first, doesn't care for himself very much. He'll put his own needs aside for you. He'll need you to watch out for him, protect his heart for him."

Sounds like he's talking about himself. And my mother. I really hope I'm not gonna fall into the trap of repeating what's been modeled for me. Thanks, Leanne, for pointing that out last week.

"Wise words, Dad. I'll keep it in mind." I kiss him on the cheek. "I'm going to bed. You too?"

"Coming up shortly. Night, Buttercup."

I climb the stairs fighting the tightness in my throat and the tears that want to fall—for him. Love can be torturous, from all angles, especially for the ones with the bird's-eye view of a wreckage in the making.

My whole body relaxes every time I enter my cozy, warmly lit room. The bed rests against the wall, draped in soft grays and blues with what some might think is too many plushy pillows leaning on a matching gray fabric headboard. Black dressers sit on a white shag rug surrounded by floor-to-ceiling silky white curtains. The whole room's like a dreamy cloud.

I hoist my pool bag onto the bed, reach in and feel

the wet bikini and towel. I'm instantly transported back to the cabana and Cole's soft lips on my neck, his arms wrapped around me leaning me back, the bikini top falling loosely around my waist—and his desire, more than anything else. It's as subtle as the winds of a cyclone.

After the cabana, we went ahead with dinner and a movie on the lawn as planned, never being more than a few inches from each other. I loved every minute of it, but now that I'm home I immediately start an argument with myself over what I've just done. What is it about him that makes me unable to stop myself? This attraction is too much, too strong, it's unfamiliar ground. But as innocent and starry-eyed as he is, the effect he has on me is electrifying—and disturbing—and irritating.

An exhale leaves my body louder than any other.

I'm committed now. It's creating a bowling ball of stress in my stomach. I'm spoken for, claimed, bound, restricted. And I *chose* it. What was I thinking? Being responsible for someone else's feelings? Pfft. I'll have to alert the others that it's over. And Jeremy? That'll have to be over too. They'll *all* have to be over. I genuinely hope I can do this. He's too sweet to hurt.

****

"Get a room!" Leanne's holler through cupped hands reaches Cole and me across the bonfire circle we've made on the sand of the beach. The town of Seaside is beautiful at night. The heavy summer humidity has finally faded, replaced by a coolness that clings to the shore under an early fall sky. About twenty of us hang out on blankets and low beach chairs surrounded by various-sized white coolers. Bryce is playing a mellow riff on his guitar but stops to join in with the erupting laughter.

I feel myself blush as all eyes turn toward us. Kissing my neck, he whisper-breathes into my ear, "Let's take a walk."

It's been weeks since the cabana, every possible moment spent together with each day further sealing the deal between us. He's captured my heart and replaced my hesitancy with certainty, my reluctance with willingness. We're equally captivated by each other, fitting together perfectly in every way.

We walk along the water's edge letting the cool foam of the waves smooth over our bare feet. The glow of the moon shimmers across the ocean like a lunar spotlight. It illuminates our path to the grouping of dunes we've been to countless times by now. The farther we walk in the soft cold sand, the more the strumming of the guitar gives way to the fizzling of the ocean sprawling across the sand. A misty, seaweed-laden breeze lifts my hair and flows into my nostrils. I love the smell and feel of the beach at night.

Cole takes my hand as we walk, recounting his childhood with his mother in this town.

He's shared little pieces of his past with me, but now more is coming out. Being back here is causing an avalanche of boulder-sized memories to fall on him. All the different streets he lived on because they had to keep moving, the uncertainty of when his next meal would be, the fear when he was left alone for hours and sometimes days on end.

"It must have been lonely for you," I say.

His head drops, and he squeezes my hand tighter.

He told of an incident involving his mother, a

shovel, and a trip to the emergency room for him and other events that would make anyone's head spin and heart break. I imagine him as a little neglected and abused boy and want to go back in time, scoop him up, and hold him in my arms. This explains so much about him—his intensity, insecurity, the up and down moods I'm beginning to notice. Even his worries, when there's nothing to worry about. It's clear when he's with me, he finally feels safe, secure, and cared for. He's happy. Losing me now is not an option. I want to be the lighthouse in the storm, a safe place for him, as he is for me.

Our feet sink into the sand as we make our way up and over the dunes, arriving at our spot. It's hidden and private. I sense the pain he's been carrying transform into something else, as if going from a state of starvation to insatiable hunger—for me. *I* can be the one to fill that bottomless never-ending need for connection inside him. I can create and build the bonding Leanne said he did not receive as a child. It's easy when the combination of his seductive eyes and smoldering grin are so intoxicating. Every time he looks at me like this, parts of me tingle with anticipation. I crave the feeling of his hands on me.

Cole gives me one side of the blanket. We lift it up like a parachute. As soon as the air has spread and straightened it, the blanket sails down onto the sand, and I'm on my back with him on top. Not sure how it happened so quickly, and I don't care. He's kissing me again in that urgent, searching way as if I might give him back whatever he is missing. We're all skin and tongue and breath. I wrap my parted legs around him, and he is no longer afraid to put his full weight on me as he had once been.

"You're everything to me, Faith. I need you to know that."

"I do know."

His hands are wrapped in my hair, kissing me softly. A calm has come over him. "Do you? I can never get enough, and I don't know what I'd do without you."

Somewhere in the back of my mind, a warning flickers that I might want to be worried about that. But I disregard it.

He pauses between kisses, gazing at me, smoothing out my hair. Our connection is way beyond physical, so much so, I can feel the words in his head waiting to pour out.

"Say it, Cole," I whisper.

And without a second's hesitation he reaches straight into my heart and tattoos the words on my soul. "I love you, Faith. I've loved you from the first minute I saw you."

"I love you too, Cole. I can't imagine a world where we're not together."

And at the moment I mean it. I mean every word.

Chapter Twelve

A temporary fixture
Cole 2012

"I'm in love with her. I thought I was in love when I first saw her, but that's nothing compared to this. Now, we're in love together, and it's completely different. It's real. Not in my imagination. This is so right. We're perfect together and—"

Bryce interrupts the bullet train of thoughts in my head. "Man, you got it bad for this girl. Maybe you should consider slowing it down a bit?"

We're jogging off the football field in our gear, and I stop dead in my tracks at his comment. He stops also, turning toward me while a sea of players pivot around both sides of us like a marching band. I look at him in disbelief and offense, which he picks up on.

"I'm happy for you, Cole. I'm just saying…you sure it's mutual?"

"Words came right out of her mouth. Even school doesn't suck as much. I was feeling invisible like, transparent sometimes, but…she's my missing piece."

We head to the locker room where the rest of the team, at various levels of undress, begin singing "Happy Birthday" to me. There is a single chocolate-frosted cupcake on the bench in front of my locker. "Did you know about this?" I ask Bryce.

"Of course. Happy birthday, man. Let's celebrate this weekend." He slaps me on the back. "You know, word has gotten out that you're dating a senior. Your status has formally been elevated to stud. Congrats, man."

"You know who's not impressed?" I open my locker and place the cupcake on the top shelf. "Jeremy. She's always been his. Now the power has shifted, but I don't know if she's really over him. Feel like I could lose her back to him in an instant even though she's promising me it won't happen. I don't trust that asshole. We stare each other down in the halls. I could literally rip his head off."

Bryce is stripping down. "I'm no fan of Jeremy, but dude, you're starting to sound the way you did a few years ago when we first met. You were this close to winning yourself a spot in juvie until the judge took pity on you."

"That was different. My mom's boyfriend was drunk and being a dick. He deserved it. Jeremy's a totally different kind of dick, an intentional, in your face, 'I'm better than you' dick. And honestly, he deserves it more."

"It's not worth it, man. Things are good. She's with you now. She moved into your locker, right?"

"Yep, it feels like we're living together." I throw my clothes into a turf-stained pile and wrap a towel around myself.

"You seeing her tonight?"

"We're going to the Lighthouse. I've never been there and haven't met all her friends yet."

"I've heard of it. Aren't her friends all older than you? You have ID?"

"Nah, don't need it."

"Sounds like you're in, dude."

"I'd invite you, but I wanna get a pulse on this group first."

"Sure, buddy. Have fun and have a drink for me. Don't do anything I would."

****

"I'll be there. Thanks for the invite!" I promise Steve Harris on my way out the door of the Lighthouse.

"We're holding you to it, Cole," Sam Moore shouts from the bar, pointing at me with both hands.

"They like you," Faith assures, taking my hand as we walk through the parking lot.

I think the night was a success. I bonded the most with Steve, but they all agreed I should come to a party they're having next weekend. They're a good bunch of guys and seem to have accepted me into their circle as if I'd always been there. Not sure if it's because of Faith or if I've genuinely earned my spot, but I'll take it. Everything's falling into place.

"So, what'd you think?" she asks as we drive out of the lot.

"I think I won them over."

"No!" She laughs. "Of course they like *you*, but do you like *them*?"

I didn't know what might happen to our relationship if I didn't fit in with these guys. And yet, she never doubted me, not for a second. Her unshakable belief in me is like an injection of self-confidence through a syringe straight into my veins.

"They're cool. Glad you brought me tonight." She told me she dated some of them. I'm dying to know which ones but don't want to seem too eager. Definitely got a strange vibe from some of the guys tonight, like I'm only a temporary fixture. Like I'm not good enough for her. Maybe I'm not. Faith has had her whole life planned out since she was in seventh grade, sets goals, works toward them, and crushes them. I'm nothing like that, have no idea where I'm headed. I only know I want to be with her.

"I'm so glad, Cole. They've been like big brothers to me and the girls, always watching and protecting us."

Except the ones that want to get in your pants, but I don't say that out loud. It would be rude.

She parks in front of my house and opens her mouth to say something, then stops. The air in the car suddenly feels thick. Something isn't right. Did I miss it? Does she have something to tell me? I'm starting to feel like I don't know her at all. Maybe I've been wrong about us. Have I misread everything? Maybe this thing between us is not as special as I thought. What is she even doing with me?

Chapter Thirteen

Doesn't actually exist on paper
Faith 2026

The offices of the Athena Detective Agency are located on the second floor of the prestigious Nassau Corporate Center, a ten-story sky-blue glass building with a soaring atrium lobby. The building is home to some of the largest corporations, medical companies, attorneys, and accountants on the island. My partner Brooke and I chose this place seven years ago. A selling point for us was the multiple entrances/exits inside the building and as well as the stairways leading to an underground and very secure parking garage.

But it wasn't until after we customized the place that we could truly call it home. This included renting the space on both sides of us, installing cameras, and a little construction work to connect it all. Labeling those additional office doors with other business nameplates was a must. Only three of us know the true size and escape routes of our office. To everyone else, the Athena Detective Agency has one set of glass doors through which to come and go.

"How did parent-teacher night go?" I ask Sarah, our receptionist, as I pass through the small waiting room we've designated as the lounge. She's one of the magicians that turn our chaotic, messy field work into tidy intelligible reports.

"How'd you remember that, Faith? I mentioned it weeks ago. Charlie's failing math, but he loves his teacher so…silver lining."

The personal circumstances preceding a visit to our office are always less than ideal. We know how stressful it can be to walk through our doors, so our lounge has been specifically designed to lower anxiety and promote tranquility with our plush couches, warm lighting, and Zen fountain. The mini fridge is stocked with waters, juices, and sodas, or clients can choose from our coffee and tea nook. What else would you expect from two female PIs?

"A great teacher makes all the difference," I say, as Sarah buzzes me in through the second door, giving entrance to a wide hallway. It leads to the conference room, my personal office, Brooke's office, and one large space for the agents we call the War Room. They come in to pick up assignments, do their prep work before heading out, and decompress between cases. It's also used for debriefing with either myself or Brooke. They don't know it, but we've decorated their workspace for serenity as well. Jury's still out on whether it's working.

I peek my head into Brooke's office on my way to my own. "'Sup? Is Makris here yet?"

"Any minute," she responds without lifting her eyes from her laptop, typing at a rate of roughly a thousand words a minute.

"Do we know what this is about?" I check my watch.

"Maybe she's bringing a fruit basket, but I doubt it."

Mrs. Makris has been a client for years, but not in the way one might think. She pays us for self-surveillance, meaning we are contracted to watch *her*. She's been cheating on her husband for at least ten years with a man who is cheating on his wife. She desperately wants to spend the rest of her life with her boyfriend, but the damn guy won't leave his wife. Mrs. Makris took matters into her own hands, hired us to follow her with the boyfriend, record everything, and I mean *everything*, then hand deliver it all to the boyfriend's wife and her own husband, forcing divorces. Insane in the membrane, if you ask me.

Unfortunately the boyfriend's wife's two goon brothers were there for the delivery. A high-speed chase ensued through the streets of Jersey before we finally lost them. Shouldn't Makris and her boyfriend be living happily ever after by now?

I head to my office, sit in front of my laptop, and finish the Englehoffer report while we wait. Client's attorney needs it asap so he can get the ball rolling on obtaining a warrant for a search and seizure of everything in Alex's warehouse. Turns out none of it came through customs.

Even with everything piling up on my desk, the faint scent of lemongrass aromatherapy lingers. It's nice. Sarah buzzes my desk phone. Andy's on line two, something about a meat truck.

"Are you calling in for my lunch order, Andy?" I'm trying to defuse him. He tends to get a bit panicky in the field.

"No," he says, like he thought I was serious. "I'm on Rizzoli in Brooklyn. Followed him to the docks. He ditched his car, and now he's driving a meat truck. I'm following him to Jersey, I think."

"A meat truck?"

"Yeah, like those big, refrigerated ones."

"Labeled?" I lean back in my chair.

"Nope, clean."

"Anyone with him?" I question.

"Not yet. But what the fuck?"

"Beats me. This is what it's all about, you're doing great. Got your EZ Pass?" I ask.

"Yep."

"You good to stay on him?"

"Doing my best," Andy says.

"Call in if you need anything and keep me posted."

All my field agents have been instructed to keep their GPS on, both phone and car, so we can see where they are at all times. It gives us, and them, peace of mind, like they're not entirely on their own out there. The bonus is we know they're not billing us for hours they're not actually working. I normally keep close tabs on the newbies, but I've been giving Andy a longer leash, otherwise I would have already known he was headed to Jersey.

On the other hand, my black ops source, Mr. X, is impossible to find. Mr. X is actually a female former black operator for the military. Which branch is still a mystery to me, but I'm fine with it because the hard-to-get info she provides is always accurate, timely, and actionable. Mr. X is buried deep under so many layers of government secrecy, security clearances, and plausibly deniable programs, she doesn't actually exist on paper. Or so she says. Ironically, I haven't been able to verify this, lending weight to its credibility.

In actuality, there's no such thing as a black op or a

black op agent. It's a catchphrase with no real meaning other than an operator or operation that's secret, clandestine, and/or covert. The black ops Hollywood tries to depict doesn't exist. The Mafia doesn't exist either.

That being said, Mr. X is the first person who comes to mind when I think about this letter writer and his potential ill intent. Part of me is having fun with this cute little mystery, enjoying the memories of the timeframe he references, but another part of me is on high alert. While this could all be in good fun, I don't take my personal safety lightly, and Mr. X has the tools to help me focus on the objective rather than the subjective in the form of fingerprint and DNA testing on the letter and its envelope.

Since there's no sample to match against, I'll only get a hit on people already in the system but that system has been greatly enhanced in recent years, extending beyond the criminal element to anyone who's ever applied for a professional license or position requiring a background investigation. Amongst the alphabet soup of the NCIC, IAFIS, RISC, N-DEX and NGI, to name a few, one has their pick of data points and biometrics.

I reach out to Mr. X through the agreed-upon channels.

"What'da ya got?" It's her standard greeting.

"A letter and the envelope it came in." I pull on the cow-licky strands of hair I sense are out of place.

"Bag it and send it."

"You still in New York? I'll deliver it," I suggest.

"Nope, have to keep moving and cultivating new sources for you people. You're insatiable." She laughs. "What's the priority level on this?"

"It's personal."

"Then it's of the highest," she says. "Toodles."

All calls with Mr. X are intentionally quick. Despite this, we've managed to build a solid rapport over the years, and I'm touched she's prioritized my safety by moving me to the front of her line. I'm also thrilled with preliminary investigatory excitement. This little cat-and-mouse game is underway.

Brooke knocks on the wall. Client is here. I make a quick note for myself and head to the conference room. She and Mrs. Makris are already seated at the oval high-shine table that spans the room. A small bonsai tree sits in the middle of the table alongside a tray containing water, paper cups, napkins, and stirrers. The walls are lined with tall potted plants. At the far end is a large screen TV connected to a variety of devices that can play any type of recording.

"That son of a bitch is working it out with her," Makris snarls.

"Come again?" Brooke squints.

"My boyfriend, Nikos. That coward begged his wife to forgive him and take him back. Again!" She slams her hand on the table. "After *all* that! We need to put our heads together and come up with something. What do you suggest?" She leans down, pulling out a legal pad and pen from her bag.

My eyes meet Brooke's across the table. It's gonna be a long morning.

Chapter Fourteen

Partnered with him on a crime spree
Faith 2012

The brightness in Cole's eyes has dimmed. What started as a great night at the Lighthouse has taken a turn. He knows I dated a few of these guys, and he's questioning his place with me. He doesn't need to say it. I can feel it, which is weird.

I'm not ashamed of my past and definitely don't want any secrets between us, but he looks distressed, wounded even. I feel it in my bones. Love and protectiveness have taken over. Those days are behind me now. A new ingredient has been added, Cole, and I've morphed once again. This time, in a good way. I can't have him upset because of me. All I can do now is help him through the damage and reassure him that all is well. The car is no place for it.

"Can I come in so we can talk?"

"Of course," he says, opening the car door.

We tiptoe through his front door. It's still. His aunt and uncle are probably asleep. As we make our way down the basement steps to his room, he's quieter than usual. I feel the heaviness in his heart settle into mine as I try to find the words he needs to hear. Cole sits on the edge of the bed, reaches back to light a candle, and flips on the music as usual. When he turns back, I'm standing in front of him, placing my arms around his neck. I know exactly what he needs—to hear nothing about us has changed.

Silently, he returns the hug pulling me in even tighter. I melt at his need to want me close, like I'm an essential element to his existence. Running my fingers through his thick dark hair, I massage his scalp with my nails as I tilt his face up toward mine.

"I hope meeting these guys doesn't change anything between us. I have a past and never want anyone to surprise you with anything about me. After Jeremy, I went a little crazy, but that's all done now. I hope you know that."

"It's hard to think about, you with Jeremy and you with these others. For me, it's only you. Jeremy still wants you. I know he does, and I'm worried you won't be able to resist him if he tries. He was your first love. You'll never feel that way about anyone else again, not even me. Are you sure it's over?"

"I'm with you now and only you," I assure, drawing him in and placing my lips on his. "I don't want anyone else."

"I love you." He kisses me.

"I love you too." But somehow, I know this is not enough.

He gently pulls me onto the bed. We've spent many nights together here, almost naked, kissing, caressing, and playing with each other. He's ready, and so am I. Not to have sex, but to make love. These months with him have changed me. His hand and heart have sculpted me into something new again, from a block of stone into a deeply caring, feeling, human work of art. Sex was just something fun to do, lacking any true emotion or connection. But with Cole, it's all emotion and connection. And I want it all the time, with him. Only him.

He always finds a new way to take my clothes off. It makes each time seem like the first. I feel both in control of him and yet out of control because of him every time. His level of desire is always the same—intense, all-consuming and overwhelming—especially tonight. But something's different. There's desperation mixed in with lust, fear almost. He kisses me in that wildly passionate way he does, but unlike the other times when it's felt like he's looking for something inside me, tonight it's as though he may never find it.

I close my eyes, inhaling his breath and his rainy-berry scent. "There's no one like you, Cole, and there never will be anyone better for me."

His gaze locks onto mine. The side of his lip curls and his eyes are devilishly happy, as if I've partnered with him on a crime spree that'll take us to hell and back.

I mirror the same back and continue, "And there's nowhere I'd rather be, than right here with you."

He kisses my mouth, then trails his lips down my neck and to my breasts as he flicks open the button of my jeans. The days of doing one thing at a time are over; he's mastered the sexual multitask. Easing my jeans and panties off, he kisses his way down between my legs, staying there in what's become one of his favorite pastimes, bringing me to a marathon of orgasms. He isn't happy with anything less.

Once his clothes are off, I pull him down directly on top of me, something we've avoided while we were naked, until now. I feel Cole inhale long and exhale deep, hugging me as our bodies come together for the first time in this position fully naked. He understands what I'm telling him, kissing me longer, deeper and slower than usual. My legs spread naturally inviting him in closer.

"I want to feel you inside me," I say, but he's already halfway there, taking my breath away.

He is gentle and rough and sweet and the thought of this moment staying with him for the rest of his life almost brings me to tears. Now I understand what he meant when he said I'll never have another Jeremy and he'll never have another me. These are snapshots in time that can never be undone. Cole wanted to be my Jeremy so we could have shared this together, and in this moment, I wish he'd been my Jeremy too. And this elicits an altogether different feeling, one in which I have no power to change.

We move together as if this is the thousandth time, not the first. His arms tighten around me, and I feel him climax.

"You're beautiful," he whispers, studying my face anew.

"You couldn't have made that any more perfect if you tried, Cole."

It was innocent and hot and pure and so much more than it's ever been with anyone else. Exactly how I expected. And now, I can never go back to anything less.

Chapter Fifteen

I know what he's doing
Cole 2013

Dear Faith,
The other day you asked me why I love you, and I couldn't answer. I'm sorry. I've been thinking about it. It's like I said tonight (last night by the time you get this), we were two stars in different galaxies who were drawn together. At least they were supposed to, they were supposed to meet in a neutral galaxy where everything was new to both of them. But instead, I met you in yours so everything is new to me and to you it's the same, just with a new star, me. So without you, I'm totally lost. I think you know what I mean. But that's not why I love you. It's because you're you and because of everything about you, your personality, your awesome sense of humor and your looks, especially your looks. What I like best is when you smile. It makes me feel so happy inside, and if what I feel isn't love, then love doesn't exist because nothing on this earth could make me happier than you. Before we met, I felt like if I disappeared no one would notice. But you filled the empty spot and gave my life meaning. So believe me when I say I love you and don't ever forget it.
This is with all my love,
Cole

PS—Steve's throwing a party this weekend. Wanna be my date?

I intricately fold my note to Faith and use a rubber band to hang it in our locker where she'll see it when she stops by between the third and fourth period, then attach a red rose to it. Everything's perfect. Hours later, we're at the party.

"Dance with me." Faith pulls me onto the dance floor of the Lighthouse and wraps her arms around my neck as mine fall naturally to her tiny waist. She looks hot as hell in the off-the-shoulder red dress she's wearing. And she's mine.

"Are you having fun?" she asks.

"I am, but I'm really looking forward to what I have planned for you later."

The place is packed tight with tons of people we know. Faith led me onto a section of the dance floor far away from Jeremy and his new girlfriend, yet somehow, they've ended up dancing right next to us. My eyes are on him. Whether this is intentional or not, I don't like him being so close to her.

"Hey," Faith says, trying to defuse this potential landmine and get my attention back on her.

"Hmmm?" It's all I can manage. I'm still focused on him.

"Did you take one of those pills tonight?" she asks.

They've been handed out like breath mints. I might have, but I'm not telling her that.

"Cole!" she snaps. I look down at her. "Imagine if I broke up with you."

"What?" Hope I heard her wrong over the mind-numbing music.

"Ah, now you're back." She continues, "Imagine

how heartbroken you'd be."

"Shit, are you…" I freeze.

"No, dumbass. This is a hypothetical scenario, listen. I break up with you and you're heartbroken. Now imagine you meet another girl who's so special, so spectacular, she sweeps you off your inconsolable feet and makes you forget all about me."

"Impossible!" I laugh.

"Well, it's what you've done for me." She kisses me, not caring who's looking.

Faith always knows exactly what to say. She's created a safe haven for me, for us—our own little bubble nothing can penetrate, and there's no better feeling in the world. I'm her ride or die, and she's mine. I have no doubt about her feelings for me at this moment. It's Jeremy who's got my blood boiling. Again. But for the sake of her and our night, I won't let it ruin us.

I caught them talking last week in the gym on my way to sixth period. I saw Faith, shaking her head at him with the skin crinkling between her eyes and him, with an urgent expression taking hold of her hand, like he was trying to convince her of something. I asked her about it later when she came over, said it was nothing and changed the subject. I know what he's doing. He's trying to get her back. Whether he wants her as his girlfriend again or only in his bed, I'm done. Not gonna lose her. Definitely not gonna let him draw her in and hurt her again. I'll keep my cool right now for her sake, but enough is enough. One way or another, this ends tonight.

Chapter Sixteen

Always the wrong time
Faith 2026

Driving to the foot of my driveway with Mrs. Eleni Markis' crazy conference room voice still echoing in my head, I get out to check the mail. It takes effort to leave work at work, and this lady and her fury are hard to shake. I peer into the mailbox. It's filled with the usual grocery store flyers, solicitations, bills, and the addition of one crisp white envelope with the same neat blue handwriting. My heart flutters, wanting to open it standing right here at the curb. I also don't want to be so interested and decide to savor this delightful little mystery a bit longer, at least until I get into the house.

Once in the garage, I carry my bag, case files, and mail inside with the mystery envelope on top. Will there be a return address on the other side this time? *You can wait until you get inside to look, can't you?* But what if there is one? The identity of the letter writer would be revealed right now. Can't stand the suspense. I turn it over. Nothing. Again. I'm disappointed, feeling a little hostile. Combative even. Who the fuck does this guy think he is?

Tossing my keys into the candy dish, my eyes meet a chocolate but decide against it. By the time I reach the kitchen, the envelope gets flung onto the counter with the rest of the mail. The best course of action is to act like it's not even there, walk away, and put some laundry in the washer.

What could possibly come from this anyway? Even if I find out who this is, end up finding them at all attractive, and it grows into something…so what? Am I even capable of having feelings for anyone at this point? Haven't I already had it all? The great first love, then the once-in-a-lifetime love, only to be lucky enough to have my first love back? What am I even thinking?

The house phone interrupts my self-analysis. I return to the kitchen, giving the envelope a dirty look as I pass it.

"Hey there, lady, long time no talk!" It's Leanne.

"Long time? I spoke to you two days ago. If that wasn't you, then I bored some complete stranger with the details of my latest work assignment." I cave and unwrap a peanut butter cup.

"Haven't the slightest idea what you're talking about. In twenty-something years, I have yet to have a boring conversation with you." Leanne sounds like she's in the car.

"Well, in that case, let me keep our streak going. I received a letter from someone, and it's unsigned."

"Unsigned? Ooh, how mysteriously delicious! Spill." We're instantly transported back to high school.

"It started out as a condolence letter telling me how sorry they were for my loss and not being there for the funeral, but then it kinda changed, saying they'd always been smitten with me, even if I didn't realize it."

"Get out!" Yep, still back in high school. "But that could be anyone, Faith. You dated a lot."

"They said they would write again and they did. The next letter is sitting on my counter right now."

"What does it say?" Leanne gushes.

"Haven't opened it yet." The peanut-buttery chocolate melts in my mouth.

"What? Why not? Open it now, while I'm on the phone."

"No!"

"Come on!" she begs.

"I'm not ready to read it."

"You're right, sorry." Leanne's pace slows. "In the excitement I forgot. It hasn't been very long."

"I'll let you know what it says when I do read it. I've been thinking back to who it could be. One person who stands out is Steve. He's the only one something should have happened with back then, but didn't. It was always the wrong time."

"I remember. You two had great chemistry, but you were always with other people and when one was attached, the other wasn't. Interesting theory."

"Or maybe Bryce Henderson. I don't know. It really could be anyone, Leanne." Finn swaggers in through the doggie door, happy to see me.

"What are you doing Saturday night?" Leanne knows there's a very good chance I will not be doing anything. It's become the new routine on the weekends, nothing, at home alone. Leanne does her best to fill the void.

"Thought I'd reorganize the pantry," I say. "It's a mess and I've been putting it—"

"*No bueno*. You can do that another time. You're coming over here. I'm having a dinner party."

"Ooh, sounds fun." Not really. "Who's coming?"

"Nice try. You know I enjoy surprising my guests with who their dining companions will be. You'll have to wait and see."

Leanne has a way of making things fun. Even when we were young, she had a knack for bringing different groups of people together who clicked. Now, I find being around people and couples difficult. It'll pass, but I'm not even sure I want to go.

I linger at the counter after hanging up, my eyes falling to the envelope again, still sitting where it was tossed. A companion might not be such a bad thing. Someone to go to events like this with might be nice. Nothing serious of course. I have no interest in that, but having someone around to have good conversations with might not be so bad.

I shake my head and pick up the envelope again, cross-examining it with my eyes. *All right, fine!*

Chapter Seventeen

All sorts of ugly
Faith 2013

Dear Faith,

How's your day been? I've been thinking about you, about us, and this all feels like some crazy whirlwind I can't explain. I need you to know what you mean to me. First, I love you—but it's more than that. When I look at you, I see a part of me, a pretty big chunk you're holding because I've given it to you. The part I want you to have and never give back. You couldn't, even if you tried.

You know what else I see? Everything. Everything I've ever wanted and could ever want in the future. If we're together, we can overcome anything. I want you to trust it. Trust me. I'll never let anything hurt you. We're at the very beginning of something eternal. And I will protect that, protect us. I would take a bullet to keep you safe.

Love,
Cole

"His notes to you are so romantic." Leanne presses the loose-leaf paper to her heart. "He writes them every day?"

"Pretty much." We're at my house making cupcakes.

"You're lucky. Evan's such an ass. I should have never given him a third chance. One minute he wants to marry me as soon as we graduate, and the next, he doesn't know I'm alive."

Leanne has a broken heart again, and this is what we do when one of us is devastated—bake. I look at her with gentle eyes encouraging her to talk, but she picks up on it.

"No, I'm done analyzing Evan and me. Let's talk about you two."

"Oh God, here we go." I roll my eyes and hand her the flour and measuring cups while I get the mixing bowl and pans.

"Yes, Faith. Here we go again. Who else is better qualified than me? I passed the AP Psychology exam with the highest score."

"So proud of you for that! At this rate, you'll have your PhD and be in private practice before your twenty-first birthday. What temperature does it say I should set the oven to?"

"Three fifty. But in the meantime, let me practice on you two. What do we know so far?" Leanne's expression changes to that of a blank-faced seasoned therapist. "Cole was neglected and abused as a child, so much so he was taken from the custody of his mom and placed with his aunt and uncle. Do you have any idea what that does to a child? Do you know what you're dealing with?"

"I'm starting to. He was so laser-focused on winning me over. He can be very intense. It sucks me right in, like I'm drowning in him, although mostly in a good way. But he got attached so quickly. He absolutely hates being away from me, and he can't stand being alone."

"It's childhood trauma, Faith. The effects can last a lifetime. It's so overlooked. We are the most impressionable during our first seven years. Early experiences set up the foundation for all our adult relations. If our core needs are not met, the result is neediness, attachment trauma, and all sorts of ugly. Hand me that bowl."

It's amazing how she can spew all this jargony lingo while measuring and not miss a beat.

"He's so intense about everything, including me, and I love it. I really do, being adored like this. It's like we've bonded into one person, but it can be too much at times. Like he's a fire ripping through a house, and I'm the gasoline. Throw some extra chocolate chips in there."

Leanne dumps the whole bag in.

"It's like I'm his whole world. You know what he said when I asked him what he wanted to be when he grew up?" I stop stirring in the chips and look at her. "A pirate! That's what he said. Hadn't given it much thought. He has no goals, no aspirations, he's not working toward building his future. He's the exact opposite of me."

"Okay, yes, but he's only seventeen, Faith. You've been an ambitious thirty-year-old on steroids since you were twelve, always knew you wanted to be an investigator. Like you're on a crusade to right all the injustices in the world and reveal hidden truths. The same truths that were kept from you growing up."

"There you go again." I return to stirring. "Look, it's not a deal-breaker, at least not yet, but what is our future going to look like if he's so lackadaisical?"

"Ooh, SAT word." Leanne pours the batter. "I'm only pointing out not everyone's like you."

"You are."

She shrugs. "Well, he's got football."

"I'd just like to be with someone who has a plan, an aspiration independent of me, something he wants for himself."

Leanne goes into full psychologist mode in a textbook manner. "You know, they've mapped the brain through imaging and found that love is like an addiction. The same neurochemicals get released when we're in love as when we're on drugs. And a new romance creates a huge neurochemical rush making us obsessive and dependent. The high we get from it makes us crave more and more of the person. Add that together with his attachment trauma, and this letter makes sense; in his eyes, there is no *him* separate from *you*. And he'll do anything to protect it. It can lead to some real dysfunction down the line for you two."

"This is either really romantic or terrifying."

"Yeah, if you think being anxious, depressed, and paranoid is romantic."

"Why does he need to fit into some diagnostic category?" I ask. "Why does there have to be something wrong with him? By that standard, most of the people we know are mentally ill. Can't he just be in love?" I slide the pan into the oven.

"I've diagnosed Evan as a raging narcissist with psychotic tendencies if that makes you feel any better."

"It does." We both laugh.

After several hours of relationship analysis, I insist Leanne take home half the leftover cupcakes. She's being overly protective of me. I love her for it, but Cole and I are fine. No, great actually. She's right about his lack of ambition, probably normal. I suppose it's natural to want him to be more like me. I won't let it ruin us. He's happy, and I want him to stay that way just as much as he wants the same for me.

Jeremy, on the other hand, has been doing everything he can to charm me back into his bed. He's not taken kindly to my repeated rejections. On the contrary, they've strengthened his resolve, but I have no intention of it. Since Cole and I consummated the relationship, our bond is stronger than ever. He's become more skilled in the love department, surpassing Jeremy by leaps and bounds. We've had a lot of practice because we've fallen into an almost nightly routine.

It starts with a phone call from Cole. I drive over and park down the block from his house, walking down the path on the side of Leanne's house, and slipping through the line of tall bushes separating their homes. That brings me directly to his basement window, which is incidentally below this aunt and uncle's bedroom window, so stealth is key. Cole will take the screen out of the window way ahead of time, so it doesn't make any noise and I don't have to wait out there too long and risk being caught. He drapes a heavy blanket over the ledge, so I don't scrape myself.

We determined climbing in feet first is best. Headfirst was a disaster almost ending with a cracked skull and a trip to the ER. Cole holds my legs, guiding me in, and catches me on the way down. I end up exactly where I want to be—in his arms. We stuff the window with as many blankets as needed to keep the weather and bugs out.

I've been sneaking into his house via that window almost every night for months. We both decided his basement was the best place for these rendezvous. Sliding in quietly is hard, but the bigger challenge by far is keeping the volume down during sex. Over time, Cole has completely mastered my body. He knows how to bring me right to the edge over and over, making the eventual climaxes more intense. He still loves giving me a marathon of orgasms before I'm allowed to do anything to him and even after we collapse into each other in exhaustion for a short nap, it doesn't last long. We start all over again.

Eventually Cole helps me put my clothes back on and, using his clasped hands as a ladder for me to step into, hoists me up and out the window so I can sneak back to my car and into my own home before anyone wakes up. No one at my house notices anymore. Having distracted parents in an unhealthy relationship helps.

Tonight, winter is showing its true colors. The window frame feels colder than ice as I slide down the ledge into Cole's arms. We haven't seen each other since the party the other night, but something's not right. I feel the tension in his body instantly.

"What's wrong?" My face scrunches.

"You don't know?" He studies my eyes.

"Don't know what?" I shake my head. It feels like he's accusing me of lying.

"Come on, Faith. Someone must have told you. Did you go visit him?"

"Visit who? What are you talking about?" He *does* think I'm lying.

"Jeremy. He was attacked on his way home from the party. He's in the hospital."

Chapter Eighteen

Remarkably high walls
Cole 2013

"Faith, did you hear what I said?" Her expression is blank. I wait for my words to connect with her brain.

"What? He's where? Why, what happened?" Now she's getting it and may be a little too concerned.

"I don't have those answers. I only heard it may have been a carjacking type of thing."

"Is he okay?" Her eyes start to fill.

"Yeah, nothing too serious, maybe a concussion. They wanted to watch him overnight."

She sits on the corner of my bed with her face in her hands. I hate to see her upset, but I also have no tolerance for people who cause pain to others. Jeremy got what he deserved. He hurt her. It was karma. I've never seen her cry before and sit beside her, rub her back, and try to be supportive but it's not easy.

"I'm not crying about Jeremy."

"Whatever it is, you can tell me. Even if it is about him."

"He left…" is all she gets out between sobs.

"Who left?"

"My dad. Moved out today. And now this."

Shit. I wrap my arms around her, but it won't be enough. The divorce is taking its toll on her. She told me all about her mother's bullshit unapologetic ways and her heartbroken dad who can't let go. I've been around her family enough to know what's going on. It's clear how much her dad loves her, but I'm not sure it's enough to make up for the damage her mom has done.

Faith's been living in the war zone for a long time. She doesn't like to talk about it, but it's eating her up. She's a combination of both of them. Before we met, she was like her mom, self-centered with little to no emotion. Once we got together, I could see that fading and her *dad* side coming out, the warm caring part, capable of being vulnerable and letting me in. In the back of my mind, I worry she could switch sides again at any time.

"I hate her," she manages to say through tears, "and now I'm stuck with her."

I hug Faith tighter, but she's inconsolable. It's killing me to see her like this. At the same time, I feel honored she's sharing it with me. She still has some remarkably high walls built around her. I understand how they came to be because mine are built on the same unsteady, broken, flawed ground. And now I sound like Leanne.

"What can I do, Faith?" I kiss her forehead.

"Exactly what you're doing now."

"I'm always here for you, and I always will be. You know that, right?"

"Yeah, and I love you for it."

Chapter Nineteen

Some alternative universe
Faith 2026

I'm almost feeling resentment toward these little white envelopes and the person penning them. Nevertheless, I stand in my kitchen and open the second one as delicately as I opened the first. Everything about it is the same, its stark whiteness, the texture on my fingers, the sound of it tearing. Even the perfect half fold of the letter. Except this time, there are two sheets inside. I close my eyes and visualize myself sitting cross-legged in meditation, thumbs touching middle fingers, directly in the center of a seesaw keeping it perfectly level between irritation on the one side and excitement on the other.

Dear Faith,

I hope the passage of time is helping you heal from this tragedy. I find myself wondering how you are and felt it necessary to write again. They say time heals all wounds, but I'm not entirely sure this is true. Being separated from someone you love feels like a thousand knives entering your heart, penetrating through to your soul.

There seems to be no end in sight, but then, over time, the immensity of the loss diminishes enough to let you feel like you can breathe again without the heaviness in the space where your heart used to be. What's left is a dull aching pain that never lets up and never lets you feel entirely free of it again. Unless, you're one of those rare and fortunate beings who is granted a miracle.

I sometimes envision myself helping you through this. Whether it be years ago or now, I have always felt and still feel the need to be there for you. Remembering those few times you felt safe enough to open up with me back then causes me to believe an association between us now could be something beneficial for you too. Although I can't reveal myself to you yet, I would like to in the future.

I don't know how you felt about receiving my first letter, and I'm equally concerned about how you're receiving this one. Please consider what I've suggested, however implausible it may seem to you now.

Until next time…

Now wait…there's something very familiar here, but I can't quite get it. The tone? Yes, it's the tone. That's what I'm connecting with, beyond the words. Still, its content is leaving me more confused than ever.

Years ago? How many? I'm pretty sure he means before I was married. I can work with that, but again I'm stuck with high school and college friends, people I worked with, people who could have liked me in high school and college I may not have known about. This category has so many people in it, I'm not sure I can narrow it down.

And he was "there for me"? I "opened up to him"? I didn't do that very often with anyone. And who knows what kind of crap may have flown out of my mouth if I was drinking.

And the way he describes what it feels like being ripped from someone you love—he's clearly experienced it in the same way I have. His descriptions, those words, the imagery, is so clear in fact, it brings me right back to how I felt about…

No. It *can't* be him. Maybe if this were some alternative universe, yes. But this person is clearly someone I can relate to, someone who's known the depths of such a love.

Steve comes to mind again. And I *did* open up to him, many times in fact, before and after…Cole. Fine, I'll let myself *think* his name. I did open up and confide in Steve before Cole came into the picture, crashing into my life like a tornado, sweeping up everything in its path, throwing it in all directions. Steve was one of Cole's closest friends. He could fit.

It could also be Bryce, another one of Cole's closest friends. Why does it keep coming back to Cole? After the incident, Bryce and I spent a lot of time together. We were two heartbroken souls with the same regrets trying to make our way through them. Yes, he "was there for me" and yes, I did "open up" to him too. Nothing romantic ever happened. Maybe he wanted it to but thought it would be inappropriate.

He can't reveal himself to me yet? Why not? What's with all this melodramatic veiled evasive shit? Am I living my life or trapped in the latest suspense thriller? Honestly, the pacing is about the same.

Meandering thoughts are interrupted by a text. The fingerprint analysis Mr. X ran is back. Good. Perfect timing. I click on the attachment and open the report:

"A search for fingerprints on the document provided using the suggested parameters has revealed no evidence of prints."

No prints? Fuck. This doesn't mean they lifted some prints and couldn't find a match. It means they were unable to find *any* prints on the document. *At all.*

Who writes a letter without getting their prints on it? You can't grab a piece of paper, write on it, fold it, and put it into an envelope without leaving prints. Unless you're trying. Unless you're wearing gloves. Unless you don't have any prints. Unless your intent is to deceive.

Sometimes no evidence *is* evidence.

Chapter Twenty

Doctor-patient privilege
Faith 2013

Dear Faith,
I hope you're feeling better today. I want you to
know without a doubt I will always be there for you. No
matter what the future brings. I never want to see you
hurting, and I will go to the ends of the earth and back
to take that pain away. Just say the word and I'll do it.
If you find yourself in a desert, I'll bring you the sea. If
you're lost, I'll be your compass. I'll do whatever you
need done, and I'll be whoever you need me to be.
Loving you always,
Cole

"Where did he leave that one?" Jen, our imaginary
friend, reaches on tippy toes into the cabinet for the
flour and sugar. Strands of blonde hair that didn't make
it into her messy bun dangle down her back. She always
looks like she just rolled out of bed, but it really works
for her.

"Tucked under the windshield wiper of my car." I
set the oven to three fifty again.

"He's so...romantic. So..." Jen falters trying to
find the right word.

"In love and obsessed?" Leanne chimes in.

"Every time I find one of his intricately folded

notes, I get butterflies," I say.

"I would too, if they said stuff like this." Jen's eyeing the recipe.

"I'm in love again. Cole's happy, and I know he's feeling safe and secure."

"Do you *need* him to feel safe and secure?" Leanne's interviewing me, or interrogating me and I know where this is headed.

"What's wrong with wanting the person you love to feel good?" I measure the flour and dump it into the bowl.

"Nothing, until you find yourself having to *manage* his emotions. It's a dangerous precedent to set." Leanne beats the eggs and mixes in the sugar.

"I *manage* everyone's emotions. Don't we all?" I shoot her a side glance.

"Yes, unfortunately. It's a bad habit our emotionally avoidant parents have passed on to us. When we had *big* emotions, they didn't know how to handle us because they didn't know how to process their own. They got angry, like we were to blame for something. And we *never* want Mommy and Daddy angry, hence we learn at a young age we're responsible for other people's feelings. We're not. But we all have a little of that generational junk." Leanne doesn't look up as she greases the pans.

"Should I go lie on the couch while you take notes?" I ask.

Leanne rolls her eyes.

"I don't see the problem," I continue. "Jen just finished telling us she went over to Tim's house to console and support him after he found out his grandmother was in the hospital. That led to them getting back together of course, and then he dumped her again, which is why we're making cake, but the point is, she didn't want him to be unhappy and alone."

"It's not the same thing." Leanne's tone is matter-of-fact.

"I don't see the difference either, Leanne." Jen's stirring the cake batter.

"The difference is Tim worrying about his grandmother in the hospital is normal. Jen wanting to comfort him is appropriate. Even Cole worrying about losing you is a basic fear in every relationship, but for him it's different. Losing you is a threat to his very survival."

"Dramatic much?" Jen says.

"Am I?" Leanne looks at me. "I've known him the longest, talked to him about you before you were even together. His feelings for you were always extreme and bordering on obsessive. And you—you've been so conditioned to take responsibility for other people's feelings, you think you need to be the one to make him feel better. You can thank your mother for that." She points a batter-covered spoon at me. "You can't be happy if he's not, so you need to make him okay so you can be okay. It's called enmeshment."

"I am not *enmeshed*. I'm only loving him the way he needs me to." I pour the batter into the pans.

"Is there doctor-patient privilege going on here? Should I leave?" Jen laughs. "She does make a good point, Faith. This could be the beginning of a codependent relationship." Jen's eyes widen.

"So you're saying I want to fix him? I won't feel okay about myself unless he's okay? Not sure I'm buying that." I smirk at Leanne.

"That's exactly what I'm saying. But this goes beyond wanting to fix somebody. The danger is not only thinking you're the cure to his ills, which right now makes you feel good. The real issue will happen somewhere down the line when you start thinking you're also the *cause*, and *that* is a problem. A *big* unhealthy dysfunctional problem." Leanne licks the spoon.

"Hmm…Maybe." I shrug. "Should I expect a bill in the mail?"

I put the filled cake pans into the oven while Leanne changes the subject. "Have you talked to Jeremy since he was attacked? He's been pretty tight-lipped about it."

"Yeah, I called him the day after it happened. I think he's embarrassed. You know, someone getting the better of him and all."

"What happened? You've heard the rumors, right?" Jen asks.

"Which ones?" I ask.

"That it was Cole."

"That's ridiculous!" My voice raises a few octaves.

"Is it?" Leanne asks.

"I heard the same thing." Jen crosses her arms.

"He was with me!" I'm beyond annoyed at the insinuation.

"Until what time?" Leanne interrogates.

"Did you pass the AP exam in detective work too? Geez, it wasn't Cole."

"Okay, okay. So what did Jeremy say?" Leanne asks.

"He was headed home after dropping his girlfriend off from the party, stopped at a red light when someone wearing a facemask appeared at his driver side window pointing a gun at his head and telling him to get out. So he did, thinking the guy would take the car and leave, but he was beat up pretty good. The next thing he remembered was lying on the ground next to his car with a good Samaritan standing over him who stopped to help."

"So I'm guessing he wasn't able to get a look at the guy? Does he have any idea who would do this?"

"Nope, and the police have no witnesses."

"Damn, that's scary. Could have happened to anyone. Has he still been on you to get together?" Jen asks.

"Yeah, but he doesn't know what he wants. I do. It's not him. I just want to make it through this year without any more drama."

Chapter Twenty-One

Not going to waste it
Cole 2013

Faith looks hotter than usual tonight in her white prom dress. Between the slit reaching high up the side of her thigh and the low scooping neckline revealing her perfect cleavage, it's all I can do to not take her back to the limo and ravish her. I'm still trying to figure out what she's doing with me, even after all the months of reassurances. She says I make her feel connected and our bond is so strong nothing will ever break us apart. Not time, not distance, not space, and definitely not another person.

It's exactly how I feel about her. No matter what happens, it'll never end between us, even if we're not together. I want to be with her every minute, and when I'm not, I'm lost. Everything feels *off*, scattered. When I was young, I would build a tent in my room and hide there when things got out of hand, licking my wounds and feeling alone. In some ways, I still crawl back into the tent of my past. I fucking hate that. Like if I disappear, no one will even notice. But Faith would. She gives me purpose, a reason to be alive. I'm doing everything in my power to set the bar so high, no one else will ever be able to come close.

"Table photos!" The prom photographer announces

himself as he approaches our table. He motions us to move in closer, pointing his camera and lights at us. The girls sit next to each other, guys stand behind.

"Okay, everybody ready? On three, say sex!"

The end of the year is here. Faith got into all the schools she applied to, of course, but decided to stay local. Maybe to be around me. Maybe to be around for her dad. Not really sure which. Could be both. The school is only forty-five minutes away. She'll be on campus having new experiences, meeting people, and I'll be here. Time to get it together, figure out what will happen after next year's graduation. I'm floundering, and she's frustrated with me. This is where we differ. Faith's priority is school, career, me—in that order. Mine is Faith, school, career. To my mind, as long as we're together, the rest will fall into place. Despite her reassurances we're good, the anxiety about what this change will do to us is killing me. Everything's perfect, and I want it to stay this way. *Need it* to stay this way.

"I'm going to get a drink. Do you want anything?" Faith asks, wrapping her arms around my neck, kissing my cheek.

"I'll go for you. What do you want, babe?" I squeeze her tiny waist with my hands.

"You stay. Jen and Tim are arguing again. I'm gonna take her with me so we can talk."

I watch as Faith and Jen head toward the buffet, joining Bryce's date.

"We're two lucky guys, aren't we?" Bryce stands beside me watching them as well.

"A great end to an even greater year," I say.

"Maybe not." Bryce motions his head up toward the dance floor. Jeremy is making his way to us. "Want some backup?"

"Na, I got it." My spine involuntarily straightens making me taller. I'm ready for anything he's got.

"Cole!" Jeremy stretches a hand out like an olive branch.

I take it, but I'd rather rip it off. "Jeremy." My voice is flat.

"Listen, you're a good guy, Cole." He leans in and an overabundance of alcohol hits me in the face. "But I'm pretty sure you're the one who put me in the hospital."

I pull back from him.

"No no no, no sweat. I get it." He's slurring his words. "You were defending your territory. It's cool. But just a heads-up, Faith knows how you really spend your time during study hall."

"What are you talking about?"

"You know, your weakness for child porn."

"Fuck you, I don't like that shit."

"That's not what she thinks." He takes several steps back, arms open with an arrogant smirk, and turns to walk away.

Is this what he's been whispering in her ear? This douche doesn't know when to let up. My heart's racing. I step forward to grab him by his neck and bring him to the ground, but a strong hand on my shoulder stops me.

"She's yours. Let it go," Bryce instructs into my ear over the music.

The tension running through me dissipates. Plus, I'm wondering if Faith is watching this exchange. What will she think if I let loose on this asshole?

"He's gonna be many, many states away at college, dude. It's not worth it."

He's right. I'll let this one go. After tonight, that will be the end of that. *Finally.*

****

We stand on the deck of the boat looking at the night sky and toward the lighted dock ahead. I'm behind Faith with my arms wrapped around her, chin resting on her shoulder, dotting her neck with kisses. She shudders when I hit the spot that tickles, cringing and smiling. The full moon is illuminating our path through the water of the Hudson Bay as the cool night air and light mist rush over us forming goose bumps on Faith's skin. I take off my suit jacket and drape it over her bare shoulders. Muffled music and laughter drift out from inside the cabin.

"Would you rather be inside where it's warmer?" I ask into her ear.

"Right here with you is perfect."

The waterway has narrowed bringing the boat closer to the towering slick black rock that borders the shore on each side. We arrive at the dock, disembark, and silently climb into the waiting van. It's late, and our party of eight is tired. I choose the long seat at the rear, and Faith leans into me, falling asleep almost instantly. I carry her in when we arrive at the cabin, put her to bed in the room I choose for us, carry the bags in, and collapse onto the bed with her.

We wake at noon to the sound of music floating through the halls of the cabin. It appears everyone's up, except us. Faith's lying on her back, golden hair spread out on the pillow, one arm overhead. Her body stirs slightly as I pull the blanket down gently, exposing her nakedness. I run the palm of my hand from her leg up her belly to her breasts and bury my head in her neck.

113

We've never been able to spend a full night together and wake up in each other's arms until now. I'm not going to waste it.

Her hand moves onto the back of my head, gently massaging my scalp. Eyes still closed, the rest of her body comes alive as she rolls on her side, wrapping herself around me. I glide my hand into her hair pulling her mouth onto mine and slide myself into her as effortlessly as water flows downstream. Faith moans with a long exhale, drawing my breath and heart into her.

She's everything to me. Has been from the first time I set eyes on her. She has a way of putting me into this crazy sexualized state where I disconnect from the world. There's only us, floating, eternal. I'm in deep, she's my drug of choice, and no one's coming to save me. Even if they were, I'd send them away. I feel her tighten around me as we both climax.

For the first time today, she blinks her lids open, trying to focus on me.

"Good morning, my love," she says.

"It is now." I kiss her again.

"I'm sorry I passed out and missed everything last night. Let's eat and spend the day together exploring."

"You read my mind."

Within two hours, we hike our way through lush green forest, across babbling brooks, and over slick black rock to the top of Prescott Peak. Faith takes a blanket out of her backpack and lays it out on the grass while I grab some snacks and drinks from mine. The views are stunning, stretching hundreds of miles in every direction, yet, despite the freeing feeling of being on this expansive, spacious peak, something changed on the way up, and I'm feeling...constricted...unsteady, anxious again. Like something bad's about to happen. I don't know why. Shit. Everything's perfect. This has been the goal, to be with Faith, in a relationship, in love with her, and her in love with me. We're alone, devoted to each other, at the top of this amazing mountain and yet, I'm terrified. With her starting college in a few months, I'm afraid this won't last. I'm afraid I'm gonna lose her...and I want to die just thinking about it.

Chapter Twenty-Two

Hear me out
Faith 2026

"Look at this," I say, pushing photos across the café table to Leanne. "The police are not done with the accident reconstruction, but the lead detective is a friend and he gave me these."

"What am I looking at?" Leanne eyes the photos, twisting her head and squinting for whatever she's supposed to notice.

"Jeremy's accident scene photos. Look at his car. It's so mangled from hitting the tree, but there are no clear shots of the left quarter panel."

"Yes?" She's intrigued.

"And now look at the one of Jeremy's car in the police impound. It was taken a few days later. It's covered with snow. No one bothered to brush the snow off the rear of the car. You still can't see the left quarter panel."

"And…?"

"And the police told me they ruled out the possibility that any other cars were involved. But how could they if they never got a good look at the left side? If someone else was on the road with Jeremy in the storm and tried to pass him, they would have passed on his left. They could have hit him and pushed him off the road into the tree. And if they did, they would have hit him on the left side. But now there's no photos of it."

Leanne shakes her head looking down at them, trying to follow along with my theory. She clicks her tongue against the roof of her mouth. "I hate to see you like this, still questioning the circumstances of this accident. But I have to admit, you have a point."

I'm grateful for the validation.

"Maybe he *was* pushed off the road." Leanne takes a sip of coffee. "But I can't believe it would be intentional. He didn't have any enemies, did he?"

"None that I can think of." I slip the photos back into the manilla envelope and slide it into my bag.

"Have they released the car yet? You could have a look at it for yourself."

"That's my plan."

"Do you want me to come?"

"No, thanks. It's too far out of the way for you."

"Did you read the second letter yet?" Leanne takes a bite of quiche.

"I did." A sip of this café's fresh squeezed orange juice is like sunlight in a glass. Divine.

"Still unsigned?" she garbles, covering her mouth.

"Yep."

"What did it say?"

"He talks about wanting to help me through my grief. Said he knows what it's like to lose someone."

"How do you know it's a 'he'?" Leanne asks.

"My spidey senses. I'll tell you, Leanne, the way he describes the pain, how it never really goes away, I feel like I know him." The rich, toasty mix of garlic, onion and sesame rises from the untouched everything bagel sitting in front of me. I flag the waiter with my eyes and mouth the words, *butter, please.*

"Well, you do, somehow. Right?" She picks up her coffee cup.

"Yeah, but it's different. Like I *know* him. It may sound crazy, but…I feel like it's Cole."

"Oh, honey." Leanne puts her coffee down, cocking her head to the side like I'm a mental patient.

"No, wait, hear me out." I put up a hand. "It *feels* like him, the words, the emotions coming through. I've always felt him around me."

"Feelings are not evidence." Leanne's shaking her head at me.

"Well, I'm almost certain I've seen him. How about that? The other day I saw a jogger outside my house. I could have sworn it was him." I pause. "I think he's watching me."

"Stop." It's Leanne's turn to put up a hand. "You know it's not possible. Don't you, Faith?"

"But we never had any concrete answers." I continue to push.

"Yes, we did. You just didn't like them." There's panic in her eyes, and I know I should stop myself, at least until I have more proof.

"How's your sleep been?" Leanne's trying to extract more from me.

"On and off." The butter is delivered with an apologetic look.

"Any nightmares?"

I hesitate.

"Tell me the truth," she insists.

"Yeah…"

"Are they about Jeremy or Cole?"

"Both." I know she'll see right through me if I try

to lie, partly because she knows me better than anyone, partly because she's a damn good psychologist.

"It's perfectly normal, you know." She resumes eating. "You've got a lot going on right now, Faith. You're running a high-stress business, you're grieving, and these letters are forcing you to think about the past. Sometimes stress can distort our thinking. The scab of old wounds we thought healed can rip off, triggering old emotions. Time can feel like it's overlapping, and we can confuse things."

"What are you saying?" I ask.

"I'm not *saying*. I'm just saying." Leanne has most definitely mastered the art of *implying* without suggesting. Her two thousand hours of post-doctoral training have ensured it.

"Do *you* think I'm confused?" The butter is finally making its way onto my bagel.

"All I'm saying is, when something happens to us in the present that's similar to something we've experienced in the past, it can easily dredge up all the feelings and emotions we had then. Trauma can make us feel like we're back *there* instead of *here*. We can perceive a threat in the present when there isn't one. It can make us feel as though things from the past are happening now when they aren't."

Bingo. But I don't say that out loud. "You're starting to sound like the Riddler," I jest.

"Are you...experiencing any confusion between the past and the present, Faith?"

"All right, look, I *am* thinking a lot about the past. But I haven't come unhinged if that's what you mean. Not yet at least."

"Stress can also trigger something called delusional

disorder. It's when you can't tell what's real and what's imagined. It's very common in women, Faith. Your doctor can write you a prescription again."

"That stuff made me foggy. I can't run a business like that." I bite into the bagel.

"You still remember how to use those grounding techniques?" she asks.

"You mean the ones that pull me away from negative memories and thoughts and help me refocus on what's happening in this very *real* and *perfect* present moment?" I smirk.

The past wasn't *all* bad, Leanne. But again, I don't say that out loud.

For the next hour, we chatter on about the letter writer, the upcoming dinner party of which she still won't reveal a thing about the guest list, and the cute waiter. Some things never change. I don't mention the possibility these letters could be coming from a subject of a prior investigation. Why worry her without just cause?

"Let me know when the next letter comes or what happens at the impound, whichever comes first." Leanne hugs me on the sidewalk outside the café, and we part ways.

I head over to the post office while I'm still down on Long Island. It's virtually impossible to track the origin, date, and time of where my letters were mailed, but what I was able to determine with certainty is that the main mail processing and distribution center uses one type of postmark while the Devenport post office uses another.

Both my letters have different postmarks. Nice work, letter writer. The second one was stamped at the main distribution center meaning it could have originated from anywhere. Dead end. The first letter however, was stamped at the Devenport post office with the date and time—bingo. It was either dropped at the box outside or put through the mail slot inside, no guarantees though. Hence my trip to the Devenport post office.

I arrive in the parking lot, take note of the cameras, and immediately rule out the drive-through blue mailboxes, not because my letter writer couldn't have dropped it there, but because the cameras are focused on the entrance and a part of the parking lot that does not include the drive-through. Shit.

I walk to the counter, choose the male postal worker over the female, and explain, quite desperately, that my ailing mother is being charged an exorbitant fee for getting her mortgage payment in late, again, when she's certain she mails her mortgage payments out two weeks in advance. I need to know if she still has all her marbles and the post office has mishandled the mail or if she's showing early signs of dementia, in which case I'll need to get her to a doctor and possibly move her in with me before she burns my childhood home down making her afternoon chamomile tea. And I just don't see how to manage it as a single mother working a full-time job with three kids under five.

Too easy? Too implausible? Not at all. I'm female, young, attractive so I've been told, nonthreatening, and in this case, playing the role of the damsel in distress waiting, no, *needing*, to be saved. It's misguided patriarchal epistemological arrogance—a feminist's worst nightmare. But not to me. To me, it's another tool in my toolbox. And they won't ever see it coming. Or going, for that matter. *This* is how the real world works. And it *does* work. Every time. This is where the feminists get it wrong; there's absolutely *no one* standing in our way. We've always had the power; some women just don't know how to use it.

Fred, my postal worker, as established by the name tag affixed to his standard-issue light-blue collared shirt, is happy to help me save my mother's life and my sanity. I hand him a copy of the envelope across the counter. He examines it and types into his terminal.

"Well, it looks like your mother walked into this building on..."

More clicking. I hold my twitchy tongue.

"...last Wednesday at 8:36 am."

"Wednesday? In the morning? Are you sure?" I feign surprise.

"That's what it says." Fred shrugs.

I'm already in the process of whipping out my phone and finger-swiping through my calendar.

"That doesn't sound right. I took her to the gastroenterologist that morning. Or maybe...her boyfriend walked in here and mailed it. Oh no! Fred, that's even worse. I never liked him, and I definitely never trusted him, and now she may have given him access to her banking!"

Using my best doe-eyed expression, I look at him in a panic for direction. "I know this is none of your concern, and there's a line of people behind me but..." My eyes lift to the camera behind him. "...is there any way I could look at your camera footage? I have to know. Fred, I *need* to know."

Fred glances over at his coworker servicing another customer. Then at me. I see a glimmer of empathy, or pity, not sure which. And it doesn't matter. He picks up his phone, presses three buttons, and waits.

"Yeah, it's Fred. Last Wednesday. We still have camera three footage?" He leans forward, resting his elbows on the counter, one hand holding the phone to his ear, making eye contact with me. I wait and watch his eyes drop down to the counter. He squints and ruffles his brow.

"What do you mean?" he says into the phone looking at me again. Pause. "Has that ever happened before?" Pause. "Huh. Okay, thanks." He hangs up. "Cameras malfunctioned last Wednesday. Lost everything."

Shit.

I compose myself.

"Damn. Thanks for trying. I really appreciate it."

"Ask your mom to make you a co-signer on her account and offer to do her banking for her online. That's what I had to do."

"Thanks for the tip."

I'm back in my car driving on autopilot. Cameras malfunctioned? On Wednesday? Only Wednesday? Is this letter writer innocently trying to reach me and this camera problem is simply a coincidence? Or is something more sinister going on? There were no prints on the letter—none. Now there are two reasons to suspect this person may have a malevolent intent. In order to destroy security camera footage on government property, you'd have to break in, either physically or digitally, and delete it or corrupt the file. Not easy. Could this person be much more sophisticated than I had originally thought? And why?

The calming sensation I normally get during the

drive up the mountain is nowhere to be found. Did I ingest too much high-powered vitamin C at the café? My brain feels wired and tense, stretched thin in too many directions. Last week's encounter with the blue van has me spooked. Between managing my field team, training the newbies, working my own caseload, and these mysterious letters engrossing me, some peace would be nice. But it's all a good distraction from the constant reminders of Jeremy facing me every time I walk into my house, like now.

No matter which room I walk into, there's something there I'm not ready to remove: his running shoes by the garage door, the book he was in the middle of on the bedroom nightstand, his razor at the sink. Maybe letting go will be easier if I got rid of everything at once instead of leaving those items and lingering on these feelings and questions. It's over, he's gone. Have I learned nothing about the pain of not letting go over the past fifteen years?

And Leanne's right. These letters are transporting me back to high school and college, compelling me to remember the people, places, and events of that time. I'm recalling things I had long forgotten, maybe for the best—my parents' divorce, my first love with Jeremy and all that came with it, then a new group of friends and the crazy times with all those people, and of course, Cole, who had come into my life next. It's all jumbling together in my head at once like clothes rolling around in a dryer, difficult to separate them and try to pinpoint who this letter writer might be.

My analytical investigative head is telling me to be cautious, but my heart knows the more I read them, the more an undeniable connection to the writer emerges—

familiar, safe. Steve and Bryce are definite possibilities because logically they fit into the clues about circumstance and timeframe, but viscerally, there's only one person who's ever evoked these kinds of feelings in me. Only one person who truly fits the emotional intensity of these letters, and it *can't* be him. *Can it?* No, Leanne's probably right. I *have* had bouts of confusion in the past. But it could be someone he was friends with. People tend to gravitate toward those like themselves. Or it's any number of investigative targets coming for me.

What I can do right now is move forward with the next investigative step, a handwriting analysis, and of course, I got a guy. While the reliability of a handwriting comparison always comes down to the expert doing the analysis, I'm not looking for perfection. I'm looking for *close*. This doesn't need to hold up in a courtroom. It only needs to be accurate enough to give me a few leads.

I'll need to submit the letters with samples for comparison. I've saved my school yearbooks and notes passed in class. That'll have to do. I text my contact, and he immediately gives the okay to send over what I have. He's good like that. I'll dig the stuff up later and send it.

Whoever you are, friend or foe, I'm coming for you.

Chapter Twenty-Three

Everything's going wrong
Faith 2013

The hike Cole and I take to the top of the mountain has been exhausting but worth every step. Prescott Peak overlooks the rolling green hills of the Hudson Valley and winding blue water of the Hudson River. From the top, trails on neighboring mountains reveal themselves while sunlight blinks on scattered tiny towns below. Cloud shadows cast themselves upon the landscape, roaming over the ridges and valleys like silky waves. It's picture perfect, and I imagine us staying, even living here someday.

The scent of fresh earth and pine fills my nose and a cool wind bathes my hot, sweaty face. The summit sinks into a motionless tranquility but not for long. I reach into my backpack, grab the blanket for us to sit on, and see the discomfort on Cole's face. The same look from our first night on the couch, and at the party at the Lighthouse. Something happens in that beautiful head of his. It turns him dark, distracted, and disconnected. It seeps into every inch of my being, triggering me to help him erase everything that's happened to make him feel this way. I can be anything he needs, friend, lover, drug, therapist. He's afraid of losing me. He worries about the past, the present, and the future, but sometimes I grow tired of convincing him I love him and will forever. He feels lost without me and retreats somewhere beyond my perception. It all gets so heavy sometimes.

I run through last night and this morning looking for the first sign that something was off with him. Was it when I fell asleep on the ride here? Did he take it as an insult? Think I'm getting bored with him? Falling out of love? But this morning…so perfect and sweet. Surely it reassured him everything is good with us.

Looking at the view, he's standing, pacing, then standing still again. He kneels to look in his backpack, frustrated by something, and paces again.

"Cole?"

He looks at me with surprise, like he forgot I'm here.

"Yeah, babe?"

"Come sit with me."

"In a minute." He rummages through the bag again, comes over, and sits with the sandwiches and drinks we packed earlier.

"Tell me what's happening," I say.

"With what?"

"You. You seem…preoccupied. Are you okay? Was it something I did?"

"I like that you noticed, but no, it's nothing you did. It's…" His voice trails off.

"You can tell me anything, Cole. I want to help." I wrap my arm in his.

"I don't know how to explain it. Sometimes I get caught in my head. Like there's an angry seesaw in there, forcing me up and down. I'm good, ready to take on the world, but then sink into a hole so deep, I'm not sure I'll ever climb out. Feels like everything's going wrong somehow, like I have no fucking control over it." He shakes his head. "But I'm good when I'm with you. The way you look at me—I don't know what I'd do if you didn't love me. I never want to go back to the empty feeling I had before you."

"I understand but…" I bite my lower lip. "I'm not sure this is what a healthy relationship is supposed to look like. For you or for me. It's why I've encouraged you to have something else in your life besides me."

"You're right, and I'm working on it. Changes are coming, and I just don't ever want to lose you."

"That's not something you have to worry about, Cole. I'll always love you."

"How can you be so sure? You're starting college. Anything can happen."

He looks over the peak to the mountains. Hopelessness invades those beautiful brown eyes of his. It destroys me, and I want nothing more than to ease his tormented mind.

"Cole, look at me." I hold his hand.

He does, and what I see is that haunted little boy, still in there, trying to trust that life won't always go to shit.

"You *have* me. I'm yours, you're mine. This love between us will never end. It's a bond that can never be broken even if, through some crazy twist of fate, we're not together. We'll always make it back to each other. No matter what happens to us or between us or where we are on this earth. Or even off this earth, in another universe, on another plane of existence." We both breathe out a hint of laughter. "Love is love, in every place, in every time. Nothing and no one can ever separate us."

The side of his lip barely curls. "There's so many other people out there you're going to meet." Voice low, his eyes drop to our clasped hands.

"And none of them will be you. There's no one like you, Cole. You're as rare as this birthmark on your hand. It's part of what makes you, you."

"I love everything you said, and I want to believe it."

"Have I done anything to make you doubt me?" I squeeze his hand.

"You haven't."

I can barely hear him. "Then believe it. Believe it until you have a reason not to."

There's a glimmer of relief in his face. He reaches into his bag, pulls out his MP3 player and spins the scroll wheel. "This song has been echoing in my head for weeks," he says.

I stretch my neck to look as he presses play. The melody is haunting yet peaceful. The male singer's voice is strong and full of emotion:

You are the vision, the breath, the flame
My reason, my rhythm, my heart in a frame
An eternal love, entangled as one
No matter how far or what may come
When gravity fails and the universe falls through
I will still be loving you
When mountains crumble to the ground
We will still be safe, still be sound
No end, no edge, no line we trace
Just timeless pull in infinite space
No finish line, no final page
Love becomes our only stage

When gravity fails and the universe falls through
I will still be loving you
When mountains crumble to the ground
We will still be safe, still be sound

He wraps his arms around me as we listen. "I've been playing this one for you for weeks in the basement," he whispers into my ear.

"I know, heard it every time." I rest my head on his shoulder. "It's perfect, isn't it?"

"It *is*. Especially right here, right now, on top of this mountain. I wish we could bottle this moment and keep it forever," he says.

So do I because in truth, he's not wrong. I'm as worried and anxious about our future as he is, but I don't dare say that out loud. New ingredients are about to be added again, blending with the old, altering me into something else. I wish I had more trust in myself, but there's no telling what might happen.

We sit, gazing over the hills. They're like him, high and low, dipping downward and then swooping upward, over and over in all directions with no end as far as the eye can see. But I can tell the song has soothed his restless, tortured mind.

And I can breathe again.

Chapter Twenty-Four

Behavior is just adaptation
Cole 2013

The summer months have flown by, each better than the one before. Faith's seen it all, my random moods and the darkness that crashes everything to a screeching halt of despair, apathy, and anxiety. The side that feels insignificant and worthless. She sees me for who I really am and somehow, stays anyway. This shit is because of my childhood, but I never understood the details. Never cared. I do now, want to do better, be better, for me and for Faith.

Since I want to contribute to Leanne's future success, I let her use me as a test subject. She won a full scholarship to Stanford, so she's the closest thing I have to an authority on the matter. We're on a video call. Leanne's in her dorm room and I'm sitting at my desktop in my room while she scores the assessment she gave me, shaking her head as she checks off each answer.

"What?" I ask.

She ignores me while comparing my test to the textbook laying open on the table, swishing the pages back and forth. It was only a few questions, what's taking so long?

"Do you know why I administered this test?"

"Because you love torturing me?"

"Psychological responses to torture would have been a different test." Leanne blinks annoyance at me. "This one measures adverse childhood experiences. You scored a six out of ten."

"Oh. Let me take it again, see if I can get a higher score."

"You don't want a high score. You want a zero. This is not good, too much trauma, not enough bonding with your primary caregivers. You didn't feel safe and cared for, and it can fuck you up."

"Great," I say. "But I'm already aware of that."

She licks her thumb, flips through a bunch of pages, and starts to read, "Insecure attachments with parent figures can cause us to become needy in adult relationships and feel physically addicted to another person, all consumed by them, and anxious when they're away from us."

"Sounds like a bunch of cerebral gobbledygook to me, but I *do* feel addicted to Faith. Can't really help it."

"You *can* help it, but first you have to understand it. The higher you score on this test, the more predisposed you become to psychological and physical health issues down the line. Things like addiction, depression, suicide, violence, impaired work performance, and chronic health issues."

"Something to look forward to," I joke.

"Not funny," she scolds. "Behavior is just adaptation—our attempt to get more of what we need or to protect us by getting less of what we don't want. Ironically, this can place pressure on both partners if they want different things. The needy one is forever insecure about the relationship while the other feels overwhelmed by it and may resist the connection."

"That's what's happening, Leanne! Haven't seen her much lately. She started college, has a whole new life there, while I hang out with her friends."

"You've become real tight with Steve and Sam, right? That's a good thing."

"I guess, but what if she wants to leave me behind?"

"Hasn't happened yet, right?" Leanne reassures.

"No, but I'm already starting to feel the effects. We're arguing, mostly about all the time she's spending on campus. She made the dance team and because they're competitive, practices are almost every day, sometimes twice a day, plus halftime performances and travel time. She also made the debate team. Class time and her social life all add up to less time with me."

"I know she loves you." Leanne closes the book.

"I want her to be happy and live her life, but I'm starting to feel deserted. If I say something, she resents it and pulls away. We never resolve anything. I'm afraid she'll revert to her old self, the self she was after Jeremy and before me."

"Haven't you two been up to the mountains a few times? Everything seems good." She sips a caramel colored iced coffee drink through a straw.

"Yeah, we loved the prom trip enough to go back two more times."

Those mountains are like me in my more optimistic moments, open, easy, flowing. But also like me when the darkness sets in, empty, isolated, lonely. I forget about everything when we're up there—makes the distance between us melt away. "Faith keeps coming back to me and that's what's important." I peer into the screen at Leanne. "But for how long?"

Chapter Twenty-Five

Altered bits and pieces
Faith 2026

I'm pointing the gun at Cole. He's ten feet away, pointing his at me. It's a standoff. The rain's pelting down on us, forcing me to squint, pooling in the divots of the lawn. "You shouldn't have come," he yells. Lightning branches through the gray sky, illuminating the darkness around us, revealing the crazy look in his eyes. He wants to kill me. He could pull the trigger at any moment, and I'm sure he will. I pull mine, but nothing happens. His outstretched arms point the gun at me, and his finger pulls back on the trigger. Hearing the explosion and seeing a muzzle flash of white light, I brace myself for the bullet that is about to rip through me but again, nothing. Not to me. Somehow, he's struck instead, by a hail of bullets tearing through his flesh leaving gaping bloody holes, exposing bone fragments and dripping internal organs. He collapses onto the wet lawn, and I run to him. "I'm sorry!" I cry, holding his head in my lap as blood soaks into my hands and jeans. His eyes are desperate, lids closing. "I love you," he says, shaking his head ever so slightly, "but you shouldn't have come."

I wake in my dimly lit bedroom, heart vibrating like the nylon of a drum. My hands are clenched in the shag of my throw pillow, still feeling like the damp bloody hair on his head.

"Jesus!" I'm in my own bed, heart beats returning to normal. I thought a nap might do me some good before heading out this evening. Wrong. I've almost come to accept these nightmares, altered bits and pieces of reality mixed with horror, random synapses firing at will. They're never quite the same. Similar to a one-night stand, they rush in, we have our way with each other, and then part company, leaving behind confusion, sorrow, and maybe even a little bit of anger. I shake it off and jump in the shower.

Tonight, I'm heading back to Devenport for Leanne's dinner party. I completely freed myself from work, at least for a few hours, by making sure my field team knows where to be and understands their contingency plans if necessary. My newbies will funnel any emergencies to Brooke.

I've decided to pay a little more attention to my hair and makeup, even wear that cute little wrap-around dress. As far as socializing goes, this is progress.

My first stop is the bakery in Devenport to pick up dessert, but until then, I'm going to enjoy this drive. For months, the viciousness of Jeremy's death on this mountain has consumed me. That needs to stop—won't change anything. It really is beautiful and should be appreciated, with its thick lush green forests, winding roads, and spectacular views, especially now in late spring, before sunset.

Earlier I was nervous about being with people again in a social setting. Now a calmness sets in as I park the car in front of the old bakery. There are so many cherished memories here.

"Faith! Good to see you again. What brings you into town?" Tim Watkins beams across the counter as I walk in. He's Jen's first love from high school who still lives in town and now runs the bakery for his father.

"Hi, Tim! Heading to a friend's for dinner and *had* to stop by and pick up a pie like only you can make."

"Well, you're in luck, there's still three in the case. Take a look. I've got to run in the back for a minute. Hey, did you hear? They caught those guys." On his way into the back, he points to the large flat screen TV mounted behind the counter.

It's flashing images of the twenty terrorists caught so far in connection with the Paris attacks, switching to footage of the destruction and clean-up efforts still underway. The city looks like a war zone. They're estimating it'll take at least ten years to rebuild. Jeremy left in the storm to go to the gym the very next morning. These two events are forever melded in my mind.

They split-screen to a psychologist who's talking about the collective trauma we all experience with tragedies like these, and ironically, how important it is to monitor our exposure to the twenty-four-hour news cycle and social media. Given all the death, destruction, and doom raining down on us for the last months, it's critical we learn to step away, get involved with activities we enjoy, and surround ourselves with those who love us. I learned that a long time ago and try to live my life accordingly. That's why evenings like tonight are so important. Pushing myself out the door to engage and connect with people can do wonders for the soul, even when it's hard.

As I look into the case trying to decide which pie

might be best and cursing Leanne under my breath because I don't know who exactly is going to be there and consequently can't decide on which pie might be the better choice, the door to the bakery opens behind me. Because the PI license comes with a set of eyes in the back of my head, I know it's a male, but still deep in thought alternating between the blueberry and banana cream, I continue to ignore the figure, now standing right next to me.

"Faith?" A male voice interrupts my vacillating. I'm frozen staring into the face of a man who looks like a stranger and a friend at the same time, studying the features of his face and rearranging them into a discernible order I can recognize. It finally comes to me, and I couldn't be more embarrassed for taking so long.

"Bryce!" I throw my arms around him. He instantly hugs back. "I'm sorry for gawking like that, but you look so different. It's been ten years! You're all grown up and mature-looking. It took me a minute."

"I know! I get that a lot. I always had such a baby face, finally outgrew it. And look at you. You look wonderful, Faith! I was so sorry to hear about your husband." He hugs me again. "You'll get through this. You're one of the strongest people I've ever met."

"Thanks, Bryce."

It isn't until this moment in our reunion I remember the letters and my suspicion that *he* is the possible author. We spend the next twenty minutes engrossed in conversation catching up, both forgetting the bakery is only a pit stop on our way to other destinations.

"Shoot, I'm gonna be late to Mike's party," he says

in response to the chiming clock on the wall. "Faith, I'd love to meet you for lunch one day when we're both back in town."

Is this simply an expression of our friendship, or is there another intention? One that matches the letter writer? In the second between the end of his sentence and where the beginning of my answer should have been, I hesitate. Should I bring it up now or wait until we meet again?

"I'd love to." I'm reviewing his face for clues. We exchange phone numbers, pay for our pies, and walk out together.

"Bryce?" I hear myself say on an impulse, after we've turned to walk in separate directions.

He spins around meeting my gaze. I have no idea what words are about to come out of me next. If he isn't the letter writer, then everything will stay the same between us, but if he *is*, what then? I haven't thought this through, very unlike me. How can I bring it up, possibly finding out he's the one with the years-long crush? The person interested in some kind of more-than-friends relations with me, and *not* be prepared with a well-thought-out decision beforehand? I owe him more than this.

"Yes?" He's waiting.

"It was really good to see you again" is what comes out.

"You too, Faith. I'll call you."

I'm still thinking about Bryce and who the letter writer could be when I arrive in front of Leanne's house. It must be the thousandth time, but even so, after all these years it still feels like a second home full of treasured moments I've never outgrown. Some of the cars already on the street are familiar to me. I shift into park and glance over at the house next door, heart aching at the sight of it.

My eyes float to the basement window, the one I climbed in and out of so many times. The cool earthy grass under my palms and butt as I slid in, Cole's hands wrapped around my legs guiding me. I'm back there again, even though I also know I'm sitting in my car watching myself. The top of my head disappears inside the window, but within seconds there's movement. Someone's climbing out. Is that…Cole?

He struggles, wiggling himself out and onto the grass, brushes himself off, and begins walking toward the passenger side of my car. I blink in rapid succession, swallowing hard. Is he really there? He hasn't aged a bit, looks exactly the same. And he's smiling at me. I'm frozen. I want it to be true. I'm pretty sure it's not.

He motions to roll down my window. I do it, but my hand is shaking and I end up pressing both buttons. All the windows go down. He leans in, casually resting his arms on the door.

"I've been waiting for you." The side of his lip curls in that devilishly attractive way.

"You have?" I might be in shock.

"Always."

"Where have you been?" But he only looks at me. "Cole! Where the fuck have you been?" I slam my hands on the steering wheel.

At that moment, I'm jolted out of myself by the quick blast of a car horn. I look left out my driver window and see Jen in her own car next to me.

"Oh my god, Faith! I didn't know you were

coming. We can catch up! Come on!" She maneuvers her car to the curb in front of mine.

I look left to Cole, who's no longer there. The passenger side window isn't rolled down either. What just happened? He was right here. Wasn't he? I stretch my upper body to peer out the passenger side of the car, but now Jen's knocking on my window. Grabbing my bag and the pie, I get out.

"Who were you talking to?" she asks as we head toward the house.

"Uh...I was singing along to the radio."

"To what? Heavy metal death rap? You seemed pretty angry. Ooooh, you stopped at the bakery! They always have the best pies, don't they? Did you see Tim? How is he?"

"Seems great." I compose myself as we walk to Leanne's door, looking back over my shoulder at the passenger side of my car and the grass for foot imprints. Nothing.

"I can't wait to see who else Leanne is surprising us with," Jen says.

I've had enough surprises for one night.

Chapter Twenty-Six

Sharp and jagged
Faith 2014

Faith,
Hi. What's up? Not much here, except I was here
(your house) and you weren't. Sorry I missed you. How
was your day? Mine was okay. I love you! You make me
so happy if I'm in a bad mood or depressed, all I have
to do is think of you and everything's cool again. What
are you doing tonight? I don't think I'm going to the
Lighthouse. I'm tired, and don't feel like sneaking out
of my house to spend money I don't have. What about
tomorrow night, what are we going to do? I don't care
what we do, just take me with you. What time will you
be home tomorrow? Early I hope. Are you performing
at the basketball game tomorrow? I love you! Call me
when you get home!
Love,
Cole

Basketball—God! I can't even think about it. I'd
rather concentrate on this note and Cole. This time last
year, we were strangers getting to know each other. He
captured my attention and heart right from the
beginning whether I liked it or not. I fought it, every
feeling, every butterfly, every ounce of attraction. But
his innocence and that crazy raw intensity pulled me in

like the gravity of a black hole where nothing escapes. And now I'm attached to him like the positive and negative charges that bind an atom.

Life with Cole is like riding a rolling wave in a storm, and the less time I spend with him the worse it gets. I start high up and euphoric, feel the anticipation of being with him, the excitement, the desire, the feeling of being so intensely cherished and needed by him. Only to be dropped down into a panic when he desperately needs to be pulled out of an unexplainable abyss of despair. The wave overtakes us, and we're both drenched in his pain. I hold onto him until the storm calms, we coast for a while, and then do it all over again. I'm afraid of what will happen if I let go of him. I'm afraid of what he'll do if I'm not there to pull him off the ledge of that abyss.

It was only gonna be a matter of time until I'd be bad for him. Before I'd fuck up. I've been holding it together all these months, almost a year now, being totally, truly, madly in love with him, while waiting for the inevitable moment when I would blow it. When I would start being the asshole I've always been. Well, that time has come. With new ingredients, comes a new Faith, like it or not. That other version of me has been creeping back in for months. The side that again wants to be free, unchained, detached.

Cole was right to be worried. Maybe he knows me better than I know myself. I don't understand it. I want him, and I want others. I want it all, and I want to be ruthlessly selfish about it. I'm torn. Leanne says this is all "developmentally appropriate" behavior, and how many high school sweethearts make it through college together?

Last Saturday night, through a haze of alcohol, I cheated on Cole. With a basketball player. I won't even name him. My dance team was spending a lot of time with the basketball team. Their practices are in the same gym as ours, and we travel with them. I'm not making excuses for my despicable behavior, but this is how it happened. And worse, I know it's gonna happen again. Just being honest.

Something has snapped in me. I wish it hadn't. I hate myself. Cole's everything I've always wanted except for those moody ups and downs, but they're not his fault. In my eyes, he's as close to perfect as there is and I'm…not. I have no control and don't want to have any either. My eyes are burning, been crying about it for days, avoiding Cole as much as possible, but I can't put this off any longer.

The weight of a thousand mountains is on me.

I arrive at Cole's house at six p.m. His aunt and uncle are out—good. He leads me into the kitchen, a space we've never hung out in before so it feels wrong to be in here now, as wrong as what I'm about to say to him. Nausea has set in.

"We need to talk, Cole."

"Okay, let's." He's casual, taking a can of soda out of the fridge. "Want one?"

"No." My stomach turns as he pops the cap. "I think we should take some time off."

"Time off? What do you mean?" The liquid fizzles, he pauses, then takes a sip.

"I think we should take a break—from each other." I draw in a breath, having knocked the wind out of myself.

"No." He's shaking his head.

144

"I need a little time…"

"Is it because of those arguments we've been having? I can fix it."

"It's not that."

"Faith, you're all I want."

"I can't be *all* you want, Cole."

"I've been researching careers like you wanted. Think I found one and a school to…"

"Stop," I interrupt.

His shoulders slump. "What happened? Whatever it is, we can work it out." He's searching my eyes for something, anything, but nothing's coming out of my mouth.

"What's going on, Faith? Is something happening on campus?" As if he already knows.

"Nothing."

"Is there someone else?"

I hesitate and he catches it. Shit.

His demeanor shifts from wounded puppy to CIA interrogator. Placing the soda can on the counter, he straightens his back and tells me to sit by motioning me to the kitchen table. I do it. He pulls out a chair and sits facing me as far away as the space will allow.

"Tell me" is all he says, voice flat.

It's time for me to own up to my lies. "I can't. It's hard to look at you." I sob with shaking hands over my face.

"Well, you better. You need to." He's not going to say another word until I do.

"It started during basketball season." My face is burning.

"Basketball season?" He practically yells because we both know that was months ago.

"I started seeing one of the players…" My voice trembles.

"Seeing or sleeping with?" The sharpness of his voice tells me he's losing patience with me, and even after a long pause, there's so much shame filling the space between us, I can't speak.

"Faith?" he demands.

I look at him, moving my head back and forth as if this is the first time even I'm hearing about it. Having to admit the truth feels like a waterboarding. My throat is closing. I stand up and turn away from him covering my face. He stands up just as fast, turns me toward him as gently as his anger will allow and takes my wrists in his hands, pulling them off my face. I still can't make eye contact.

"Look at me, when was the first time?" He only wants information now, without the drama. I can't put him off any longer.

"Two months ago."

"How many times?"

"A few."

"With him? The basketball player?"

"Yes."

"How many others are there?"

"Two."

"Two plus him or including him?"

"Including him."

"Are you sure?"

"Yes."

"When was the last time?"

"Two weeks ago."

"Fucking Christ, are you serious?"

"I'm sorry, Cole." My knees begin to buckle.

"Do you love any of them?"

"No!"

I can't stand up anymore, literally collapsing under all this truth. He lets go of my wrists and I fold over, hands on both knees supporting myself like I sprinted a ten K, crumbling into a ball of hysterics. When I look up, Cole has his hands on his head turning around in a circle, trying to process. I stay quiet and small, huddled in a ball. I'm afraid of what he's going to say, what he thinks of me now.

"Oh my God, is one of them Jeremy? Are you going back to him?"

"No!"

"I would fucking kill him, Faith. I'm such a dumbass over here thinking it's been only you and me." His eyes are on fire as he paces the room. "I've been so patient with you, and for what?" The muscles in his jaw are clenching, but his steps slow to a stop, and he looks directly at me. The fire has dimmed to an ember. He sighs, and his face softens.

"I don't know what to do with any of this, Faith." Cole starts opening and closing drawers like he's looking for something. "I've never felt like this about you before. I'm so angry, but then I wanna wrap my arms around you, force you to forget anyone else exists."

"It's not as bad as you think, Cole." I stay in my spot on the floor because I feel like I should.

He takes a long swig from the soda can and slams it down on the counter. "Please explain to me how it's not!"

I can't.

He puffs out mistrust. "Who are you? How could

you do this to us?" He's opening and closing drawers again, yelling now. "How could you spend all these months lying to my face? You're throwing it all away, Faith!"

"Do you think I want to be like this, Cole!"

Frustrated, he turns away and punches the wall. A surge of adrenaline makes me want to hug him, but I've never seen him like this before. Leanne might say he's manic.

"Please don't do this," he mutters over and over, hands on hips. I'm not sure if he's talking to me or the wall he's still facing.

"Cole, it's just a break. It's not like we're never going to see each other again." My voice cracks as I wipe away tears.

He sits back down on his chair, gulps the last of his soda, and focuses downward on the empty can. I don't like the sudden silence that's taken over the room.

"This is bad for both of us," I say gently. "I'm so busy with school, dance, and debate, there's no time for anything else." Blaming my own time management skills is the strategy.

He says nothing, partly because he's heard this speech before and partly because he's focused on the can he's twisting back and forth. The grinding metal tears and rips apart.

"I wish we'd met at a different time in our lives, Cole. I don't know what's wrong with me. Life is taking me in a different direction. I'm just trying to figure myself out. I wish we could skip ahead a bunch of years and start there."

He's not responding. My eyes dart from the can to his expressionless face. By now, he's ripped the can in two, both ends looking sharp and jagged. Panic explodes in my stomach as he brings the jagged edge to the flesh of his inner arm. He drags the uneven metal across his skin, slitting it open the same way you'd butterfly a chicken breast, except with more blood.

My eyes blur with tears. The thick, oozing redness forces my stomach into the back of my throat, and my heart beats out of my chest. "Cole, please don't. We'll still see each other!" I plead.

The moment is surreal. People think they know what that word means—they don't. *This* is a nightmare. *This* can't be happening. How could I hurt him like this? How could I do this to someone I love? And why does he feel so worthless he'd do this to himself? He continues his assault. I feel every slash to his arm as if he's carving into my own heart.

For a second I'm frozen and afraid, wondering if the next slice of self-hatred will continue on his own body or turn into a rage transferring onto mine. He continues in silence with another slash. His entire inner arm, from wrist to elbow, is filled with tiny cuts, blood dripping onto the floor, then splashing back up. He's in some kind of trance with a far-off look on his face.

I jump up and put my hands on his shoulders, shaking him. "If you don't stop, Cole, I'm calling 9-1-1."

He's not listening. He's looking through me, but his body eases, face softens, and his eyes focus on me. Words evade me, as if they've never existed.

On autopilot, I take the can out of his hand, grab the kitchen towels hanging by the sink, and wrap his arm. "Let's sit you on the ground." I guide him off the chair, a few paces away from the blood pool and onto the kitchen floor, placing his arm on a chair to get it elevated. "Hold the towels." He complies, and I grab the phone.

"I don't know what I was thinking." A weak grin emerges on his face. "I'm sorry you saw that."

"9-1-1, what's your emergency?"

"Suicide attempt, 534 Grove Street, Devenport." Can't believe I'm saying the words, but what else should I call it?

"Can we sit here for a little while together?" He looks woozy, eyes not fully focusing.

"Of course," I say, while staying on the line.

I get on the floor and maneuver us so my back is against the cabinets and he's leaning on me, arm still up on the chair. I wrap my arms around him. "We'll be okay, Cole. It'll be okay," I say, but will it? Blood seeps through the towel, and I follow the trail of red drops to the spot he was sitting in when he made the cuts. Kissing his forehead, I apply pressure and listen to the birds chirp outside the window. Help can't come fast enough.

I want to stay with him, and yet, I want to be free of him. I want to erase from my mind that first kiss in the car with the rain pounding down, and yet, I want to go back and freeze us in time right there. I want to never see him again until he finds a way to release himself from this never-ending cycle of worthlessness, and yet, I want to save him from every drop of pain he has ever felt and will ever feel in the future.

"I just need more of this," he whispers. "More of you."

"I know." Sirens wail in the distance. "I know you do, babe."

Chapter Twenty-Seven

All the shit Leanne talks about
Cole 2014

The sight of Faith walking through those hospital doors brings both relief and shame. She still cares enough to come, but I'm embarrassed by what I've done—to myself *and* her. I promised to never let anything hurt her, and now I'm a hypocrite. I've betrayed her in the most painful way—farewell via suicide. It was a moment of weakness. I should have ridden it out. The thought of losing her and being alone, brought me all the way back to the tent of my past, the place I used to hide to avoid the beatings.

I was afraid my attempt was gonna make everything worse between us, push her even farther away, but as she walks closer, there's a softness in her eyes. It's obvious she's been crying, and when she gets close enough, I stand. She practically collapses into my arms sobbing.

"It's okay, Faith, I'm fine," I whisper, supporting her weight and pulling her in close.

"I would have never forgiven myself, Cole." Her voice is muffled into my chest.

"This is on me. It was a stupid mistake." I usher us to the couches where we sit.

"I tried, I really did." She moves her head side to

side. "But every time I go out on campus, some other Faith takes over. The one I was before you. But when I'm with you, it's different. I'm the person you've turned me into, kind, caring, patient. I don't even know which one is the real me anymore. Now you know about this dual personality of mine. I'm doing the same thing to you my mother did to my father, and I hate myself for it. You shouldn't be with me. Look what happened. And it'll happen again. You'll die trying to hold onto me, and I'll let you because that's what I do. I'm gonna destroy us both."

"Don't do that, Faith. This is not only about you."

"It's my fault, Cole. You were upset about us, about what I said."

"It's *not* your fault." I don't know what to do with my hands, clasping them in front of me, then circling my thumbs around each other. "I was upset about our conversation, but this wasn't *because* of you. I can't have you thinking that. This was about me feeling the way I did growing up. Trauma, abandonment, all the shit Leanne talks about. It's true. It all came crashing down at the same time. I didn't handle it the right way, but I'm fine now."

"Are you?"

"I am. I promise."

"How's that possible? A few days ago, you didn't want to be here."

"Hard to explain. It comes and goes. Remember that hole I told you about? When I fall in, nothing matters. I didn't want to die, and I definitely didn't want to leave you." I cross my arms just to move them. "There's no one in there with me driving me to do it or stopping me either. It's me versus my demons. I can

152

usually get myself out, but this time I couldn't."

She looks down at her hands pushed together between her knees. The side of her jaw clenches. "And this time I put you into that hole, didn't I?"

I can barely hear her. "You didn't. Please don't do that. Fuck, I'm not explaining this right." I run my hand through my hair. "It's like a pot on a stove. Even if the flame gets turned up higher, it doesn't matter. Eventually, the water is always going to boil."

"When can you come home?" She looks up at me with those eyes.

"Wednesday, I think."

She takes my hand in hers. I can only hope this is a good sign.

Chapter Twenty-Eight

Some kind of inconclusivity
Faith 2026

The front door to Leanne's house is unlocked. It's customary to walk yourself in without knocking just like on our old board game nights. The house is bubbling with chatter and laughter, but I'm on edge after the event at my car. Cole stood there saying he's been waiting for me. Was it a waking dream, wishful thinking, real, or some form of psychosis? My normal MO is to analyze what just happened until my brain short-circuits, but now is not the time.

Jen and I enter and a round of hugs ensues, as it always has. Leanne has picked a charming variety of friends and…Steve. She invited Steve. She's at it again! This is what Leanne does. In all our years of friendship she's always loved playing Cupid. She purposely invited Steve to see what happens between us. I want to hug her, and maybe stab her, at the same time.

"Faith!" He says, stretching his arms toward me. "How long has it been? Eight years?"

"Steve!" I match his enthusiasm and hug him back. "Maybe longer."

I had an even more meaningful bond with Steve than with Bryce. While I was tortured with regret for not being there for Cole when it all unraveled, Steve was riddled with the same guilt and remorse for being there. He had watched Cole spiral, was part of it, and by the time he tried to step in and help, it was too late. The two of us remained friends for years afterward, the only two who really understood how this level of guilt felt, looking for an absolution that's never come.

"It's so good to see you, Faith." Steve's sandy hair and blue eyes haven't changed a bit. "I'm sorry for your loss. Didn't know until I came back to Devenport. I missed the funeral."

Steve had met a woman, fell in love, and relocated to a different state some years ago. No one knows much more about it. Word is it didn't work out, no kids involved. He's in the process of moving back. After the initial surprise of seeing him, I'm recalling the letters and realize he fits the profile even more fully now than he had before. A twinge of excitement comes over me, just like it does out in the field when I'm working.

"Don't give it another thought," I say. "You've had a full plate."

We chitchat and gravitate to the dining room. The night is filled with lively conversation, jokes, stories new and old, and occasional concerned glances from Leanne checking to see how I'm faring, half because I'm in a large crowd of old friends without Jeremy and half curious to see what, if anything, is occurring with Steve.

"It's got to be him," Leanne whispers in the kitchen as we set up for dessert. "I see the way he's looking at you. It makes so much sense! Think about it. You and he had a spark before you met Cole. And then afterward, the two of you spent so much time together, but he knew it would be wrong to start anything. When enough time had passed, Jeremy came back into your life. Steve never had his shot with you. I bet he's been waiting all this time. And"—her eyes widen—"he missed the funeral."

"You should've been a trial attorney."

I involuntarily check my phone to see if the DNA or handwriting comparison is back. Nothing. Could Steve be the one mailing these letters, but with no prints on them? Why would he go that far with it?

"Are you going to ask him tonight?" Leanne reaches for the silverware.

"Not sure. I mean, where would it go? Do I *want* it to go anywhere? Honestly, I'm exhausted from the last twenty years, always being with someone or getting over them."

Leanne nods and doesn't push any further. "Well, if you do ask, you've got to let me know." She hands me a serving platter with the pie I brought on it.

As the night progresses, I study Steve. I'm not sure of anything when it comes to this letter writer, but a romantic relationship is definitely not in the cards, nothing of the sort right now. It's nice to know it might be there in the future if the author is in fact Steve, the Steve I've known all these years during the best and worst times of our lives. Then again, leaving him hanging, perhaps even pining away for something that might never come, is not right either.

At the same time I decide that I will in fact ask him tonight, the phone in my pocket pings. My heart vibrates like a bell in a boxing ring. It's Mr. X. The DNA results are back. She wants me to call. That's highly unusual and can only mean there's some kind of inconclusivity she needs to explain. I excuse myself to the back porch while placing the call. It doesn't even ring, she immediately starts talking.

"A tiny fragment of hair was found stuck to the adhesive on the inside of the envelope. Now listen, there's some controversy over DNA hair matching when the sample is from the shaft and not the root. This sample does not have a root. It's only a tiny segment of hair that broke off from the rest. There's plenty of DNA in it. However, in samples like these it's highly degraded. Stuff like this can never be used in court, not reliable enough. But I suspect you're not looking for courtroom evidence?

"Correct."

"So I went with what we had and cross-referenced it with GVPs, which are even less reliable in court, and this is where things get weird."

"Wait, what's a GVP?"

"It's a protein in the hair shaft. Some new next-level genetics shit they've recently started using when there's only a partial DNA sample available."

"And?"

"And I got a hit, but here's the thing. The DNA profile is in the system without identification."

"What does that mean?"

"It means it *was* in there, but it's been taken out. Flushed. Expunged. Scrubbed."

"Human error? A data entry mistake?" I ask.

"It doesn't work that way. The system is designed to catch mistakes. This was intentional. Someone came in a back door to do this, probably in a rush, and didn't wipe it all."

"Seriously? Are you telling me we have a highly degraded sample, partially matched using a new and even more unreliable method, to someone who can't be found? What the hell am I supposed to do with that?"

"I don't know what you're into, Faith, but I'll tell you one thing, be careful. If this sample is an accurate match to this missing file, and I mean *if*, this is some high-level shit. This is somebody who doesn't want to be found. Who shouldn't be found. Do you understand?"

"Yeah, but this is bullshit." I look to the sky in frustration.

"Most of what we do is. Call me if you have anything else."

"By the way, what color is the hair?" I ask.

"Black, natural black." True to form, the line goes dead.

I immediately work to integrate the new info with the old. A post office camera malfunction, no prints on the letter or envelope, and DNA that's suspicious and...*irregular.* Between the CODIS system and all the other private genetic databases Mr. X can access, there are millions of samples available for comparison. It's hard to hide in this day and age. There's one thing you learn right away in this business—there's no such thing as privacy. But somehow, my letter writer has managed to stay behind the veil. Somebody who doesn't want to be found and shouldn't? This brings things to a whole new level. I'm still digesting when Leanne pops her head out.

"I think Steve's getting ready to head out."

I blink myself back to the present moment. "Be right in."

****

"Faith, can I get your jacket?" Steve opens the

closet door. The night's coming to a close, and until this point, I haven't found any way to get him alone to bring it up. And with this new info from Mr. X, I'm looking at him anew, with suspicious eyes.

"Yes, thanks. And I'll walk out with you."

Leanne raises an eyebrow, smiling at me.

"Great night," Steve starts as we walk down the driveway. "I'm glad Leanne included me, and I ran into you again. I've really missed everyone."

"I'm happy to hear you're moving back. It's always good to be around familiar faces. But Steve…" A surge of adrenaline burns. "Is there anything you want to tell me?"

"That's a strange question. I think I've poured my heart out to you enough times in the past that you already know everything there is to know about me. Maybe a little too much." He laughs.

I'm not sure what to make of *that* answer. Is he not ready to tell me it's him or is it not him? In the pause we stare at each other, waiting to see who's going to speak next. It's oddly uncomfortable.

"Sorry, am I missing something, Faith?"

But at this point I know. I've been trained to know. The look in his eyes, the curve of his lips—he isn't trying to be difficult or mysterious. There's no tell here. He really doesn't know what I'm hinting at. I'm almost sure he's not trying to hide anything.

"No, you're not. Sorry for the confusion. I've been receiving these letters lately. They're unsigned and from someone in my past, our past. I wasn't sure if…if maybe it was you." There, I said it.

"Oh!" He breathes a sigh of relief, seeming genuinely concerned he might have been upsetting me in some way without knowing it. "I was worried there was something I was supposed to remember." His expression changes. "You're receiving letters from someone? Unsigned? What do they say?"

"Yeah, since Jeremy passed. There've been two so far. He said he would send another. They're kind of mysterious, hinting at the timeframe we knew each other, saying he had some kind of crush on me."

"Are these letters coming to your house?" His brows scrunch downward.

"Yep."

Almost instantly, Steve's face morphs into something I have not seen in a long time. The look he and the guys used to wear whenever someone uninvited came near us. Like a silent warning—back off, or things will get ugly.

"I don't like the sound of that, Faith. You don't know who it could be. And I don't like these letters coming right to your door. He knows where you live. You're up on that mountain alone now. I know you can handle yourself, but still…Would you humor me and let me stop by, check up on you every now and then?"

"Of course, but I think it's harmless."

"It'd make me feel better," he says.

"And you can stay for dinner when you do."

"I'd like that."

"Good luck with the rest of your move." I head to my car. "You have help?"

"Plenty. Drive safe," he says.

I get into my car. He closes the door for me as if we'd just been on a first date.

Chapter Twenty-Nine

Not looking for perfect
Faith 2014

Did Cole really try to kill himself because he thought he lost me? What if he'd *died*? My life would be over. I knew it, I was uneasy about breaking it off but did it anyway. What's wrong with me? Jesus, it *is* my fault! Since visiting Cole in the hospital, I've spent most of my time crying with Leanne and Steve, trying to make sense of it.

"His early life makes him more susceptible to suicide attempts," Leanne explained. "For someone to reach the point of an attempt, the slow burn of pain and struggle will have reached its peak, and all emotional reserves have been exhausted. At that point it's an acute state, not unlike suffering a heart attack."

Steve said there's not a single cause but a perfect storm of many little things that align at once. They did their best to convince me this isn't my fault. I'm pretty sure it is, despite all the psychological mumbo jumbo.

Cole spent the remainder of his time in the hospital meeting with doctors, being questioned, examined, and evaluated, while I spent my time berating myself for not listening to my gut when it told me something bad was going to happen. It's clear to me now my actions have real-life consequences. Ever since that day in his kitchen, I've felt like I'm being followed by a towering, faceless, hooded presence that's violently shoved its hand into my chest, suffocating my beating heart with its fingers—guilt. And it hasn't let go since.

What's made things worse is everyone, and I mean everyone, has an opinion about Cole's attempt and what I should be thinking and feeling. Leanne is the only one with anything constructive to say. "Both your parents want you to stop seeing Cole?"

"They told me separately of course, like they have any idea what real love and commitment is supposed to look like."

"They're worried about you, Faith. And so are we." Leanne looks across the café table at Jen and back at me. It's covered with one of every type of pastry and cookie this place has to offer.

"I'm okay." I scan the sweets.

"Really?" Jen says, reaching for the black-and-white cookie. "How's that possible? You break it off with him, and he tries to take his life?" She leans in. "In front of you?"

"I know, I know, but it's complicated. *He's* complicated. Cole was in a dark place, knows he shouldn't have done it. He's getting help."

"What are you going to do when he gets out of the hospital? He's definitely gonna want to see you. You're going to stay away, aren't you? Please tell me you are. You don't need that in your life," Jen announces.

"Of course I'm gonna see him." What a stupid question.

"Seriously, Faith? What he did was selfish. You should be mad at him."

"No, I shouldn't. You're wrong, Jen. And way out

of line for saying it." Leanne leans forward and squirms in her seat wanting to jump in, but I continue. "Cole's been through a lot in his life. He struggles with it. Who wouldn't? Does that mean we should give up on the people in our lives who are going through a rough time? He needs me more than ever, and I'm gonna be there for him."

"Seems like much more than a rough time." Jen shakes her head in protest. "It's not like the therapist can wave a magic wand and fix him right up. This is him, how he is, and you're still gonna have to deal with it right alongside him, walking on eggshells, wondering when and what the next thing is that'll set him off. I couldn't be with someone like that. Someone so…"

"Unpredictable?" Leanne can't hold back any longer. "Look, you're right. The breakup triggered some of the trauma he's suffered in his early life, but Faith knows it's not her fault."

Leanne looks at me nodding, but I don't nod back. I can't. She continues.

"When people are in that much pain, they have blinders on, not thinking about anyone else in the moment. They want to make the pain stop, but they don't have the tools to do it in a healthy way. You're right, Jen. This is not going to disappear. It will take time to work through with the therapist. What will come out in time is whether this was an impulsive act or the symptom of an underlying mental health issue. With treatment and sometimes even medication, people can lead very happy lives and have healthy relationships. They can even heal."

"Remember when Tim broke his arm at football practice?" I say to Jen. "Did you stop seeing him because part of him was broken?"

"Not the same thing." Jen smirks.

"It is, actually." I reach for a Boston cream donut. "Pain is pain. Physical or emotional. They both need attention. If you got cancer, is it your fault? Are you selfish? Of course not. I wish people could see that emotional issues are the same. There's no blame here. No one should be made to feel like they're a burden or defective."

"I guess." Jen breaks off the white side of the cookie.

"And it's not Cole's fault he's this way." I sip my drink. "It's one part of him, it's not all of him. I see him for who he is—*all* of who he is. And he lets me. I love him for that. I'm not going to abandon him. I'll support him any way I can."

"What if it happens again?" Leanne asks, choosing a chocolate croissant.

"We'll deal with it. I'll admit it's hard feeling like I have someone's life in my hands, but no one's perfect. I certainly am not. Are you? And I'm not looking for perfect. There's no such thing."

Jen continues. "Sounds like a lot of work to me. We're so young, there's a million other boys out there."

"Really? Look at our friends and so many of our parents' relationships—total bullshit. Ignoring their issues, hiding their true selves, more concerned with projecting the picture-perfect life inside a white picket fence. It doesn't exist. Life's messy. It can be heartbreaking and cruel and raw. Cole's not hiding who he is. He's real and able to be vulnerable with me. Not everyone can handle that. Or wants to. When things are good, it's better than anything I've dreamed of."

"You know…" Jen takes a bite. "They say suicide is anger turned inward. What if he turns it outward, toward you or someone else? Then what?" she garbles.

I tilt my head at her, irritated, and chew my donut. She already accused Cole of attacking Jeremy a few months back.

"It just seems like he goes to the extreme." Jen looks at Leanne. "Like he's obsessed with her instead of being in love with her. It sounds codependent to me. What about you and what *you need*, Faith? You don't need to be put through an emotional wood chipper."

I roll my eyes, swallow and answer. "Maybe it *is* codependency. But isn't there a little of that in every relationship? Your partner always needs something from you and you from them, and you give it because you want them to be happy, feel supported, and loved."

"Agreed." Leanne breaks off a piece of croissant. "But relationships are muddy. Be careful, Faith. I warned you about feeling responsible for his actions a few months ago, remember? You're not. He's getting the help he needs to stand on his own, but it's gonna be easy to fall back into being his crutch."

"Honestly, I'm exhausted most of the time. I keep replaying it and seeing the can and the blood and the…" I stop myself.

"And you should talk to someone also, Faith. What you witnessed can cause PTSD with long-lasting effects."

"Why? I have you." I laugh it off even though that day is seared into my brain forever. "You're right. Maybe I will. And Cole…" I push out a breath. "I'm going to support him, not fix him. That's got to come from him."

"Spoken like a true therapist."

****

Cole was back home Wednesday. His father, aunt, and uncle have been spending more time with him now, which is not only an annoyance to Cole but also a hypocritical slap in the face more than anything else. According to the doctor, I have too much influence over him. His family is blaming his attempt on me. They don't want us seeing each other, but we find a way.

On Thursday, Cole skips lacrosse practice and comes to my house instead. We aren't going to have much time. He has to get back to school by the end of practice for his dad to pick him up. He walks through the kitchen door like he has so many times before, but this time is different. This time I feel like I broke him. The force of the words I said to him are clamped around my heart so tight, I can hardly breathe.

What have I done to him? Why was I thinking anything on campus could be more important than us? My heart's racing as he walks in. Has his time with the doctors made him see what a terrible person I am? Does he hate me as much as I hate myself? Can this be fixed?

All my worries melt away as soon as he comes in and hugs me. We've always fit together perfectly, and today is no different. His body feels the way it always has, strong arms around my waist and back, my hand on the back of his head feeling the softness of his hair again. Just breathing. Our connection is restored, washing away some of the distance between us. The tension I was carrying lifts. The quiet surrounding us is the kind that comes after a hurricane has ripped through town, throwing everything in all directions, leaving people's lives in ruins. It's time to stand together amid the destruction, take a deep breath, and rebuild.

"Are you okay?" I ask, pulling back to look at him.

"I am now. Are you?" His eyes reflect a combination of shame for himself and concern for me. Still, after everything I've said and done, he's worried about me.

I shake my head, lowering it to hide my watering eyes. "I'm trying, Cole. This thing between us is so big and intense, it scares me. Sometimes it's like I'm drowning in you. I feel things for you I've never felt for anyone. It has power over me. *You* have power over me. I'm out of control with you sometimes, and I don't like it. I know how much you need me. You've told me over and over you could never live without me, you're addicted to me—"

"Faith—" He tries to interrupt, but my words are pouring out.

"—that I'm the only one who truly understands you, and I love being that person for you, but it's too much sometimes, so heavy. I never wanted to hurt you. I'm not trying to make excuses, only trying to explain what's going on in my head. And now you know everything. Everything I've been afraid to show you about myself because I've been sure once you know, we'll be over."

He's quiet for what seems like hours. I wait silently for him to process. He turns to me but then closes his eyes, like it hurts too much to see my face. "What do you want?" The pain in his eyes is shredding my heart.

"I want you…" I sob.

"You want me *and* you want your freedom?"

"I don't know how to answer that. Are you asking me to choose?"

"I'm asking if you want both," he says.

I still don't understand.

"Every time I look at you, I see the future. And you know it." He takes my hand. "I don't want to be without you. This is fucked up. I hate what you've done, and I'm gonna be mad at you for a while, but I can't lose you. Not now. Not if you still want to be with me. Do you—still want to be with me?"

"Of course I do," I manage.

"Then if you want to see other people, do it. I'll give you that. But I want to know about it; you can't lie to me."

Can't believe what I'm hearing. Is he forgiving me? "It's going to be too hard for you, Cole."

"Let me worry about that."

"I can't. What if I'm not able to be the person you need me to be? Are you going to do this again? I'm afraid you'll destroy yourself trying to hold on to me while I die a little every time I pull away. We should take some time to think about this."

"I don't need time," he says softly.

"We'll ruin each other if we can't get this right," I say. "You should be with someone else."

"I don't want someone else. I want you." He brings my hand to his lips and kisses it, solidifying his place in my heart. He never ceases to amaze me. He's a much better person than I am. The fact that he even wants to attempt a relationship like this is crazy, but he's always had a way of making crazy feel normal.

"I don't know how to get past the guilt I feel every time I look at you." I drop my head.

"Faith…" He holds my face and brushes away the tears. "I can't have you do that. It was my fault and mine alone." His voice cracks. "I never meant to hurt you, and if you need your freedom, I'll live with it."

"*You*...never meant to hurt *me*?" I say in confusion. "I swear, Cole, sometimes I don't understand you. I'm the one that started this problem. I don't know why I thought I wanted to be apart from you..."

The rest of the words I want to say never make it out. He kisses me through my apology, his way of telling me he's heard enough. Lifting me in his arms, he carries me to my room and places me on the bed. Our clothes come off in a frenzy, torn away from my body and replaced with his hands and mouth. Our desperation slows to a more tender pace, breathing into each other. Like the calm an injection of heroin brings to an addict, the feeling of skin on skin consoles us both.

The bandages are gone from his arm, and I immediately need to see what it looks like. Rolling on top and straddling him, I lift his arm toward me. He resists, but I continue until the inner flesh is exposed, forearm facing me. There are cuts in different directions, and my stomach turns, remembering with crystal clarity how they got there. Most are jagged and shallow, covered with a few well-placed thin bandage strips that look like they don't need to be there holding things together anymore. For a split second a wave of relief washes over me, but two of the lacerations are deeper, required stitching, and still look red, swollen, and angry. Flashes of the prior week's conversation and the look on his face come bursting back into my head.

I close my eyes and drop my face down into his forearm. He sits up so we're facing each other and wraps his arms around me.

"This is why I didn't want you to look," he whispers.

"Do they hurt?"

"No."

He wouldn't tell me if they did.

"Look at me," he says, brushing the hair from my face. "We can move forward from this, can't we? I'm sorry, Faith. I wish I could take those couple of minutes back. I love you. Please forgive me…and forgive yourself." His voice trails off.

My entire being aches for him and for what I've done. His hands move up and down my body, warming me wherever he places them, healing every inch of pain that's in me. Cole lifts me up and onto him, both of us breathing a soft moan as he slides into me. I kiss his cheek tasting salty tears and drag my lips onto his warm waiting mouth.

Leaning me back, his tongue runs down my neck to my breasts. He is getting larger inside, one hand on the small of my back, pulling me into him as he moves in deeper. There's nowhere I'd rather be, and the thought of the basketball player in his place creates a new ripple of self-loathing.

The first waves of pleasure wash over me. He knows and slows the rhythm, holding his own pleasure back during what becomes a blur of multiple pulses. After the fourth…fifth…sixth, I'm trembling with exhaustion.

We're back, and I'm not gonna let anything come between us again.

Chapter Thirty

I would fucking kill him
Cole 2014

"I gave Faith the option to see other people a*nd* me. Not ideal, but I'll take it for now."

"What? Why?" Bryce is mystified as he lifts the fifty-pound plate and places it on the bar.

"She's been right all along. I have this intensity for her. It's too much sometimes. *I did this.* I caused it. I pushed her right to those other guys. My emotional thermostat is set too high for her."

Bryce shoots me a look of confusion.

"Sorry, man, it's a therapy term."

Bryce lies on the weight bench. "Are you seriously gonna sit here and blame yourself for her bullshit?" He pushes the words out, muscling the weight up.

"Even you've told me I can be *extra*. Can't help it. With her, it's all or nothing. It's who I am." I'm keeping a close eye because this is too much weight for him. "No matter how hard I've tried to lose the ghosts of the past, they still show up, like they're holding a gun to my head forcing me to say and do shit. My sessions with the therapist have made that clear. It's no different for Faith. Look what she's coming from, can't help it either. But both of us can do better, change. Love doesn't have to be perfect, it just has to be real."

"Cole…" He finishes his set and stands up. "We're young, got our whole lives ahead of us. Maybe backing off for a while is a good thing."

"Did we just meet yesterday? Not gonna happen. As long as Faith knows I'm here for her, she'll always come back to me. We just need to get past this rough patch. Isn't that what commitment is, loving someone through their faults?" We move to the free weights.

"I guess, but there has to be a limit to how much shit you should take, right?"

"Does there?"

"Dude, not sure how to say this but…" Bryce presses his lips together. "I know it's not something you like to think about, but your mom…how she mistreated you. Things are different now, you don't have to put up with that from anyone."

"That's *not* what's happening, Bryce." I grab the fifties and start some curls. "Faith loves me, but it's not the same for her as it is for me. Her first love was…someone else. I won't even utter his name."

Bryce finds the forties and works his triceps, scrunching his face. "Do you think she's been seeing him too?"

"I don't know what to believe anymore." I put the fifties down and take a breather. "I would fucking kill him. He'll only hurt her again. I'm so angry at her, and yet, she's the one trying to figure out if we should move forward like this. *Her*, not me."

"Sucks, dude."

"I wish we could skip all this and get to the part where we live happily ever after. Wild horses couldn't drag me away. This is a nightmare. We'll get through this. We have to."

Days turn into weeks. On my way home from class, I drop off my usual love letter to Faith, still not knowing where she and I are going. I only know we love each other. Our new normal is a dysfunctional mess—together yet apart. The ache that comes when I'm not with her is deep and constant, but letting her go is not an option. Faith has insisted I keep seeing my therapist as a condition of our relationship. Can't blame her. I have things to work on.

Like today, coming home and seeing my neighbors' dog still chained up on the front lawn.

Poor thing was out there when I left early this morning, shivering, with no food or water. And now it's five p.m. This dick leaves him out in the cold all day and night. People like this make my blood shoot straight up to a thousand degrees. I've already mentioned it to him. What kind of *motivation* does this fuck *need* to take proper care of this innocent dog who's done nothing to anyone but give love and want to be loved in return? I know how that feels. People think they can get away with anything. They can't.

When I head over with food, water, and a blanket for the little guy, his tail wags. I pet him for a bit and ring the bell even though dickweed doesn't get home from work till later. No answer. He's lucky. Faith would be a hundred percent behind me on this. She loves dogs. We've even talked about getting one in the future, but for now, we're leading mostly separate lives. Mine is spent on the field as a starting varsity senior, and researching colleges for computer engineering programs like she encouraged me to do. Faith's is on campus, occupied with dance, debate, studying, and God knows what else, *who* else.

We get close, she pulls away. We get closer, she pulls away again. I wait for her to come back. She always does. I know her better than she knows herself. She can't be with me but she can't be without me either. She's mine, I'm hers, no matter who else might be on the periphery. I'm trying to believe in her, in our future, and accept who she is right now, giving her the freedom she's clearly craving. But I have to admit, this cycle we're in is a slow ride to insanity.

I want more. I *need* more. And she knows it.

Chapter Thirty-One

Arguing with myself
Faith 2026

I always appreciate time off, but it looks like the shiz hit the fan, and it's blowing squarely on me today. Our client, Mrs. Finola Hughes, was arrested last night for breaking and entering a hotel room, disorderly conduct, destruction of private property, and assault with a deadly weapon. Sarah welcomes me back to the office with a call on hold from the arresting detective on line three. Great.

"Good morning, Detective. What can I do for you?"

"You can start by explaining what in the hell your agents think they're doing out there."

"Whoa, hold on, Detective. I just got in. Can you fill me in?" I ask, having to move the phone away from my ear.

"Since when do your agents call the hell-hath-no-fury wives with the exact location of their piece-of-shit cheating husbands in real time? We have your client Mrs. Hughes here, about to be arraigned on a laundry list of charges. Somebody could have been killed."

"Right. We're all on the same team. That's not how we operate. Won't happen again, sir." I remember the intake meeting with Mrs. Hughes and how she insisted on being notified when we caught the "son of a bitch" which I had no intention of doing. There *may* have been notes in the file to that effect. The case was on last night, and no one informed the agent *not* to call her. Oops.

"This is a courtesy call. Don't let it happen again." The detective emphasizes *don't* and hangs up before I can reassure him. Rude. I have half a mind to go down there, find him, and wring his neck.

I walk into the war room to find Andy, poor guy. He's got gold star potential. It's just going to take some time to polish him. He's in the back of the room, head buried in his laptop.

"Andy, come to my office when you have a minute," I say.

His head pops up as do the heads of three other agents in the room. "Ooooh, you're going to the principal's office…ooooh, you're in trouble."

"Let me finish mapping out this…case." His voice catches.

Returning to my desk, I work on the final draft of the X-rated Miller report while I wait. It's a perfect example of Andy's creativity in the field. He managed to get video of Mrs. Miller and her boytoy straight through her bedroom window without ever setting foot on the property via a tree he climbed in the park next door. They're in court tomorrow, and now it's a rush. Mr. Miller had the court date moved up because his five- and seven-year-olds were home the evening Mommy had her *friend* over. The kids heard the whole sex thing. He's had to explain to them over and over that, no, Mommy's not hurt, no, she was not attacked, and no, this will never happen again because he'll have full custody starting yesterday to protect them, just as soon as our video is blasted up on the courtroom widescreen with our accompanying report for the judge.

"You wanted to see me?" Andy's in the doorway.

"Do you like working here?" I motion him to sit.

"Love it."

"You're doing a bang-up job, no pun intended, but I'm sure you know why I called you in. The detective is pissed, and we never want to be on the radar with our police. Calling Mrs. Hughes was a no-no. Just don't do it again."

"But it was in my file to call her."

"Clerical error. Even so, it was a judgment call, and your judgment was…off. Do you understand why?"

"Yes, ma'am."

"Investigative discernment will come in time. Nothing to lose sleep over. I've done worse. Carry on," I say.

Andy leaves with his tail between his overly motivated legs.

Before I ditch out early, I finish the report, return a few messages, and set up a new client meeting for myself in the a.m. I'm booked solid tomorrow, so the hours will even out. I head out with a bunch of case files and grab a coffee for the ride. Midday is the best time to drive anywhere on Long Island, but it's always a crapshoot. There's too many damn people on this island. I'm relieved to see little traffic on the Meadowbrook Parkway. Flipping on the radio, I settle in for the drive and the bottleneck I know I'll hit at the Queens border. It's okay though. This is where I do some of my best thinking.

I'm debating the pros and cons of placing Andy in

his first undercover situation while wearing a wire for a new case when my analysis is interrupted by a chirping text. It's an attachment of the handwriting comparison with the message, "Bingo!" Excitement fills my chest cavity. Wasn't expecting it to come back this quickly. Between the notes passed in class I saved and the samples in my yearbook, there's lots to compare. I want to open it right now, but I also just drove past a "Stay alive, don't text and drive" billboard.

Both the car and my brain go into overdrive as I speed to the next rest stop. Before getting too carried away with the name in this report, I remind myself how handwriting comparisons are not always reliable. Not everyone is identifiable, especially in this scenario where the samples are from teenagers who are now many years older. Developmentally, people change, but their handwriting tends to stay the same, although this is not true for everyone. More recent samples would have boosted reliability. Plus, if my letter writer intends harm, he probably tried to disguise his writing, further muddying the waters.

I pull over and skip past the standard section of the report displaying blown-up images of words and letters comparing the "questioned writing," which is the letter, to the "known writing," which are the samples I provided. Right now I'm not interested in the examiner's interpretation of letter height, width, spacing, stroke angle, curve, and pressure. I scroll right to the conclusion:

"After a thorough examination of the questioned document, it is this examiner's opinion that the known writing provided in sample two and the questioned writing were written by the same person."

Oh God, who's sample two? I scroll back through the pages like a contestant spinning the wheel on *The Price Is Right*. Sample two…where's sample two…

Squinting, my eyes focus on each bolded heading after bolded heading, as I scroll backward, page after page. I turn down the radio because everyone knows you can see better when it's quiet and there—sample two. My thumb skids the scrolling to an abrupt stop. Sample two is…

Cole?

Eyes blur on the page, going out of focus like someone has turned the tube on my kaleidoscope. Thoughts collapse inward.

No.

It can't be.

Can it?

Of course not. *Don't even go there, Faith. The science is not a hundred percent, and you know it.* I click the phone off, throw it onto the passenger seat, and put the car in drive.

Cole?

The rest of the ride home consists of me arguing with myself over sample number two. I've only used this forensic company a handful of times, but they've always been dead-on balls accurate. Then again, if this report's wrong, at least a few people have been ruled out. But if it's correct? Cole's out there, somewhere, maybe close by…trying to reach me? Ridiculous. Cole's dead. I was at his funeral. I was *at his death.* Wrapping my thoughts around this result is impossible, as if the neurotransmitters in my brain can't make the jump between synapses.

So ridiculous.

I walk into the house through the garage, letting the door slam behind me. Wait, did I turn off the car? Can't remember and peek my head back in…yep. Tossing my keys into the bowl, I grab an entire handful of peanut butter cups, feeling no willpower at the moment, and throw my bag and files on the kitchen counter. Finn follows me as I head into the closet on robo-pilot, change clothes, inhale all the chocolates, and head to the backyard.

If I share this with Leanne, she's going to say exactly what I'd expect. I'm stressed, overthinking, confusing the past with the present. She already pretty much hinted at it during our last lunch, didn't she? Leanne knows me better than anyone. Her assessment is probably right. Still, I can't help but play out all the possibilities. It's what we do as investigators, work through all the potential scenarios to their conclusions, no matter how far-fetched and implausible.

I slip on my work gloves, grab my supply bucket, and look around the backyard. I'm way behind in my landscaping duties. It's a big piece of property. Jeremy and I used to do the spring cleanup together. After he was gone, I didn't care much about the foliage.

I don't care much right now either, but feel compelled to get it done, and this, like driving, helps me process. Finn likes to assist, so he's right beside me as I clip dead branches, rake, and move earth for new flowers. Working outside in the fresh air and sunshine makes everything else fall away. It's one of the only times my brain can go quiet. I find it calming.

Finn apparently does not. He's as bothered as me today, on alert, pacing and growling. Jeremy brought him home one Christmas, and he's been part of everything ever since. Jeremy always thought we'd grow up, get married, have two point five kids and a Lab. Turns out he was right, except for the kid part. Wasn't in the cards. And now Finn's looking up the mountain into the trees barking a protective, as opposed to interested, yowl. Something has him spooked. And with all these thoughts about the letter writer and the new piece of data ricocheting inside my skull, I'm spooked too. I left my gun inside with my clothes. Maybe I shouldn't have.

Walking to the edge of the lawn, I look up into the dense trees and shrubs. Don't see a thing. I give him a pat on the head and go back to the plants but hear some rustling and Finn goes into a frenzy again. Still, nothing is visible. Probably a squirrel or rabbit with its babies. There's loads of them up there. This *is* a mountain.

The inside of my head feels like a pinball machine. There's three possible scenarios pinging my brain now regarding this letter writer. One, it's truly an innocent flirtation from someone I've known who's reaching out to me now. Two, it's someone with malicious intent with a plan I'm not aware of that might not end well for me. Three, the examiner is correct, and Cole is reaching out to me.

So ridiculous. But…

I've always felt him around me. At first, I thought it was a spiritual thing, like his energy was there. But sometimes I actually *see* him. Do I just want to? I'm not crazy. Not delusional. I'm *not*. It was right there in black and white in the report. These letters are coming from him.

A fourth possibility occurs to me. What if this letter writer is trying to disguise his handwriting? He's either trying to hide himself or he's trying to make it look like Cole. But why would anyone do that? He would have to know me, like *really know me. And Cole.* But again, why? If this is someone I've pissed off with my work, why would they want it to look like Cole? How would they even know him or want me to think he's alive?

There's no scenario where that makes sense, so I strike the fourth idea, but it's immediately replaced with a fifth that's even worse. What if it's one, two, *and* three meaning it's Cole, he's alive, and he currently both loves me *and* hates me?

The doorbell rings. Another round of barking ensues from Finn who gets to the front door before me. I can't see clearly through the frosted glass window, but I'm able to get a blurry view of the visitor, dressed in brown, which means it's likely my UPS carrier, Ben. After all the barking in the backyard, I hesitate but trust my gut and open the door.

Ben is carrying a large package with my regular mail, nice enough to walk it up to the house today.

"Thanks, Ben," I say, taking the package.

"Sure, Faith. I like to ring the bell and check on you sometimes. How's things?"

"Moving along, thanks."

He turns and hurries off in his usual way.

The package is so oddly shaped and awkward to hold, I drop it. All the mail cascades onto the floor as soon as I turn from the door. Everything scatters across the hallway floor. The last letter to stop sliding is another crisp white envelope with blue-penned writing.

My heart burns and splits in two. One side is enraged with this asshole who's clearly trying to get under my skin. The other's aching with anticipation over what Cole has to say next. In my neurotic bifurcated brain, there's room for both these possibilities.

The letters are coming closer together now, this one only two weeks after the last. Either way, I'm now staring at yet another and wondering how long this will go on.

Chapter Thirty-Two

One wrong move
Faith 2014

Dear Faith,
You're not returning my calls—again. All this time together and this is where we're at? Don't know what you're thinking. We are SO right for each other. You know how I feel about you. I'm not trying to make you feel guilty, but if I didn't have such strong feelings for you, would I forgive you? Why this is up to you, I'll never understand, but I really don't care because I want it, I want you. We should give it another shot. What could we lose by trying? I know you're scared, but do you really think I'm not? Look what I went through because of you, and I'd be willing to do it again if it meant we could be together. I miss you, I really do, and hate not being with you. Please don't give up on me—on us. I just want to be with you, what's so wrong with that? Why won't you let me love you?
Loving you always (no matter what you say),
Cole

Leanne looks at me after reading Cole's letter like her own heart's been ripped out.

"I know," I whine. "Every time I pull away, he delivers one of these. It's not that I don't want to see him. I do. But this isn't the right time for us."

We're seated at the Pastry Palladium's free taste-testing event. If there's one thing I'm good at, it's finding sweets.

"Don't be so hard on yourself." Leanne hands me the menu. "You're caught in the middle of your school life and him. It's perfectly normal."

"Feels like I'm two separate people. It's killing the Faith that loves him, who wants nothing more than to be content in his arms for the rest of her life. It's also the perfect situation for conquest-seeking Faith, the Faith who loves to have her cake and eat it too."

"You do like your cake. Look where we are." Leanne looks at the menu.

"We don't need to pick, Leanne. They're going to bring *everything* over." I lay mine on the table. "There's so much about Cole that makes him the perfect guy, romantic, devoted, sweetly vulnerable. What's wrong with me?"

"Fuck if I know."

"Seriously? You've been analyzing me for years."

The waiter, oddly dressed in pink from head to toe matching the store logo, arrives at our table. "Anything to drink?"

"Two cappuccinos, please." I look to Leanne for confirmation. She bobs her head, and the waiter takes the menus. "I love feeling like the sun rises and sets with me, but it's not easy to feel like you're holding someone's life in your hands. At what point do I put myself first?"

"You think if you walk away, he might not make it?"

"Exactly. There's a fine line between love and desperation, and every woman decides where that is for herself."

"We live in a culture that romanticizes dysfunctional relationships." Leanne leans in, resting her elbows on the table. "We're drawn to love stories that are fast in the beginning, intense in the middle, and tragic in the end. *The Notebook*, *Titanic*, *A Star Is Born*, *Heathers*. They all feature men who are passionate, devoted, and charming but also wild, brooding, and overflowing with intense feelings. They can be reckless, dark, and moody, with elements of repressed rage, unresolved abandonment issues, and self-destructive tendencies who, in the end, sacrifice themselves for the ones they love."

"Exactly," I nod. "And women eat this shit up. Are we watching romance or psychosis?"

"Researchers say to a brain in love, there is no difference."

"And what about all those drippy song lyrics, Leanne? 'I can't live without you,' 'everything is pointless if you're not around,' 'I would die for you'? What do you do when it's actually true? When one wrong move or change of heart can mean life or death? How does the one on the other end of those lyrics navigate such a relationship?"

The waiter places the coffees and a large tray of delightful-looking bite-sized samples on the table.

"Thank you," Leanne says.

I scan the tray for my favorite and continue. "We all think we want the intense, spin-your-head-around love, until it actually happens. I can tell you in reality, it's tragic in more than one way. It's soul-crushing and disorder-producing."

"So what are you going to do?" Leanne sips her

coffee and takes the Black Forest square. Damn, it looked good.

"I don't know. It's all so normal sometimes, and then it's not. Since his attempt..." I bite into the raspberry truffle. Heavenly.

When I don't finish my sentence, Leanne stops chewing. "Oh no, you can't leave me hanging. Continue, please."

"I saw how angry he was at his neighbor for leaving the dog outside all day, and one time up at Prescott Peak, I hinted at spending a little less time together. Cole jumped off a cliff. Literally. Thought I was watching him die in front of me again. There was a lake below, but the chance of injury or death was real. Was he being fun and spontaneous or sending me a message? My nerves are frayed."

"Oh giiiirl." The waiter is wiping the table next to us. "That doesn't sound good. More napkins?"

"Please," Leanne says. The waiter places them down and leaves. "And you're right, Faith. Your nerves should be frayed. Why didn't you tell me this sooner?"

"I don't know. Forget I said it."

"No, it's important. Reckless behavior is developmentally appropriate for our age group. It's how we express our desire for independence, but he also could be crossing the border into dangerous territory."

"How do I know which it is?"

"Shit, I don't know. I didn't get that far in the DSM."

"The what?"

"The book of mental health disorders." Leanne snags the pistachio macaroon and uses it to point at me. "The reality is, you both know what you're doing to each other. His reliance on you creates too much pressure. You think you need to save him, so you pull away. This makes him anxious, so you, in turn, give him just enough of yourself to keep him hanging on." She pops it into her mouth. "Classic codependency."

"I can't let go of him, and he can't let go of me. Why can't we just be done? We're like the frayed edges of a rope, still one, still connected, but holding on by a thread. Sometimes I want to end this rollercoaster I've put us on. But he loves me. It brings me back to him over and over, like waves that pull away from the shore during a tsunami and rush back even stronger. He just won't walk away."

And secretly, if I'm being honest with myself, I don't want him to.

****

At two a.m. on a Saturday night weeks later, Cole comes through the door of my dorm room like the tornado he is, hugging me with a desperation that lifts me up, forcing me against the wall. My legs automatically wrap around him. My roommates are out and not expected back anytime soon, which is good because nothing could stop this storm, even if they sat here and watched.

"I missed you so much," he whispers, gently pulling my head back by my hair to kiss my neck. He runs his tongue to my mouth kissing me, igniting a fire like only he can. Carrying me to my room, Cole closes and locks the door with one hand, never letting his mouth leave mine, and places me on the bed as he has thousands of times before. We never tire of *us* and all that comes with it. We undress each other in seconds, and he's inside me before my head even touches the pillow.

When things start like this, it's gonna be a long night. Anytime we have sex in my dorm room, it's as if he's reclaiming his territory. He doesn't know the details of what I'm doing on campus, and he's stopped asking, but I know his imagination easily runs away with him. He needs to erase whatever may have happened in here, wipe the slate clean, reset the room—and me. He dominates my body and soul so completely, there's never a trace of anyone else left, and no real desire remaining for them either.

The rush to get inside me stops the second he's in. We've merged as one now. It soothes his aching soul and tames my wandering heart. Only when he is with me, in me, does he feel safe, loved, secure.

On top, his face is inches from mine, eyes burning holes straight through to my heart reconnecting us. I lift my head to him, but he returns it to the pillow gently with his palm on my cheek. He's making me wait knowing how much I love his lips on mine, aware this intimate distance he's putting between us will only increase the desire. Motionless and still in me, he's focused only on my mouth, not because he needs to do one thing at a time anymore but because he wants this to be a slow, simmering, loving torture for me.

He's teasing me, and he loves the control. But I love control too. I swing my leg around and over him simultaneously, rolling us over, placing myself on top. Never underestimate a dancer, no matter how petite they are. I pin his arms over his head, exposing the soft flesh of his inner arms, revealing the faint trace of scars from his suicide attempt months earlier. It binds us together like cause and effect, one event contributing to

189

the other, where the cause is partly responsible for the effect and the effect, partly dependent on the cause. We're in a never-ending loop of Groundhog Days we can't escape.

His arms tense beneath mine, but he lets me kiss him long enough to drop my guard, flipping me over to my back again, holding both my arms overhead with his one. He's all hands and tongue, everywhere at once as my body molds to his and melts under his touch.

Cole slowly releases my wrists. "Leave them there, babe," he growls in a low raspy voice filled with sex.

He runs his tongue down my neck to my breasts, belly button, and beyond. He has me right where he wants me, and my body responds within seconds. The sound of his voice and the complete control he has while bringing me to climax over and over has kept me coming back to him. But it's not only the physical connection; it's the emotional bond that makes my heart jump to be with his every time. This love we have is real, it's messy and raw and complicated, but it's also tender and unconditional. It's not perfect, but it's ours. I love him. I've loved him every day of the last few years whether I've wanted to admit that to myself or not. I just haven't been very good at it. But here, in this realm, where the body meets the mind, heart, and soul, time stands still and none of that matters to either of us.

His lips land on mine, and he is instantly sliding into me again, and again. How many times have I been right here in this exact position, feeling the same unending passion and love for each other? And yet, each time feels like the thousandth and first wrapped into one.

"Are you ready?" His voice explodes inside my

head, making me want to gather up each piece of him and hold him together for the rest of my life. I can be anything he needs me to be if it will keep his beautiful soul intact and at peace.

"Yes." I can barely breathe.

"I love you more than you'll ever know," he says. And as if he had been waiting for me to give permission, we reach the summit together.

Lying intertwined, his warm breath flows over the nape of my neck. I think about all the times over the years he's come to me like this. I know the therapy's helping him, but not fast enough. I also know I'll pull away again. Soon. How many more times will we repeat this cycle? Can't live with each other, can't live without each other. We both know it. How much longer can I drag him along? We can't go on like this forever.

Can we?

Chapter Thirty-Three

You never really know anyone
Cole 2014

Through the passenger window of Faith's car, the jagged mountaintop of Prescott Peak rises above the clouds like a headstone in the mist, a sharp contrast to the lower portion where a rolling green carpet invites you in. I love it up here. *We* love it here. After arriving at the cabin, I start a fire, and we head to the balcony for the view. I'd like to hike up to the top again, but a recent storm has made it impassable by foot.

Mountains form where two continental plates collide. If both plates have a similar thickness and weight, neither will sink under the other. Instead, they crumple and fold, forcing the rocks up. The more pressure, the taller the mountain. At this point, *we* are the highest, most magnificent mountain I've ever seen.

I fall off Faith's radar sometimes. Weeks, even months, go by without hearing from her. She never falls off mine. I keep in touch with phone messages and letters. Sometimes she responds, sometimes she doesn't, like she's measuring how much attention she gives me—not too much, not too little, and I'm not privy to which calibration system she's using.

"I'm so glad you suggested this trip, Cole. I can imagine us living here someday, can't you?" She snuggles into me as we stand here.

"Ah-huh." How can one thought cause delight and despondence at the same time?

"What is it?" She looks into my eyes like only she can. "Tell me."

"I…" I lift my head to the mountain.

"Wait, look at me." She turns my face toward her. "Are you drunk?"

"No."

"Well, you're something. I can tell. You were pretty quiet in the car."

"I swear I'm not drunk."

Her eyes narrow.

"Okay, I'm high."

"You're what!" Her warm breath pushes a cold mist out. "I'm glad you've been spending more time with Steve and the guys, but they're older, Cole. You don't have to do every dumbass thing they do."

"It's okay." I downplay. "Not a big deal."

"Is that right? No big deal. Do you know who you're talking to?"

"It's just a little and only on the weekends."

"A little what?" Her eyes widen.

I ignore the question.

"Cole, there's no such thing as a little of anything with you."

"I'm fine," I say, accentuating the *ine*.

"With your history? Your parents? Your genetic predisposition for addiction?"

"My what?" I pull her into me. "Come on, Faith. No college-level psychobabble tonight, okay? You sound like Dr. Martin. I just want to be with you." I run my hand along the outside of her thigh.

"It's good that you're still seeing him, and if I'm being honest, we could both use some help. Should I get the book Leanne gave me? It's all in there."

"No, not the book. Don't get the book." I try to lighten the mood and feel her tremble against me. "It's cold out here. Let's go inside."

Faith takes my hand, sitting me down on the couch in front of the fire. Climbing onto my lap, she curls herself around me, hugging me tighter than usual. It's nice. She kisses me in that sweet and tender way of hers. It's always drawn me to her, like a mosquito into an electrified trap. It confirms that despite our separations, nothing has changed between us. Nothing ever does.

Faith's cell rings in the other room. She jumps up to get it, and I hear garbled words. She sounds surprised. I rearrange the wood on the fire as she returns to the living room with the phone still glued to her ear.

"I'll call you when I'm back on campus." She hangs up and stands next to the crackling fire, staring at me. "Did you hear what happened?"

"I don't know. What happened?" I sit back down.

"A student was attacked on his way back to his dorm room from dinner," she says.

"Yeah, I may have heard something about it."

"He's in a coma." She crosses her arms with knitted eyebrows. "Can't believe it. Allan, he was my criminology study partner. We spent a lot of time together."

"Sorry to hear that." Faith's eyeing my face in an odd way. "What?"

"Did you know he was my friend?"

"No. I don't know. What does he look like?"

"Come on." She tilts her head. "You met him the night we all went out for Halloween."

I shrug, waiting for more. Is she accusing me?

"You even said you thought he was flirting with me."

"What are you insinuating? I did something to him?"

"I don't know, Cole. You're like a different person lately. Using drugs now? And this is the second male friend of mine who's had some really bad luck."

She *is* accusing me. "Are you being serious right now?"

Faith blinks, waiting.

"Well, I'll tell you one thing." I blink right back. "Bryce knows someone on the force. They think your friend attacked a few women, may have been a serial rapist. Someone must have taken matters into their own hands, lucky for you. You might have been his next target."

"Shit, really? That doesn't sound like the Allen I know."

"I wish you hadn't been affected by this." I stare up at her. "But can't say I'm upset."

She bends one leg under and sits next to me. "I guess you never really know anyone." Her face is deep in thought. "I've been so stressed with finals coming and papers due. I'm sorry I haven't been around lately. I'm always apologizing to you."

"You don't need to."

"You know, people use drugs and alcohol to numb pain. Is that what you're doing? Is it because of me and this rollercoaster I've put us on?"

"That's not what's happening."

"Seems like it is."

"Okay, listen. Sometimes it does feel like I'm on your back burner, but you're the reason all my broken pieces haven't completely scattered. You should keep doing the school thing while I get my shit together." Dr. Martin has become something of a lifeline for me. Makes me realize I still have a lot of work ahead of me. Faith has no idea exactly how much.

She stares into the fire. "Sometimes it feels like I'm pushing you onto a ledge and then pulling you off it over and over." Her voice is low.

"I've kind of forced you into being that person for me. The kind who needs to be pulled off a ledge."

"No, you haven't." Faith looks at the ceiling as if the answers are somewhere up there. "You've never forced me to do anything. I've wanted to be there for you the way you've always been there for me. I owe you for every time I promised to be what you needed and fell miserably short."

"You don't, Faith." I hold her face in my hands, looking directly into her eyes. "Listen, it's been a two-way street with us."

"I may have made you a little…unstable." Her voice is low again.

"How do you know it's not the other way around?" I bet she hasn't thought of that.

Faith sits up straighter and changes the subject. "How do you think we'll meet in our next life?" She always does that when she's upset.

"I don't know, and it doesn't even matter because"—I sing way off key—"when gravity fails and the universe falls through, I will still be loving you…"

"Our song, Cole. It runs through my veins. It always will."

"And what color roses would you bring to my funeral?"

"I hate it when you say that." She punches my arm.

"What color?" I tickle her while she wiggles around screeching.

"Okay, okay, red! Deep red!"

"That's better."

Chapter Thirty-Four

A very talented psychopath
Faith 2026

As Ben hurries back to his running UPS truck, I pick up the box and mail that fanned out across my hallway floor. The newest mystery envelope has me intrigued. The backyard seems like a good place to read it. I take my laptop with me and sit on the couch in the shade, noticing the postmark says Devenport, which means it's from the distribution center, not the post office. *Nice work, you're getting smarter.*

Everything about the note is the same, the print, the color, the lettering, and no return address. I do like the consistency. It makes me feel connected to the author. It's intimate. Like we're the only two with a secret, twisted or otherwise.

But this time when I pull out the neatly folded in half, matching white paper and unfold it, I find several photos tucked inside. One is a large, majestic cruise ship. Another is of brightly colored homes on a beach and the third I'd recognize anywhere. It's a great shot of Montauk.

Dear Faith,

Once again, I hope this letter finds you well. The more I write to you, the more you're in my thoughts. I wonder if it's the same for you. We needn't be anything more than friends if that's what you'd prefer. I remember always wishing we were more, but you were not ready then. You may not be ready now either, and this would be perfectly fine with me again. Well, not perfectly, but seeing you and spending time with you would be enough.

I'm worried about you and sure you're struggling with Jeremy's death. It's nothing to be ashamed about. I'm on your side no matter what, no judgment. If there's anything I can do to help, I would do it. I took a trip recently and wanted to share these photos with you. Every time I look at them, I feel peace. Maybe they'll do the same for you.

Yours—

Yours? Jesus Christ, again?

Without judgment? Judgment of what? And he's on my side? Is he implying I've done something worthy of judgment, and he's okay with it?

If it's Cole, this could be his cryptic way of telling me he's alive and asking me not to judge him, wanting me to be on *his* side. It would make sense. He was accused of some pretty crazy shit before his death. Is he telling me he actually did those things and to withhold judgment until he explains or to withhold judgment because he didn't do them? I've never believed he was capable of any of it.

God, it's so easy to fall back into thinking Cole's alive. I guess it's normal after a tragedy, but I need to stay grounded, here, in reality, in the present. Breathe...If this is someone fucking with me, they're doing a great job.

Finn's bark draws my attention to the mountain. He's a quarter of the way up, weaving in and out of trees like he's on the hunt. Can't figure out why he's become so interested in the wildlife this year. I have half a mind to climb up there myself, but it's too densely wooded. It's got to be some type of nest. I want to call him but decide against it, feeling guilty for not walking or running with him as much as usual. Plus, he's having fun.

"We needn't be anything more than friends if that's what you'd prefer…I remember always wishing we were more, but you were not ready." Could be Bryce or Steve. *Or Cole.*

Moving on to the photos, the large ocean liner named *The Santana* cuts its way through crystal clear blue water. I flip open my laptop and search the name of the ship. It's from the movie Cole and I both hated, *Key Largo*, starring Lauren Bacall and Humphrey Bogart, who happen to have one of the greatest love stories of all time, both in and out of the movies. That stupid movie we bonded over is in these photos?

Next, I examine the Bahamas photo. Nothing's coming to me so I move on to the Montauk picture. You really can't get a good shot of Montauk without getting the lighthouse in. Cole and I were never there together, but the lighthouse…Jesus, it's not the Montauk lighthouse. It's *the Lighthouse*—the bar.

Oh my God.

I want to believe it. I so very much do.

No.

Get a hold of yourself, Faith.

In an investigation, one should not rule out one's own bias and subjectivity, which means I'm forced to acknowledge myself as a contributing factor in this case.

No, this person took a trip somewhere and wanted to share the photos. That's all. Steve has been gone for years. These could simply be his. He did say he was worried about me. He did miss the funeral. He is from my past. He did have feelings for me. Most of the same could be said for Bryce.

New scenarios take shape. One, a *living* person is the author, either unidentified or identified as Steve or Bryce, or a very talented psychopath. Two, I am wishing Cole back into existence and am in need of mental health assistance.

I'll tell you one thing, when I do find out who you are, and I will, I may just send you back out to sea.

Finn returns and leans against my leg, panting. Without looking up from the letter and pictures, I rub the side of his belly but feel something wet and pull away. What did he get into up there? My hand is covered in red. Nausea sets in. Holy shit did he get into a fight with something? I didn't even hear anything. But as I inspect Finn closer, it's not blood. It's paint. Spray paint. Someone has marked Finn's side with a large, round, red target. My hand moves to my gun, eyes lifting to the mountain. Eyes that are ready to kill.

Chapter Thirty-Five

A feeble attempt
Faith 2014

"Why did you want to meet me here?" Cole's walking from his car to mine.

The parking lot of our high school was the safest place I could come up with to end what little of us is left. My freshman year is almost over, and this barely-there relationship is the best I can give him right now. All I'm doing is hurting him, while I wait on eggshells for the next crisis. Can't do it anymore. The pressure is too much.

I picked a public place that's familiar to both of us. Somewhere I can get in and out of fast. Not anywhere we could end up lying down. Not his house, not my dorm room, and not sitting in a car somewhere either. Not the beach or the mountains where too many memories could get in my way.

An hour ago I called him. Five minutes earlier, I drove into this lot, parked, got out, and laid my keys on the roof. And now, leaning against the car door watching him approach, my stomach feels like the net at a soccer practice warm-up getting pummeled.

"Is everything okay?" His scent, the smell of rain and berries, conjures up too many flashbacks.

My shoulders tighten, and I start to shiver even

though it's not cold. Why is this going to be so hard? Am I making the wrong decision, fighting him and this relationship for all the wrong reasons?

No. It needs to be this way. I've gone over it in my head a million times. This is not healthy. We need a break, and I'm just gonna say it.

"We need to stop seeing each other, Cole." I'm instantly nauseous and sure my stomach is going to fall right out of my mouth.

While everything on my body tightens, his visibly shrinks at my words. Cole closes his eyes, looks up at the sky, and sighs.

"Again? Faith, you don't mean that."

My throat's burning, closing. I suck in a deep breath, hoping it's enough to hold back the tears *and* my feelings for him all at once. I cannot cry this time, or I'll never get through this.

"Yes, I do. Trust me. This is the best thing for us."

"No. It's not." He walks closer to me. "You don't realize what you're doing." He's closer than I want.

"Yes I do."

"Then why?"

"You know why."

"Stop worrying about me," Cole says. "I'm fine waiting for you."

"Waiting for me?" He'll never understand. "Cole, what do you want to be when you grow up?"

He parks his hands on his hips. "What does that have to do with anything? Is this about the college fair I missed?"

He doesn't give me time to answer.

"Is there someone else? Are you falling in love?"

"No!" I bow my head, crossing my arms in front of

me further separating us, a feeble attempt to stop him from even thinking about coming any closer.

"Look at me, Faith."

"No. I'm not staying. Only called you here to tell you this."

He reaches in my direction while I close my eyes, bracing myself for his touch. The minute he makes contact, this attempt to end it will be over. But it doesn't come. Instead, I hear the jingling of my car keys. He's taken them off the roof behind me.

"You can't go yet."

I avert my eyes to anywhere but him. "Don't make this worse than it already is."

"I can't let you leave yet." He pulls his MP3 player out of his pants pocket.

"Give me the keys," I plead.

"Just wait." He's scrolling like mad. I know what he's looking for.

He presses the play button and lifts his eyes to meet mine. What I see in them is a calm resolve. Either he's decided this won't last, or he's as worn out with us as I am.

The first chords start.

"Do you think love ever ends?" he asks.

"I don't know." I'm silently pleading with him in my head to show mercy.

"Well, it doesn't." He pauses. "I know I'm not gonna be able to stop you this time. Fine, if this is what's gonna make you happy, I'll let you go. But there's something you should remember." Cole holds the MP3 player up between us as the song plays. "Nothing will ever change for me."

And he hands me the keys.

"Can I get one last hug?" he asks.

"No." There's no way I can let that happen.

He steps back, allowing me into my car. I start it up, back out, and put it into drive, tears falling before my foot is even on the gas. In my rearview, he's standing there watching me as I pull away, hands in his pockets, looking like the loneliest soul in the world. I imagine him as the little boy he described, filled with trauma and fear, and realize I'm one more person abandoning him, the only one who promised she wouldn't. This by far, is the worst guilt yet.

As months go by, I feel lighter, but the aching and longing for him remain. I've broken my own heart along with his. Little traces of Cole continue to linger around me. One night, he showed up at the campus bar. I left immediately, not at all ready to be anywhere near him. I'm determined to stay away for now.

On the other side of campus while returning to my car from class one afternoon, there was a red queen of hearts card on my windshield with the words "I love you" written on it. I've even seen him watching me from his car driving slowly two aisles over in the parking lot as I walked from class to my dorm. I use everything as a distraction—school, debate club, dance, boys. It's working, sort of, but he's always on my mind.

His calls and messages slowed as did the notes left at my dorm room and on my car, all of which I let go unanswered. They eventually dwindled to a stop.

I find myself missing them. Missing him. This isn't the end. I need him to believe that though. It's not—we're just taking a breather.

Chapter Thirty-Six

I'm not surprised
Cole 2014

Dear Faith,
Hey, what's up? Nothing here except I miss you! A lot. I don't like this no-talking shit. You still mean everything to me. The only reason I let you drive away was because I knew you didn't know what you wanted, and it will never work unless we both want it. So great, now we're not going out, and we're not friends either. Why? Still want to be part of your life, but if you don't want that I have a few things to say to you. I love you, and nothing will ever change that. I don't regret a thing. You gave me more happiness and good times than anybody else ever has, and I want to thank you for it. Even the bad times weren't that bad, I just blew them out of proportion, but at least we were together. I don't understand why we can't be friends. You mean too much to me to forget about you.
Love,
Cole

Steve's bent over the pool table looking for his next shot. "Are you writing her again?" We're hanging out at his house. I'm on the couch, hunched over the letter on my lap while Sam waits for his turn on the table.

"It's my last one," I say.

"Have you heard from her?" Sam asks.

"No. It's been eleven weeks and three days. Where's the stuff?"

Steve nudges the cue ball into the seven, but it doesn't fall into the corner pocket. "Cole, you need to slow down with that shit."

"You're right." Still, I look around for the little baggie of white powder.

"Look, I know you," Steve adds. "You've had a lot to deal with, but this isn't gonna solve anything."

I find the bag and pour some out.

"And what the hell happened to your neighbor?" Sam sinks his ball.

"That asshole? I'm not surprised," I say.

"What happened to his neighbor? Steve looks at Sam.

"Someone tied him up in his backyard naked. Put a dog collar on him and chained him to the spike," Sam explains. "Guy froze to death."

"Didn't you hate that guy?" Steve asks me, looking at Sam.

I take a long sniff.

"And every time you come back from work you're worse. What the hell's going on at that job of yours?" Sam asks.

My college applications fell by the wayside. I found a job instead. "I fucked up. Got sucked into something I shouldn't have."

"At Greybridge Global? Isn't it a software company? What could you have gotten sucked into?" Steve's cue ball smacks the nine, but he misses the shot again.

"I signed a contract. I have obligations—you know how it is."

"No, actually, I don't. What kind of part-time job involves this much of a commitment and drugs? Look, I know it's none of our business, but we're worried about you."

"I never meant to get involved. I'm getting out." I fold the note to Faith.

"Out of what exactly?" Sam squints.

"It's better if you don't know."

"Damn, Cole, how deep in are you?" Steve maneuvers around the table.

"Too deep and these are people you don't wanna make angry." I tuck the note into my pocket.

"Dude? Seriously?"

"I know," I say.

"Job contract or not, you don't owe them anything. You need to look after number one." Sam sinks the eight ball.

"Whatever it is, you have to get out of it, like right now." Steve agrees.

"Working on it," I say.

Chapter Thirty-Seven

A little voice in the back of his mind
Faith 2026

Jeremy and Cole are in the car on the mountain in the storm. I'm in the vehicle too, yelling at them to get out of the car. Jeremy's driving. I watch Cole lean over from the passenger seat and slit Jeremy's throat with a long, slow, deep cut. Blood splatters onto the windshield, and Jeremy involuntarily jerks the wheel to the right. High-pitched screeching fills my ears, and all I see is a yellow and black explosion of fire.

I wake to a painfully quiet house feeling paralyzed, the side of my face planted into the pillow and soaked with sweat. Tangled in the sheet, I roll toward the clock on the nightstand. Five a.m. Time to get out of bed instead of lying here replaying it because that's what I'll do.

Finn is sleeping on the bed next to me. After seeing the target on him, finding nothing, and bathing him, I've decided to lock the two of us into the bedroom at night. The house alarm is always set, but still. We head to the kitchen, me to the coffee pot, him to this food bowl.

The more I believe Cole is alive, the more nightmares come. Cole would never hurt me. Would he? He definitely wouldn't harm a dog. I know what

Leanne would say if I chose to let her in on any of this. My grief for Jeremy is bringing up the past with Cole. I'm confusing and conflating. Guilt for not stopping Jeremy that morning is entangling with the regret of the past. I'm feeling responsible for both deaths, making me think Cole's alive when he's not. Leanne would be more eloquent, but the intent would be the same.

But something *is* going on. Some crazy chick tried to run me off the road, and now this. I'll need to be more vigilant. What matters more at this moment is the trip I have planned to the impound. The police let me know they have released Jeremy's car. The pit of my stomach is not looking forward to this, but lately my personal life has been a series of new doorways I have not wanted to walk through. I'll head there first, then to a new client meeting with a Mr. David Shulman who's almost positive his wife is *not* cheating on him. He just wants a professional to verify it.

The letter writer's latest installment of "Guess Who?" is still sitting on the counter. Maybe I'm making more of this than I need to. I take the coffee and continue into the closet. What to wear to an impound yard—it should probably be black.

The tension in my stomach's keeping me away from a solid breakfast. Seeing where Jeremy spent the last few minutes of his life is not something I would ever choose to see again, but I need to get a look at the left rear side of the car. Maybe it'll put an end to the spinning my mind has been engaged in. I grab my bag and head out.

The attendant at the lot comes out of his command station and motions me to pull closer to the gate. I do, and roll down my window, letting drippy humidity inside.

"Here for Jeremy Moore's car. I'm his wife. I'd like to see it and sign the paperwork to release it."

"Sorry, ma'am, closed today. We reopen tomorrow at nine a.m." He points to the large red and white sign posted outside the gate like I should have seen it.

"Damn, thanks." All that mental preparation for nothing. I'll be early for the meeting instead. I need some time to sit still and work on reports anyway. This has been the hardest part of owning a growing business, lots of field work but little office time to get all the action into a coherent format to match video. The paper end of this job is not what anyone gets into it for, but it needs to get done just the same.

I sit inside Mort's Deli in my usual private corner with a pastrami on rye, my notes strewn around my laptop. Mr. Shulman walks through the door twisting and elongating his neck like a crane to find me. I ID him the minute I have eyes on him. He matches his voice on the phone, thin and nervous. I wave him over.

After just under an hour of playing investigator slash therapist, he signs a forty-hour contract with me for upwards of ten thousand dollars. That's two hundred dollars an hour with some extras on the side. It may seem like a lot, but it's not. Even though Mr. David Shulman doesn't really believe Mrs. Rachel Shulman is up to no good, there's a little voice in the back of his mind refusing to let him forget she's already had an affair. It's long over, of course, but she is, however, spending extra time at the gym and going out with her girlfriends more often. It's all part of their marriage "reboot," allowing her more independence to follow her passions and live her best life.

As requested, he provides me with photos of her. Mrs. Shulman is hot. Not "hot" as in attractive, but "hot" to me and my team as in difficult to surveil because, one, she's a woman and women are much better at lying and cheating than men. Two, she's already been tailed. Three, we'll be following her in the city, which presents logistical challenges. And four, my spidey-sense tells me there's absolutely something happening. How? There's a saying in P.I. work—if you think it's happening, it probably is. We'll need three two-person surveillance teams, maybe four.

Mr. Shulman leaves for his bank around the corner to make a withdrawal out of whatever side account he's set up because no one walks around with that kind of cash, even in New York. Unless you're a criminal. Or a jeweler.

I stay put. Not so much because he's coming back but because I've already set up shop here. I'm organized, well-fed, and comfy. I've learned to supervise and manage my cases right where I am, monitoring and directing the field agents, making client calls and utilizing our resources to the fullest.

Shulman pops back in minutes later, sits, and places an envelope on the table. I put it in my bag and assure him we're ready to start as soon as we receive the go-ahead from him regarding which night she's going out. Texts light up my screen like mad, practically vibrating my phone off the table. Shulman notices and stands to excuse himself so I can get back to it. I'm thankful because it saves me from playing psychologist to him again which, I'm sure, since we've concluded our business, is why he sat down once more. I nod a goodbye and check my phone.

Andy's texting from the field and needs to review trespassing laws with me again, never a good sign. Brooke wants to set a time for caseload reviews. And our biggest client, attorney Dave Hutchins, is looking for a few hours with me to complete our trial prep on Englehoffer.

Normally I'd be fine with the onslaught and chaos. I thrive in it. But today, I'm off. Distracted. Anxious. And why not? I'm going about my life as usual except my husband just died. And the accident is suspicious. And someone is watching me. And I think my dead ex-boyfriend is not dead. And he's writing to me.

It's time to admit I *might* need some help. I text Leanne.

Chapter Thirty-Eight

He's lying. It's obvious.
Faith 2014

Three months post Cole break-up, I wake on my birthday to a ringing dorm room phone and consider letting it go to voicemail, but what if it's Cole? He's been on my mind lately. A lot. More than usual. Shouldn't these feelings be fading by now? This is the longest stretch we've gone without communication. I worry about him. Still.

It's emotional quantum entanglement. When tiny, subatomic particles get tangled with each other, what happens to one particle always has an impact on the other, even at great distances. It's the same for us. *I feel it.* The space between us means nothing. Something's not right. Trying to ignore these feelings has not worked. They creep in and swirl around my head interrupted only by the continual ringing of my dorm room phone.

"Happy birthday!!" Leanne, the only one who calls on this number, sounds way too alert and happy for this god-forsaken hour of the morning.

"Thanks, you pain in the ass! Who calls this early?"

"Oh, did I wake you? It's two p.m. Your cell must be on vibrate again. You know you love me anyway.

I'm guessing you went out last night. Have fun?"

"Yeah, I think…not sure I remember it all."

"Then it was a success."

"Jeremy was there last night, but I stayed away. And what have you been up to?" I rub my sleepy eyes.

"I partied in our old stomping grounds last night."

"You did not! Who'd you see? Tell me everything." I sit straight up in bed.

"We started out at Steve's, made a stop by the Venue and ended the night at the Lighthouse. Evan breezed in after breaking up with his girlfriend on her birthday. Remember, her birthday is the day before yours? What kind of dumbass does that? He spent the night trying to convince me he's a changed man. The boys wouldn't allow it. And neither would I."

"Evan *is* a dumbass. After all this time, does he really think you give a shit? And honestly, Leanne, I'm so glad you don't anymore. I'm really proud of you. I know how hard that whole shitshow was."

"Thanks. Hey, I have some news about Cole."

My heart thumps like the pop-o-matic button in the center of a board game.

"Him and Steve got a place together. Steve said Cole got a job at Greybridge Global."

"The software giant? That's a great company." I'm up and trying to get the mini coffee maker started.

"But they think something shady's going on there. Cole won't say exactly, but he's been working all kinds of odd hours and spending more time with them instead of our friends."

A shot of adrenaline surges through me. Shady? That doesn't sound like something Cole would involve himself in. It's setting off all kinds of alarms. I knew it.

Something in his life has changed, for the worse. "Did you see him last night?"

"They said he hadn't been there in days. Was working."

"I don't like this, Leanne. It's not good."

"It doesn't sound like much to me."

"Nope. Something's not right." The coffee is finally dripping.

"Why do you think that?" Leanne asks.

"My spidey-senses. I don't know, I just know something's wrong. I'm gonna call him."

"But you've come so far. Don't. Wait a while longer. I'll see what else I can get out of the boys," she suggests.

I reluctantly agree, and we decide to meet later for dinner. Picking up my cell phone, I find eight voicemails and thirty-nine texts waiting for me. At first, I panic but then remember today is my birthday, and it's already two in the afternoon. Leanne was correct. The phone was on vibrate. I switch the sound on. My hangover head hurts as it tries to focus on the notifications filling up my screen. The phone unexpectedly tickles my hand while stabbing its ring into my head. Jeremy. I need it to stop doing that, so without thinking I answer, still sounding groggy.

"Well, well, well, if it isn't my little sleeping beauty. Happy birthday, Faith!"

"I'm not your little anything, Jeremy. But thanks."

"Oh, I don't know about that. The last time I watched you sleep you seemed pretty content in my bed."

I wish he hadn't said that. "You must have me confused with someone else."

"Nope, it was you, but if you want to play it this way, fine. There've been 'someone elses' for both of us, but look, the way I see it, we needed that. You know, to be separate, experience the world a little. But the truth is, you've never left my heart, Faith."

"Good lord." I sigh from the place in my chest he just touched.

"Okay, I can tell you're not ready. It's fine, but listen, I meant what I said last night. I'm home for the weekend. Let me take you out for your birthday. We can catch up."

"Not a good idea, Jeremy."

"Why not?"

"Because I know what your idea of catching up is."

"No, no. I heard you ended it with him. I want to be here for you. Or are you too afraid to be alone with me?"

Maybe he's right. It's easy to fall back into old habits, but Cole and I are not over. "Look, I appreciate you calling, but it's gonna be a no for me."

"I've never understood what you saw in him. But if you change your mind…"

"You'll be the first to know," I finish his sentence.

We hang up. I check the calls I've missed. The first one is from Cole.

Two a.m. "Happy birthday, Faith. I know, I know, not supposed to call you, and I'm a couple of hours early because you were born at 9:36 in the morning, but this feels so wrong. I can't ignore the day and pretend it's not your birthday. Can't not think of you, and before I knew it, well, now I'm talking to your voicemail. Don't blame you for not answering if you saw my number pop up. It's fine. You don't have to call back. I only want you to know I'm thinking of you and I still…" He pauses. "I hope you have a good day."

The sound of his voice tugs at my heart unraveling it. Damn it, Cole. Is it supposed to be this hard?

The next voicemail comes at 2:55 a.m. from the friends I was out with last night who called to wish me a happy birthday while they were standing right next to me buying shots. Dumbasses. After that, it's Cole again.

3:17 a.m. "Hey." Then breathing. "Sorry, I shouldn't be calling again."

3:32 a.m. "I really didn't want to do this, Faith, but I need someone to talk to. Someone I trust. And that's you. Something's come up and…I'm not sure what to do. Call me, but only if you want to. I mean, it'll be fine. You don't have to. I shouldn't have called."

I knew it. Something *is* happening, and I'm sure it's not good. Shit. I listen to the next messages from friends and one more from him, but he only hangs up without saying anything.

9 a.m. My dad followed by Aunt Emily.

12:30 p.m. "Happy birthday, officially. Look, I'm sorry about the calls last night. I know I'm making another call to apologize for calling, but I want you to know there's no reason to worry about me. I shouldn't have done that to you, put you in a position again. I always do that, make you feel like you have to save me. It's wrong. You don't. Everything's okay. I mean, I'm sure it'll all work out. No matter what happens, the time I've spent with you has been the best of my life. I really mean it. No regrets. Have a great birthday, Faith."

He's lying. It's obvious. He's backpedaling, trying to make me feel better about not returning his calls.

Jesus, what has he gotten involved in? I want to call him, but this is why I've stayed away. It's all coming back. I've been focusing on the good, the echoes of *us*, but it's too much pressure, too hard to keep pulling him off the ledge. He needs to get it together without me. I have little to no control when it comes to him and don't want to get sucked in. Who knows what I might let him drag me into. But if I stay away? Already know what the result may be.

Can I live with it?

The next hour is a combination of physical detox and emotional gymnastics. My brain has been in overdrive since Leanne's call. Why can't we just end? It confirms what I've known in my quantum entangled gut—he needs me. Something's going on.

Covering my face with both hands, I massage my aching temples. Fuck it. I still love him. I can't *not* help. It's not who I am. It's time to break our silence.

I splash water on my face, gargle, dab on a little makeup and look for some fresh clothes. Spring in New York is so unpredictable I never know if I should wear a sundress or a snowsuit. I choose jeans and a lightweight sweater. Knocking back some pain relievers for the splitting headache, I grab my coat to head over to Cole's and open the door. I'm stopped cold in my tracks.

"Well, well, well. If it isn't the birthday girl in the flesh. And what nice flesh it is."

"Jeremy, are you kidding right now?" I slump where I stand.

"I won't take that personally." He hands me flowers pulled from behind his back.

"That's really thoughtful, but I'm heading out."

"Um, I don't think so." He pushes his way past me and into the room, closing the door.

I'm seething. "Jeremy, I don't have time for this shit. You and your gigantic ego need to leave."

"I'm not here to woo you into fucking me. I'm here because I heard something in your voice, and now that we're face-to-face, I'm glad I came. It's worse than I thought."

I roll my head to the ceiling in annoyance. The mental torment must be showing, and I don't like it.

"Tell me." He touches my hand.

The familiar empathy in his eyes, the tenderness in his face. He's genuinely concerned, and I can't hold it together any longer. The thought of what's going wrong for Cole, whether I should stay away or help, what will happen if I don't go to him and now this. Jeremy, who I've held at arm's length all this time, rejecting every effort he's made over the years to reconnect us. Maybe I should stop pushing him away. It's so easy and comfortable with him. Maybe it's time to leave Cole and all the drama in the past. I break down, even though it's the last thing I want to do.

"Faith, let me help." He holds me in his arms while I sob. "What can I do?"

I don't know how to answer. I'm stuck. Frozen, and for the first time in a long while, I need someone to take care of *me*. Jeremy's doing a good job, stroking my hair, rubbing my back, patiently waiting for me to cry it out. I start to pull away, but he doesn't allow it. He seems to know what I need more than I do.

"We don't have to talk, Faith. Just let me be here for you." He kisses my forehead. Alarms go off in my chest because I know exactly what's going to happen next.

And it does.

Hours later, I wake tangled in my sheets and Jeremy's body to yet again a ringing phone. I'm grateful for all the messages on my birthday but also highly distracted today, or destructive, not sure which. Probably both.

"Faith! You were right." Leanne's panic shoots through the phone into my ear.

"Why? What's happening?"

"I don't know. Bryce just called. Something's going down at Cole and Steve's place. It's bad. I'm heading over now."

"Meet you there." My stomach has already left the building.

"Where are you going?" Jeremy stirs out of a sound sleep. I throw on some clothes and head out without even answering him.

I race over to Cole's house with the intensity of an Indy driver in second place. It's dreary, wet, and icy. I wonder if the chill in my bones is making me shake or if it's anxiety. As I round the corner into this normally quiet suburban neighborhood, I'm forced to slam on the brakes. The car skids sideways, palms and elbows locking hard on the steering wheel. At first glance, there's a ton of activity ahead. Squinting, I see flashing lights. The roadway is crowded with cars—police cars—parked in every direction with doors open as if they stopped and ran somewhere in a hurry, emergency lights left flickering and pulsating.

My chest begins thumping hard. All these police cars are in front of Cole's house.

My trembling foot moves from the brake pedal to

the gas as I maneuver my vehicle, squeezing between other cars. I need to get closer and discard this machine. It's suffocating me. Peeling my body out of the car, the cold misty rain bathes my skin. Sirens are echoing off the inside of my eardrums. Everything's in slow motion.

There are men and women in police uniforms, some visibly armed and some not, some wearing bulletproof vests and some in plain clothes, darting here and there on the street. On his front lawn. Lightning flashes in tandem with police lights while a uniformed male with his head turned to the side talks into his shoulder-mounted radio about the "scene."

Scene of what?

"Ma'am, you need to step back." The words enter my left ear first, then my right, as the officer flies by me unrolling police tape that will cordon off the area.

"Step back from what? My friends are inside," I say.

"Who do you know in there?" Another voice pings the inside of my head from the left.

"My ex-boyfriend."

"What's his name?" That voice is connected to a woman in plain clothes with a gun holstered underneath her open jacket.

"Cole."

"Cole what?" she demands.

"Cole Anderson. What's happening? Is he okay?" My panicked and confused tone matches my insides, which feel like they're about to drop out of me and be vomited up at the same time. Steve is rushed out of the house by an officer. He comes toward me.

"Faith, what are you doing here? How'd you

know?" His eyes are wide.

"Steve! My God! Know what? What the hell's happening?"

"He's in there, Faith. The police stormed in out of nowhere. They say he's holding a gun to his head."

"Wait, what? Why?"

"I heard them talking to each other saying he's the suspect…he confessed to…killing someone…they're trying to talk him out of it…"

Steve's eyes are bulging out of his head. We're both trying to reconcile what's going on inside the house with the chaotic scene out here on the lawn.

Thunder crackles in the sky above, and at the same time we both hear a pop from inside the house. Steve and I grab each other.

"Was that thunder or…"

My eyes fill with tears. I double over, wrapping my arms around my stomach in an effort to hold my body together and prevent it from falling into a million tiny pieces.

Frantic activity ensues around us. Gravity appears to be pulling every responding officer into the house as Steve does his best to stop that same force from dropping me to the ground. I go down anyway and hear my own voice asking the question over and over, not really wanting the answer. An answer I already feel draining the life out of every cell in my body, just as that same life is emptying out of his.

Chapter Thirty-Nine

Distracted
Cole 2014—Twenty-Four Hours Earlier

"Do you know what encroachment means, Cole?" The boss turns off the car.

"Yeah," I say as we get out, still hoping to get myself out of this mess.

"And noncompete clauses?"

"Sure," I answer. My phone vibrates in my pocket.

"There's a subset of unwritten rules in our business. The sooner you learn that the better."

"What are you getting at?" I pull the phone out as we walk to the door.

"This meeting you set up—he's breaking the rules. Ring the bell, Cole."

"But he's a potential cash cow." The dim glow of the doorbell feels smooth and warm under the pressure of my finger. "And he'll be under your banner," I explain as I open the text from Steve.

"Too late. He's been warned."

"Let's lay it out for him, give him a choice to come on board," I suggest. It's a picture of Faith. With Jeremy. At the college bar.

"I'm done bullshitting. We're sending a message, tonight. Take the gun…"

"I don't want it." I put my hands up in protest, but

I'm too distracted by the photo. Of them. Together. Jesus.

"This is your mess. Fix it," the boss demands.

Rage pulses through me, blood rushing to my face. "Give me the fucking gun."

Chapter Forty

Queen of hearts
Faith 2026

My philosophy on life is this—there is no pure good or evil. Not one of us is all light or darkness. We are gray, with shades of both, depending on conditioning and life circumstances. The most brutal and heartless killer can redeem himself, rising to the highest levels of morality and virtue while the most decent and holiest of us can fall into depravity and disgrace. We're fluid, ever-changing beings. Behavior is simply adaptation. We're either protecting ourselves from pain or grasping for and hoarding as much pleasure as possible. Our thoughts and actions follow suit. The question is, which state is my letter writer in at the present moment?

Between putting in a full day's work in my makeshift deli office and the mounting evidence that Cole is alive, I'm disjointed and emotionally scattered. I want to put more thought into this analysis, but it's possible my objectivity has diminished. Plus Leanne agreed to come over. Not sure how much to share, but I need to talk, even if it's only half-truths. I pack up shop and head to the market on the way home to pick up the makings for dinner.

Hurrying down the aisles, my mind goes back to

what it does best, wandering and circling over Jeremy's accident, the car at the impound, which I will try to see again tomorrow, the past, the memories, Cole, the guilt, and my sweetly romantic or psychopathic letter writer.

Hoping my autopilot split-brain bought everything needed for dinner, I head to the car and see Steve driving into the lot. We wave. I wait for him to park but notice something on my windshield. It's too small to be a flyer. Leaning in, it turns out to be a playing card sitting face down under my driver's windshield wiper. Odd. I pull it off, feeling its smooth coating, and turn it over.

Wait...

My brain tries to keep up with my eyes, but from this moment forward, time moves in slow motion. At first, I recognize it for what it is, a simple playing card. But upon closer inspection the card is not a red king of diamonds or a black ace of spades, but a red *queen of hearts*. I freeze, my brain revving into overdrive, swirling back and still farther back. There's no stopping it.

The last time I pulled this card off my windshield was twelve years earlier—when Cole left it there. Everything goes dark.

****

"Are you okay, Faith?" Steve's bent over me.

The image of the red queen of hearts surges in my mind, and my head hurts.

"Steve?" My blurry eyes look up at him. "What happened?"

"You fainted. You were leaning toward the windshield with your back to me. Then you fell over."

"It was this, on my windshield." Looking up at him

227

from the ground, I raise my right hand to show him the card. My hand is empty. "Shit, where is it?" I sit up, looking around. It must have fallen.

"Whoa, slow down. Don't get up yet, Faith. You're very pale."

"You don't understand. It was right here." Patting myself down, I scan the ground. Maybe the wind took it.

There is no wind today.

"What are you looking for?" Steve asks.

"There was a card on my windshield, under the wiper blade. Do you see it anywhere?"

"I didn't see you holding anything. What kind of card?" Steve's searching with me now.

"A playing card, the queen of hearts." My throat tightens.

Neither of us find it. I try to stand despite his protests. He helps me up, noticing how flustered I've become.

"What is it, Faith?" Steve hugs me. "I want to help."

"I swear it was here."

"I believe you. You probably dropped it when you fainted. Anything written on it?"

"No." Maybe it was some kind of notice or advertisement, but none of the other cars have it on their windshields. "Who would do this? It wasn't you, was it? Please tell me it wasn't." My voice is unrecognizable.

"It wasn't me. I never even saw it." Steve's eyes are still scanning the ground. "What's got you so upset?"

"I almost can't say it out loud. It's going to sound

ridiculous, like I'm crazy."

"Try me," he says, in a tone filled with empathy.

"The last time this card was on my car was...when Cole put it there."

Steve freezes, then shakes his head with a quick jerk, seeming to throw the thought off with it.

"Faith, I told you I didn't like you getting these unsigned letters and now this? Whoever it is, it's not cute anymore. It's upsetting you and pissing me off. We're gonna have to find out who would do this. It's cruel."

"There's absolutely no one who would know about this card but me and..." My brain feels fried as I try to keep straight what I've told him and what my investigation and heart are leading me to believe.

"Unless he told someone about it," Steve suggests.

I exhale long and slow. "You wanna come home with me? Leanne's coming up for dinner. I'm making lemon chicken and picked up a pie. We can catch up."

"I was planning on following you home anyway to make sure you're okay, so sure, that would be nice."

We return to our cars. He never saw the card? I was holding it when I fell, *felt it* in my hand. Didn't I?

Steve waits for me to pull out of my parking spot and follows. I'm caught a little off guard by how nice it feels to have someone here for me. Maybe I could get used to this.

Chapter Forty-One

Time as a variable
Faith 2014

Words pour out through a nearby officer's radio. "Suspect has expired in his bedroom…"

It *has* to be a mistake.

"…from a self-inflicted gunshot wound to the head."

Nope, no mistake. He couldn't have survived that. Is he really dead? No—he *can't be*. We have things to talk about. I *need* to talk to him. I'll wait here until everything calms down and see him like I planned.

"Faith, I'm sorry." Steve's tone is low and shaking.

"But I just got here." My voice cracks. "I knew something was wrong. I can fix it…"

"This is not your fault, Faith. Do you hear me? Cole was in over his head."

I'm still down on the wet grass where I collapsed. "With what?"

"People he should have stayed away from. Damn it, Cole!"

"What are you saying?"

This must be what shock and confusion feel like. My brain is malfunctioning. I can tell. I'm scared, can't think, can't move, and detaching from everything around me, yet feeling every second of this nightmare as it ticks by. Time jumps in flashes. Not everything is fully coming through, as if it's moving through a filter in bits and pieces.

"...don't go in there, ma'am...you can't leave, the road is blocked"...Leanne's face..."come on, let's get you out of here"...rain drops streaking down the car window...nausea that won't go away and vomiting out the car door...the inside of Steve's house, I think...someone handing me dry clothes...crying uncontrollably until I vomit again...Leanne putting me into a bed...crying myself to sleep...

****

The first few moments of wakefulness are like any other, calm, serene, peaceful. But as my brain reboots to full consciousness and I realize I'm not in a bed I recognize, it all comes back. I have awakened to a nightmare, one in which there can be no end.

"...has expired from a self-inflicted gunshot wound to the head."

I'm woozy, in a state of suspended animation. Pushing the covers away, I feel like I've gained a hundred pounds overnight. I pull myself up and sit on the edge of the bed. There's talking outside the door. People are here, somewhere, Leanne, Steve, Bryce, others. How long have I been asleep?

Don't want to see anyone. Don't want this to be real. Maybe if I sit here a while, it won't be. If I don't go out of this room, there's a chance it might not be true. I can stay right here where it feels safe. I can live in this moment, the moment that feels like the middle, the in between of when he was alive and when he was dead.

I need Einstein and his Special Theory of

Relativity right now, his concept of time where the past, present, and future are nonlinear and relative. I really want to believe when I look up into the universe, I'm seeing the past. I want to experience time as a variable so I can insert myself into the exact right moment in time to stop this. To reverse time. Where I can unhear the gunshot still ringing in my ears. If I can unhear it, maybe I can undo the sound. And if I can undo the sound, maybe I can undo the death too. Because none of this can be real.

So I stay put, on the edge of the bed watching drops trickle down the window like cosmic rain because it's the only thing I can do to stop time. To stop the next moment from coming, and the one after it. To stop the future from happening—a forever without him.

"Faith?" Steve's standing in the doorway. "Wanna come out for breakfast?"

"I don't think I can eat." Nausea wells up at the thought of food.

"Some coffee then? Two days of isolation is enough. We're all worried about you. Come on."

While my mind insists on staying stuck in a loop of *whys*, I pull on some borrowed clothes and sob again. Had I ever really stopped? And what did Steve say? Two days? I have no sense of time and no idea how to face anyone without falling apart. Or how to go on with this day, or any day after today—the year, the month, the week. Even the next minute. I really don't care either.

Leaving the safety of the bedroom, I find Steve, Leanne, and Bryce sitting in the living room. I stand barefoot in the doorway in borrowed shorts that are falling off me and an oversized button-down shirt with sleeves so long I'm handless. They don't notice me. They're talking about how everyone descended on this house, in shock and disbelief, questioning, gossiping, and arguing over what happened during the last few days of Cole's life. No one seems to know.

I'm instantly distracted by the overwhelming feel of the room itself. Memories made here flood back. All the nights hanging out with everyone during high school, the bar in the corner serving as the meeting point to begin the night on countless occasions. Cole and I, sitting together at that very bar, him looking into my eyes, feeling the heat of his hand as it rested on my leg.

There's a clear delineation between everything before he died and everything occurring now. I'm straddling the border of time with one foot in the past and the other in the present, simultaneously. My brain jumps between the two. Both feel solid. Both feel real. Figuring out which one is true, is unnerving.

They all stop talking and look at me. Leanne's sitting on a stool at the bar and jumps up at the unexpected sight of me. "There you are. What do you need? What can I do? I picked up some of our old standbys, cake and cookies. They help in times like these."

"We've never had times like these." My voice is flat as I sit on the couch, pulling my knees to my chest.

"No, I didn't mean it like that. It's what we always do in a crisis—head straight for the sweets."

"Sorry, I know what you meant. I'm…"

"In shock, Faith," Leanne finishes. "We all are, but I can't imagine how hard this must be for you. I'm so sorry, this is horrible."

"I just missed him—literally. I was on my way over. Knew something was wrong. Didn't I tell you something was wrong?" I break down again, or still, not sure which.

"I know you did." Leanne hugs me, crying too.

We've been through broken hearts before, but this is gonna be the mother of them all.

"You always felt responsible for him, Faith," Bryce says, meeting my watery eyes from his spot on the couch. "And on your birthday…" He shakes his head. "Don't go thinking any of this was your fault."

"But it *is* my fault. It's obvious. All he ever wanted was to feel like someone cared, like someone was there to listen. He always said I was that person. He had all of you, and you were great friends to him, but it's not the same. I was the one he counted on when things got hard. And I pulled away. I wouldn't talk to him. And now something really bad was happening, and I wasn't there."

"You couldn't have known," Steve chimes in.

"But I *did know*. That's the thing. I felt it and *still* stayed away. Wasn't there to pull him off the ledge. I thought I was helping him by keeping my distance."

"You did the right thing, Faith. Don't doubt yourself now," Leanne adds.

I can't turn off my brain, or my mouth. They let me continue to vent.

"I never wanted us to end up the way we did, and now look where we are. He's in the morgue, and I'm here crying. He said one day I'd be sorry. When I was free, I'd remember our love was meant to be. Not in a mean way, but like he was worried about what would happen to me if the day ever came. Well, this is that day. My God, this is that day. It hurts so much I can hardly breathe."

"Faith, I'm so sorry." Steve comes from behind the bar and hugs me. "There are no words for this."

Leanne cracks open the plastic cookie container. "This was bigger than both of you. You know what his life was like before he came to Devenport. He was struggling with things that had nothing to do with you. You did all you could."

Her logical advice evades me. Especially after the mistake I made with Jeremy, even after I listened to Cole's voicemails. They were calls for help, and I ignored them. How could I do this to him?

"I *didn't* do all I could. Suicide is preventable. Isn't that the catchphrase these days? I could have helped him. Could have stopped all this. You don't always know what goes on between two people, and I'm telling you, I know what I know. Down deep in my core, I'm sure this did *not* have to happen. It was completely preventable. And I'll know it for the rest of my life."

Leanne hands me a cookie with a cup of coffee. I let the warm liquid coat my stinging tender throat while I work up the courage to ask what the hell happened during these last few months. My entire body feels like I've been run over by a tank, and the nausea won't let up, but I need the gaps of information filled. I *have* to know.

"Tell me everything, and don't leave anything out."

So they do.

The guys started playing around with drugs. Recreational use only, but for Cole, it got out of hand. No surprise there. Cole told them he fucked up and got sucked into something at Greybridge Global, didn't want to talk about it. He was working odd hours and was high a lot. The guys offered to help, but Cole said he had it under control, would do one more job, quit, and go into rehab. But then he called the police from his house and confessed to a murder. When the police arrived, Cole was holding a gun to his head, apologizing. That's when I showed up. They tried to talk him down, but he pulled the trigger.

"Is this true?" My voice doesn't sound like my own. "Why would he do this?" I look at all of them. "I told you long ago he needed to stay away from that shit."

"I know." Bryce shakes his head and leans forward from his spot on the couch. "And Cole knew it too, but he wasn't thinking straight. Said he was working directly for Jordan Russell."

"Jordan Russell?" I twist my head toward him. "The CEO of Greybridge? Why would a billionaire need Cole?" This makes no sense but then again, not much does right now.

"We really didn't know what was going on." Steve's eyes are brimming with remorse. "The problem was at that job, Faith. It wasn't us. I promise you."

"I never thought you guys were the problem."

"I tried." Steve inhales a long breath and blows it out. "I really did. It wasn't enough. I should have paid closer attention. Cole was getting more stressed and using too much. He'd go away on work assignments, come back so high, he literally would not sleep for days and then crash."

My heart breaks at the image of him going from one high to the next, not wanting to come down and *feel*—his childhood, his parents, losing me. I contributed to his pain. No one's going to talk me out of believing that. It's all coming at me way too fast, what I'd been worried about all along, him getting in over his head. His obsessive, addictive personality transferring from me to something else, something worse. I understand now. It's perfectly clear. I'm more certain than ever, this is my fault. After I left, he went into a total spiral. It all started with me. Then he reached out for help and I...*let it happen.*

What I really want to say is "why the hell didn't you call me?" but also don't want them to feel worse than they already do. I know why they didn't call. Everyone knows. It took so long for Cole and I to untangle ourselves from each other, no one wanted to start the whole thing up again without an incredibly good reason. Well, if there was ever one, this would have been it.

"Cole would never murder anyone," I say, not sure if I'm trying to convince them or myself. Steve sits next to me and looks at Leanne and Leanne looks at Bryce. I sense there's more.

"Just say it," I demand.

"Okay," Bryce says, short and quick as he stands up in front of us. "The police say they have Cole on a house camera. He's at the victims' house knocking with two other people. They can see the gun in Cole's hand."

"Who are the other two people?" I ask.

"They don't know, can't tell. The door opens, and all three go inside. A commotion is heard and shots are fired, then it goes dark."

The sick feeling is mounting again.

"I don't want to believe Cole killed anyone, but he did have a history in Seaside, you know, with juvie and everything." Bryce reaches to the table for a cookie.

"What history?" I sip the coffee but can barely swallow.

"He defended his mom from one of her boyfriends, put him in the hospital, and got arrested."

"What? He never told me that."

"And there were rumors Cole was the one who attacked Jeremy after the party." Leanne looks at Steve.

"Oh my God, he was with me! I told you." I glare at her but at the same time remember questioning Cole about Allan, who's still in a coma.

I try putting myself in Cole's shoes in each of these scenarios, imagine the thoughts that must have been going through his mind, but can't. I have no point of reference for *this* Cole, whoever he was, if any of this is even true. It *can't* be the Cole I've always known.

Am I wrong? Did the drugs change him? Did he have some other personality inside all along waiting to come out? I did see it once between him and Jeremy and when he cut his arm in front of me. He was like a different person. Could my judgment have been so far off as to not have seen it? I don't even care, just want him back so I can ask.

"Well, if it wasn't Cole, who do we think pulled the trigger?" Bryce returns to his spot on the love seat.

"It wasn't Cole. It couldn't have been," Steve announces. "We all know who he was, even on the drugs. Whoever did this wanted to send a message."

This kind of thing happens to someone else. Not me. Not our little close-knit group. Reality is hitting hard. I imagine Cole with a gunshot wound to his head, brains spilling out, the bloody murder scene, a limp body crumbled in a pool of blood. It's getting worse, and I don't have the stomach for any more of it. I run to the bathroom and vomit.

"Please tell me that's it." I look at Leanne when I return to the living room.

"That's it. I'm sorry. We wanted to make sure you heard it all from us before you left this house."

"I appreciate it. Now what? I don't know what to do with myself."

"They're doing an autopsy. They have to, considering the circumstances. After, they'll release his body for the funeral."

Funeral. The word hangs in the air. This is unreal. A funeral. For Cole. I just want to see him. Wrap my arms around him and feel his heartbeat against my ear, his strong arms tight around me. My stomach flips, and I'm in the bathroom again.

Chapter Forty-Two

Whatever the hell *this* is
Faith 2026

My head's aching and spinning from hitting it on the ground when I passed out and from the shock of seeing the playing card on my windshield. Steve follows in his car, but my brain won't stop racing. I want to be transported back in time to when this would have been possible. I *so, so* want to believe Cole put it there. But I must not—cannot—allow my mind to go there because sometimes when it does, it's very hard to get it back.

We get to my house, and I introduce Steve to Finn. The two of them walk through the entire house and property. Steve returns to the kitchen where I'm preparing the chicken. He seems satisfied that everything's been inspected. He's admiring the view from the windows. I hand him a beer.

"It really is beautiful here. You did a great job with the house," he says, walking around the kitchen island, scanning the space.

"Thanks."

"Hey, you have one too?" Steve points to the large framed photo on the wall I hung a few months back of rescue workers raising flags on top of the piles of Eiffel Tower rubble. "Just bought myself the same one."

"Yeah, a client gave it to me, framed and everything. All I had to do was hang it."

"It's become quite the iconic photo, hasn't it?" he asks.

"You really can't go anywhere without seeing it." I place chicken cutlets on a roasting pan.

"Faith, can I ask you something?" Steve takes a swig of his beer.

"Sure."

"You still think of him?"

I know he means Cole and not Jeremy. "Of course, don't you?"

"Yeah." He looks away.

"What we could have done differently?" Oil, bread crumb, and seasoning blend onto the chicken.

"There's a whole different ending in my mind. If only I would have jumped in sooner to help."

"I know, me too." Except a whole different ending may now be possible, but I don't say that out loud.

"Regret's a funny thing," he says. "Makes you think everything's been one big detour with no way to get back on the main road you're supposed to be on."

"That's exactly how I feel some days." I slide the pan into the oven.

"Yeah, like the road has been erased somehow." He leans back on the counter.

"Sometimes I'm proud of how far I've come." I face him. "Went on with my life, built a career, fell in love again, got married. But other days it all feels like one big joke. Like I'm a fraud and right back there on my knees on his lawn. Nothing has changed, and I'm still just as broken as I was then." My eyes start to fill but I resist.

"Alcohol helps." He tips his beer toward me.

"Amen to that." We click bottles.

"Are you sure you don't mind me busting in on your girl time with Leanne?"

"Not at all. You should both see these letters." What I really need is two clear heads to balance out my delusional one. I excuse myself from the kitchen leaving Steve with his drink and Finn, and go to my bedroom to retrieve the letters, but I'm not feeling right. Maybe it's the stress of the last few months and now this—whatever the hell *this* is. A simple playing card has turned me inside out. A card whose existence can't even be verified.

A car is making its way up the gravel driveway. Walking to the front door, I see a figure through the blurry glass surrounding it. I'm sure it's Leanne. I don't hesitate to open the door.

"Steve texted me to come right away." Leanne steps into the house and hugs me. "What the hell's going on?"

"He's in the kitchen—come on. We'll fill you in."

I break out some hard liquor as Steve gets her up to speed.

"So you're telling me, you think the mysterious letter writer is connected to the queen of hearts card left on your windshield today?" Leanne asks.

"Maybe. Yes...no. I don't know." I really *don't* know what to tell them anymore.

Leanne's looking over Steve's shoulder as he flips through the letters, reviewing them and the envelopes.

"And you had the envelopes and letters tested for prints and nothing?" Steve looks up at me.

"That's right." I get Leanne a glass out of the

cabinet.

"Well, that right there is suspicious, don't you think?" Steve points out. "Whoever wrote them would surely leave prints, unless they were intentionally trying not to. I mean, who does that?"

"Someone who wants to hide." Leanne looks worried. "Yeah, Faith, this has gone way past a friendly note. Somebody's playing with you. Couldn't this be someone you've investigated? Some crazy lunatic?"

"I've considered that." I pour Leanne some wine. "But it's never happened in my career yet. Why now?"

"I don't think we want to find out." Leanne blinks.

"And they have her address!" Steve looks at Leanne. He's very stuck on that point.

"You ran other searches too?" Leanne takes the glass I slid to her.

"I ran DNA on both the envelope and the letter and you know what? It came back with a DNA match but get this—there's no name in the database for the match."

"So this person isn't in the system?"

"No, this person *is* in the system, or *was* put into the system at some point, but their name was taken out and the DNA sample left in."

"What does that mean?"

"It means either someone made a clerical error with the full database entry or someone's trying to hide something," I say.

"Damn." Leanne takes a sip of her drink.

"What about the postmark from the Devenport post office? Can you do anything with that?" Steve asks.

"Already done. I asked the post office if I could view their surveillance cameras on the days these letters were physically brought in and dropped there. Cameras malfunctioned."

"This is getting creepy," Steve says.

"I also ran a handwriting comparison using my high school and college yearbooks."

"Why didn't you tell me any of this?" Leanne asks.

I tread lightly here, keeping in mind Leanne and I have been working on who this letter writer is for months with Steve as one of our suspects. I look her way with discretion. Of course, I leave out the part about it coming back as a match to Cole.

"No matches," I decide to say.

"That stinks," Steve says.

"Remember, the FBI spent millions trying to track down the Unabomber and the anthrax letter senders." I pour three shots. "It's not an easy task."

"And it seems like this person knows it." Leanne's looking over the letters.

"Faith, would you consider installing some surveillance cameras?" Steve asks. "It would make me feel better."

Leanne is nodding at me with great enthusiasm.

"Okay, okay. I'll put the cameras in." Not a bad idea, especially after the Finn incident.

We finish our drinks and reminisce about the many nights spent at the Lighthouse drinking these same Jägermeister shots, forgetting how we ended up in our own beds and how we're still alive to laugh about it.

I'm glad I told them. Bouncing all this off other people is exactly what I needed. There is *no* good explanation for these letters. At least not when we consider all the *normal* possibilities. And now, my theory is making all the more sense.

I keep us focused on the good times and back off all the negative creepy talk. I don't want them too worried about me. If Cole's trying to reach me, he's doing it covertly. He must have a reason.

Chapter Forty-Three

Look at her
Faith 2014

I wake to the morning sun flooding my dorm room. Another day is dawning without Cole. Memories of us camping on top of the mountain to catch the sunrise take hold. He'll never see the beauty of the morning sun again.

My body hurts. Tiny knives pierce my heart from all directions as if someone's holding a voodoo doll of me. I'm continuously queasy. The pit of my stomach aches more now because today is the day. It's going to be a closed-casket funeral.

Of course it is. Cole doesn't have a head. There's not much a mortician can do with that. In a few short hours, I'll be standing in front of it, knowing he's in there, headless. His beautiful face is gone. I want to see him again, one more time. I want to see something real, some part of him that I'll recognize, even if it's only the birthmark on his hand.

It's still dreary and raining, like the sky is crying for him too. I dress myself and get into Leanne's waiting car, floating and not fully here. My brain has been on autoplay where it wants to be, in the past with him, running through our relationship over and over, pinpointing when I could have done something different, *should* have done something different.

Time is skipping. I find myself seated in front of the coffin, a glossy light brown wood with beautiful silver detailing on the corners accented by silver rods. Totally him, couldn't have picked a better one myself. Floral in the air clings to me, the scent of lilies and roses, too fragrant and alive for this place. My eyes drift to the large photo of him on top of the closed coffin, his high school picture in a beautiful frame. The smile on his face is all too familiar because I was there the day it was taken. *Look at her*, the photographer said. I remember looking right back at him with a smile that matched. We were happy.

The grief, regret, and guilt are pulling me toward a slow death. It's not just the memories of photo day. It's the fact that this is the first time I'm seeing his face since it happened. And worse, this is the *only* way I'll ever see him again—in a photo.

Haven't listened to any of the sermon. Time is starting and stopping, dragging me along. I find myself standing in front of the casket with Leanne on one side of me and Steve on the other, unsure how I got there. My knees easily give way to a kneel, barely able to hold myself up. God, how I wish I could open it. I don't care what terrible shape his body is in, I need to see him, touch him, feel his skin on mine one last time. Morbid thought? Not to me.

Our relationship flashes through my head as I straddle the boundary of time—our first kiss in the car when it rained down on us, the beach at night, the love letters, our mountain trips, Cole rolling on top of me, him at the hospital, the rekindling of our feelings over and over, his bloody arm.

How could I have let months go by without a word? I want to go back, tell Jeremy to fuck off because if I had I would have reached Cole in time and stopped all this from happening. Tears are falling, landing on the brown leather of the pew's armrest. There are so many. Will they ever stop?

Before I know it, we're in the procession line following the coffin outside. Sam, Bryce, Steve, and Cole's father and uncles carrying the coffin. The gray sky matches the day, and the crisp air feels like a reprieve to my burning face and swollen eyes.

The pallbearers place the coffin on top of a gurney outside the open rear doors of the hearse. Everyone is handed a red rose. They all approach one by one, taking turns giving him the rose and their final good-byes.

"What color roses will you bring to my funeral?" he whispers into my ear, as he had so many times before. "What color roses will you bring…"

Lifting my eyes to the sky, I wonder where he is, despair and anger overflowing at myself. I didn't bring him flowers. They're giving them out, but *I* didn't *bring* any of my own. I hate myself even more. How could I have forgotten? I can't even do his funeral right.

Rose in hand, I walk to him for the last time, tears dripping steadily onto the coffin.

Where are you, Cole? Don't leave me here to do this on my own. Our mountains are crumbling.

****

Everyone who knew Cole instinctively gravitates to the Lighthouse. They toast him and hug and cry all around me, but I barely notice. I'm not even sure whose car I rode in to get here. The old familiar corner of the bar comes into view with all its stinging memories. It soothes my aching head and hurts my heart simultaneously. Every location I go to for the first time since he died has this effect. The familiarity temporarily restores the feeling of security I had about the world, but then it's yanked away with the echo of the gunshot ringing in my ears. Nothing can ever be the same.

Images of the past are so raw, they rip at my insides. So fresh, they're almost real to me. He was *just here*, in this very spot, the warmth of his hand holding mine while ordering drinks for us. How can this be? Maybe it isn't. Maybe *this* is the nightmare, and I'm actually awake with him at another bar somewhere. In an alternative timeline, we've worked everything out, and we're happy because the feeling of his hand in mine seems much more solid than the current reality playing out in front of me.

"What do you feel like tonight?" Leanne appears next to me with Steve, Bryce, and Sam. They could have been standing there all along, not sure.

"Hell. I feel like hell," I say.

"What do you feel like drinking, is what she meant," Sam restates.

"Whatever you're having. I plan on drowning the flood of memories with a flood of alcohol. Doesn't matter to me what the flood tastes like."

A continuous stream of friends and acquaintances fill in behind us armed with words of regret and sorrow for our loss with the occasional pat on the back. I see kindness in their eyes, or pity, not sure which. Do they blame me? Do I care?

"Did you find out anything?" Steve asks Bryce.

"I talked to my friend on the force." Bryce leans toward us. "There's a rumor in the department that some other agency stepped in, made things look the way they needed them to, because now a shit ton of arrests are being made. Like high-level arrests, but no one's supposed to question anything or they get shut down, or worse."

"Or worse? What does that mean?" Steve asks.

"I don't know. Every time I ask, he's cryptic and closes up. Said to let it go. Shouldn't have even told me anything. He can get in real trouble."

"So what the fuck then?" Leanne says.

"Is this how it's gonna be now?" I say. "Rumors? Constant gossip? News reporters twisting who he was, every day hearing some new horrible piece of information about the guy I thought I knew?"

"No, Faith." Steve rubs my back. "We all know how drugs can turn you into a different person. Maybe, in the absolute worst-case scenario, he was in the wrong place at the wrong time, but no one believes he could have been so violent as to have actually intended to do it."

"Jesus! Do we?" I down my shot, whatever it is. "Do we really know anything anymore?"

"Yes," Steve continues, "we do, Faith. We know Cole struggled with some things in his past, but we also know he was the kind of guy who'd do anything for his friends, the life of the party, always making us laugh, and we know he loved you more than anything. Nothing's ever gonna change that, especially not what some dumbass reporter says. We all know who he really was, and we shouldn't be letting these last few months define him or his life. He was so much more."

"Did he hate me?" My eyes meet Steve's.

"He could never hate you. He'd get angry

sometimes, yeah, but he could never hate you. He was like a ship in a storm, you were his anchor. He missed you a lot."

I feel the tears coming. Again. Still.

"I'm sorry, didn't mean to…" Steve starts.

I interrupt. "It's okay."

"All Cole had to say was he needed help, and we would have jumped in." Steve's voice trails off as his head goes down.

"How did it come to this?" I rub my forehead. "I always thought we'd end up together. I thought I had time, *we* had time. I made *so many* mistakes. Can't breathe under the weight of it all. I don't know how to go on from this."

I can tell Steve hates himself as much as I hate myself. He picks up the two shots of Jägermeister the bartender poured, handing one to me. "This is how."

We raise our glasses, and I can feel Cole sitting right next to me, smiling.

Chapter Forty-Four

The most important case of my life
Faith 2026

I wake to Finn's hot breath panting on my face and the sun streaming full on through my bedroom window. After Leanne and Steve left last night, I was up for hours thinking about the queen of hearts card, mulling over all the possibilities again.

Last night, I fell into the black hole of Cole memories I've so carefully managed to sidestep for years. It seems Jeremy's death and these letters have broken ground on that twelve-year-old sacred burial plot of mine, exhumed the remains of the past, and resurrected the beautiful disaster that Cole was back to its former glory. It's clear no amount of denial or regret-laden dirt is going to fill this hole back in.

I'm back to my old pattern of playing and replaying the whole thing over in my head, looking for reasons, clues, explanations as to why it all ended the way it did. None of it has ever helped me process and *integrate it* into my present life, as Leanne would say. Until now. *Now* he may be out there. Somewhere. Maybe.

I let Finn out because for an unexplained canine reason he won't use the doggie door today. Putting on some coffee, I keep checking on him through the window and look over the pile of letters, forensic DNA, and handwriting comparison still on the counter. My eyes wander to the other side of the kitchen where I left the manilla envelope from the police department—the one delivered yesterday containing everything about the last moments of Jeremy's life. Haven't opened it yet.

As an investigator, there's only one thing left to do—lay it all out and look at it again with fresh eyes. Coffee will give me those. My fingernails tap on the counter as I wait for the pot to chime, looking out the window at Finn and the mountains. It's quiet, peaceful. I remember all the time spent up here with Cole, and how after he died, I *needed* to be here to feel closer to him, to us and what we were. I recall all the mornings Jeremy sat at this kitchen table with me. He liked the view from the chair closest to the stove. Can't help but imagine what it might be like if Cole and I sat here together having breakfast…in the future…

God, I'm losing it. I really am.

I pour a fresh steaming cup, let Finn in, and see a flash of Cole's face the day I drove away from him all those years ago. *Damn you, Cole. If it's you, why would you do it like this?*

I need to be more logical than the emotional wreck I was last night. Surely with all my years of investigative experience, I can put these skills to work on the most important case of my life. I tell myself it's not him, but who else would put that card on my windshield and why?

It's possible Cole told someone he was going to put it on my car all those years ago, but it would be so insignificant to anyone else, why would they even remember? It's *got* to be him.

Stop it, Faith! It is not. He's dead. My heart breaks into a million pieces again.

But what if it's not mere wishful thinking, and my gut has been correct all along? I've felt him around me all these years, even though I tried to stuff those feelings because it was too ridiculous to be true. There was no direct evidence of him, only the intuitive connection we've always had. That quantum-entangled bond of energy flowing between us has never left me. I can't think straight, but at this point it doesn't even matter. The train is already barreling down the track.

I retrieve a box from the garage containing Cole's original letters and miscellaneous mementos from our time together. Everything, old and new, gets laid out on the floor of the living room, spread out in chronological order as if I'm creating an evidence board. From the manilla envelope, I spread the pages and photos of Jeremy's accident over to the side because, although it seems to be a separate incident, I have not yet ruled out the possibility that somehow Jeremy's death is connected to the appearance of these letters.

Picking up each piece of evidence, I study them and pace and walk myself through a maze of possibilities, hitting dead ends, turning around, trying other routes. Leanne would tell me this is the brain's way of processing, pushing thoughts and memories down pathways, over and across synapses and dendrites until the right thought with the right memory in the right order connects, tying it all together.

This time I allow myself the possibility that it can *only* be Cole to placate myself and prove the pieces won't fit.

Not at the funeral—check. Years ago—check.

Opening up to him a few times—check. Always wishing we were more—check. The ship in the photos was in the movie we saw on our first date—check. The Lighthouse is definitely us—check. But those brightly colored homes continue to throw me off. Definitely seen them somewhere before. *Think, Faith...*

I bite my lower lip, scanning the floor and everything on it.

And there it is, the ticket stub to the movie at the pool. Our community pool where Cole and I went at the start of our relationship. Oh my God—the cabanas! They were painted in almost the same bright colors.

It's all here and with the addition of the queen of hearts card, I can no longer deny it.

It's him.

And he's out there, right now?

It can't be...

But I feel my brain make the connection, hear myself gasp.

I *am* right. It can't be—it can't be anyone *but* him.

Chapter Forty-Five

Catastrophic
Faith 2014

I'm chasing a ghost. My brain keeps replaying it, trying to get to Cole in time, to stop him from doing it and heal both our hearts at the same time. Months have passed. Spring rains have transmuted into summer humidity. I barely notice. My world continues to crumble. Nightmares dominate sleep giving way to mornings filled with painful flashbacks spinning on a continuous loop of the best and worst moments in our relationship.

I'm straddling the line between past and present, sometimes feeling like the present will disappear altogether, leaving me in either a past that no longer exists or an imaginary world where he is alive. A world I have created where he is with me, and we get to do it all over again, except better this time.

Physically, Cole's gone, but psychologically, he is everywhere. Is there life after death? Where is he? We talk every day. Is this really him sticking around in some form, or have I lost it? There's no way to know for sure, but they say the dead are always with us. I believe it. I *need* to.

"We're worried about you, Faith." Steve takes a beer from the minifridge in his living room.

"I could have saved him." I don't dare tell them what really happened the day he died, Cole's voicemails making it clear what I needed to do but didn't. What I was actually doing instead of what I *should* have done, the choice I made.

Leanne eyes the box of tissues on the coffee table, motioning to Steve. He passes them to me.

"Thanks." I dab my eyes gently. The skin around them is continuously raw. "I'm so tired of feeling like this."

"Are you getting much sleep? I know I'm not," Bryce says.

"Too many bad dreams. I always hoped his life would go in a positive direction without me. It didn't. Did I make it go that way?" I shrug. "Could I have made it go the right way? Yes. I'm absolutely sure of it. Sometimes all it takes is one person to make a difference. No matter how hard anyone tries to convince me otherwise, it's the truth." I blow my nose. "It doesn't matter now. All this talking and crying won't change a thing. I'll have to live with it. Or choose not to."

"You see, that's it! This is why we're so worried," Leanne cries. "When you say things like this it scares me. You'll have to live with it or choose not to? What does that even mean? Do you want to…die?" Her voice catches.

"It's *my* fault, *I* did this to him, *I* pushed him down that road straight to his death. It's too hard to live with. I can't stand the feeling of being in my own skin."

"You did *not* do this to him," Steve counters. "His unbalanced state of mind did it to both of you at the same time."

"But I feel…like I'm going crazy," I say. "Like, literally, crazy. Like I should be committed to an institution."

"We can't stand by and watch you do this to yourself, Faith." Leanne leans forward. "It's been months." She grabs a book on the coffee table. "Look, I've been doing some reading. You're *not* crazy. Listen…'The American Psychiatric Association ranks the trauma of losing a loved one by suicide as "catastrophic"—on par with that of a concentration camp experience. The grief process for a suicide is like no other, and the grieving can be especially complex and traumatic.' "

"Damn." Steve swivels his head from side to side.

" 'After a suicide, the "what if" questions may be extreme and self-punishing, unrealistically condemning the survivor for failing to predict the death or to intervene effectively or on time. People who've recently lost someone through suicide are at increased risk for thinking about, planning, or attempting suicide.' "

"You see," Bryce adds. "What you're going through is normal, but you need help, Faith. We want you to feel better."

"Stop interrupting." Leanne scowls. "Listen to this. 'You may have recurring thoughts of the death and its circumstances, replaying the final moments over and over in an effort to understand—or simply because you can't get the thoughts out of your head.' " Leanne looks at me.

I raise an eyebrow.

" 'Some suicide survivors develop post-traumatic stress disorder (PTSD), which can become chronic and rewire the brain, leading to permanent personality alterations and damage if not treated.' "

"Is this some kind of intervention?" I smirk.

"No. Yes. I don't know. We're concerned." Leanne puts the book down.

"I bet you'd feel a lot better if you went for some counseling," Steve agrees. "There are support groups for survivors too. I think we could all use it."

"It won't bring him back, but maybe it'll bring me back."

I take my friends' advice. Leanne set me up with a grief counselor who specializes in suicide loss. I was diagnosed with complicated grief syndrome and PTSD due to what the counselor explained are my "intense feelings of loss, powerful yearnings that Cole's still present, intrusive memories, flashbacks, nightmares, deep-rooted feelings of shame, guilt, and fantasies about him."

I reread the material the therapist gave me explaining how trauma can destroy the victim's sense of time, causing them to perceive threats in their environment which are not actually occurring in the here and now because a common symptom of PTSD is confusion between the past and present. It made sense.

Leanne did her best to make sure this did not happen. She encouraged me to check myself into the hospital. Said she came over one day and watched me have a full three-way conversation with her *and Cole*. I don't remember any of it, but stayed in the hospital voluntarily for thirty days—let them work their magic with therapy and drugs. I think it helped.

But I'm still enjoying the visits from Cole, hallucinatory or otherwise. The therapist didn't ask, so I didn't say. Just trying to keep myself out of the loony bin. My brain is fragmented between two worlds—one where I go about my life and daily activities, and another where Cole and I are together. I tell him all the things I need to say and he needs to hear and can finally, *finally*, be everything he needs me to be. No one else needs to know. After such a trauma, is it so unimaginable my mind would create a happier ending?

This new split-brain of mine continues to question every detail about the events leading up to Cole's death. My role in it is at the center of my attention while every other part of my life is held in the periphery. But time doesn't pause, not even for grief. It moves forward, even when you think you're standing still. Graduation is upon me. I've been present enough to start an internship with a private investigation firm. It suits me. Needing to know every detail of things is key in this profession.

At two years post-Cole, I'm driving to work and swear I see him through my rearview mirror in the car behind me. I'm so desperate for it to be real, when I see someone who even remotely looks like him, my mind puts him there. Maybe. Therapy's helping, sort of, but how can I heal if I can never know what really happened?

"Happy Birthday" takes on a whole new meaning these days, I mean, happy? Really? Birthday calls and messages go unacknowledged while I stay holed up in my apartment. Leanne's the only person I allow around me on that day. The date I was born is the date he died. That's got to mean something. Maybe if I was never born, he never would have died. I'm certain Leanne would do her best to change those thoughts if I ever said them out loud.

The grief doesn't scream anymore. It's just there. It simply settled in. Even in happier times, a deep river of pain flows in the undercurrent. And something else. Anger. At myself. A rage so strong, I don't even know what to do with it when it comes. The guilt and regret are tattooed on me, rolling over in my mind and the depths of my soul. Quietly. Secretly. Continuously.

But one thing remains concrete about Cole—his letters. Each time I read his words in his own handwriting, it brings him back to life, back to me. Especially the letter with those lyrics, now more tragically peaceful than ever:

"When gravity fails and the universe falls through,
I will still be loving you,
When mountains crumble to the ground,
We will still be safe, still be sound."

Chapter Forty-Six

Much-needed rest
Faith 2026

My brain swirls and races around a faded ringtone coming from somewhere. Still frozen on the floor of my living room, I'm stuck inside the impossible realization I've had about the letter writer. Cole is alive. My eyes dart from letter to letter to forensic test to police report, all strewn around me. How long have I been sitting here? The ringing in my head stops, then starts again louder, clearer.

It's not in my head. It's my phone. Whoever it is, it seems important.

Brooke's panicked voice slices through. "Where are you? You're supposed to be in court today testifying on the Englehoffer case."

"Shit!" The past swallowed me whole, and I totally forgot. "Leaving now."

"I'll tell the attorney to ask for a two-hour adjournment so you can get your shit together. Is that enough time?"

"Yeah. Damn it. Thank you."

This has never happened to me where work is concerned. Forgetting a court date? So much time and effort goes into making a case, for us as the investigators and for the attorneys. Now I've forced everyone involved to wait—for me.

I jump up from the floor, throw on suitable clothes, wet my uneven part, and race out of my house into the car. My eyes burn from the lack of sleep. Should be reviewing the case in my mind, preparing myself for the blitzkrieg of questions I know I'll get on cross-examination from that prick of an attorney Englehoffer's husband hired, but I'm not. There's no space in my head for it.

Speeding my car down Route 9 along the Hudson River, under the George Washington Bridge and into lower Manhattan, my past has just become my present. Cole's not a ghostly memory anymore. He's real. Alive. Right here, right now, in the letters, in the card left on my windshield, somewhere out there. Waiting? Looking up at the same sky as me, wondering about me as I've been wondering about him?

Not sure I can trust this, trust myself. It's too implausible, too fantastic to accept as true. Two worlds are colliding—the happy fantasy one in my head and the real one I normally walk around in as my brain fights to accept what my heart already knows to be true.

"Are you all right, Faith?" Dave, the attorney for our client, asks as I step out of the elevator.

"Yes…no, well, yes, a little frazzled today, Dave. Sorry to have put you in this position."

"It's all right." Dave's been kind and patient with me since I returned to work after Jeremy's funeral. He's no different today despite this fuck up. "You look a little pale. You want to sit? We have a couple of minutes."

"Sure." We move to the hardwood bench. "Am I up first?"

"Yep."

"Good," I say.

"I don't have to tell you, testifying on undercover work is a special skill." Dave adjusts his glasses. "You're already the enemy for misrepresenting yourself. I know you can handle it, but that deadass is going to do everything he can to discredit you personally."

I know this attorney's game. He's the kind of guy I'd like to drag into a dark alley, tie up, and smack around just to see how he'd react. "Comes with the job." We stand as the doors to the courtroom open.

"You ready?"

"Always."

The judge looks particularly annoyed today, probably because I made him rearrange his docket. Great, I'll be facing Mr. Deadass Attorney doing his best to make me look like the devil and a judge who'll probably let him.

The court is called to order. I flip the switch in my brain off Cole and all the madness that has become my personal life, on to the job at hand. The next hour and twenty minutes consists of me defending my work and myself. I've been paid to make a case for my client and as such, she is my priority, not my ego. At the same time, I can't let anybody take me down in court by making me look like an unscrupulous dirtbag investigator. I must defend myself.

It went something like this. *Didn't your client withhold sex from Mr. Englehoffer?* To which I responded, *Not my purview, I wasn't paid to investigate that.* To which he asked, *Didn't you lie to my client every time you set foot inside his store?* To which I responded, *Yes, that is, in fact, what I was paid to do because liars respond best to other liars.* To which he yelled in high dramatic fashion, *So Mrs. Ansley, were you lying then or are you lying now!*

Same old, same old. It's always a balancing act. At least that's what I think happened, can't really remember.

I come off the witness stand like a soldier walking off a battlefield, battered and exhausted and lean into Dave. "If you don't need anything else from me, I'd like to go." I should sit for a while, but I'm too restless to stay in one spot.

"Sure, Faith, but call me if you need anything. I'm worried about you."

"Thanks, Dave."

Back in my car heading up Route 9, I'm focused on two things, my impossible thoughts about Cole and the mechanics of driving my car properly while in this distracted state. Home is the only place to be right now, alone with this imaginary reality in my head so I can get to work proving its validity. I text Brooke letting her know a mental health day is needed. She immediately responds with a thumbs-up, which means she'll rearrange my entire schedule. I've done the same for her in emergencies. Shit happens.

The Stone Mountain exit leads to Main Street where I make a left on River and a right on Bay, eyes lingering on the pedestrians. Any one of them could be him. What would he look like now? After all the times I wished to see him, all those times I saw his face in someone else's, now the possibility exists any one of them might actually *be* him.

No. You've gone too far with this, Faith. Is this

what a psychotic break feels like? Would I even know I was having one? I shake the whole idea off and continue to drive as usual, pushing it all out of my head.

Stopping at the red light on Sunset behind another car, I consider bringing someone else in on this. Someone like Leanne, who won't think I've gone mad. Even if she does think I've come unhinged, she knows me and loves me enough to at least hear me out before she decides to check me into a hospital for some much-needed "rest."

A long, slow stream of anxious air exits my lips as I wait for the light to change, eyes scrambling from people walking on the sidewalk to others crossing the street, to my rearview where they become fixed on the driver behind me. I squint, making direct contact with those eyes staring back at me, and the face surrounding those eyes and…I stop breathing. My stomach lurches upward. Time stands still.

It's him.

It's Cole. I'm sure of it.

Our eyes lock. His car quickly blows by, passing me on the shoulder, making the next right turn out of sight. *No way* is he getting away from me now. My breathing restarts with a pulse so fast, my heart might explode.

It's him. *Isn't it?* And was he following me?

There's no denying this now. No reason to keep all my wild thoughts in check and no time to question what I *know* I just saw.

I speed off just as fast, making the same right turn, catching a view of the tail end of his car. He's making a left turn two blocks up. I mirror his acceleration pattern, turning the same way within seconds. He's nowhere in sight.

Speeding to the next corner, my head whips left and right. He's there, to the right—I follow. Another left, shit. He's heading toward the parkway entrance. From there, it's anybody's game. He can hop on one of the four roads converging there, curving and winding away from me. There'll be no opportunity for me to fix a wrong turn if I make one. He could get away. And I *can't* have that.

I slam my foot down hard on the gas. He's so far ahead, don't think I'll make it. The car rockets forward forcing my back into the seat, flying around the curve coming dangerously close to the guard rail, but I can't find him. All I see are endless looping roads and spurs. I have to choose. Did he head north upstate? Or did he head west into Jersey? No clue.

I go north on Route 202 and hit it again, speeding around the ramp. The cars up ahead don't have tail lights that match the shape of his. Did I misjudge? Make the wrong choice?

As I drive farther without seeing him, it becomes clear. Yes, I did. How ironic. When it comes to him, I did make the wrong choice. *Again.*

Chapter Forty-Seven

A smoothie of raw emotions
Faith 2026

I drive up the mountain and putter into my garage feeling defeated, in shock and emotionally exhausted. What to do now? Nothing else matters to me except him, alive and close by. Walking through the garage door into the house, I drop my keys into the dish and take most of the mini peanut butter cups left in the bowl.

Will he reach out or did I scare him off? What's going on? I swing my bag and briefcase onto the kitchen counter. How did this happen? Is he okay? Who else knows he's alive? I open a chocolate and toss it into my mouth.

Finn runs over from his bed for kisses and a rub. And where has Cole been all this time? Who knows what his life's been like all these years or how time may have changed him. He could be married with kids.

I walk back to the key dish and gather the rest of the mini chocolates.

Wait—who was in the coffin I stood crying over? Did he fake his own death? How? The police were there. *I was there*. Did someone help him?

The phone interrupts my internal chain of questions, chiming out a text from an unknown number.

—Faith, I'm sorry I ran from you—

Adrenaline rushes through my veins like the rapids of an angry river dammed up for too long. The first words between us in years, and I clearly hear his voice saying them. The text becomes blurry, like trying to see through an ocean. My mind races with a million different words. None of them seem right. Another line of text comes in before I can do anything.

—Please let me explain—

And another right behind it.

—and don't tell anyone you've seen me—

I can hardly place my fingers on the right keys to answer. I'm euphoric, scared, and cautious all at the same time. Is he going to explain over text? No way. I need to see him. Right now. He must know where I live, didn't end up behind me by accident. I text back.

—I'm home, get here as soon as you can—

—On my way—

I'm giddy, like we're in high school again. He's coming over, and I can't wait to see him. The butterflies are back. But we're *not* teenagers, and this is *not* high school. I'm antsy, anxious, agitated, jittery. A smoothie of raw emotions. And a little afraid.

Where is he? Probably not far. How long have I got before he walks through that door? *My door*. The door of the house I sketched years ago and gave to the architect imagining it could have been our home. *Should* have been our home.

He'll walk in and stand in my foyer. Then what? You'd think after all the time I spent longing for this very moment, I'd know what to do next.

I don't.

Looking into the mirror, I pull the cowlick down

and fluff my hair like I'm waiting to be picked up for the winter formal. Should I change clothes? Fix my face? Who cares, there's no time anyway. My knees feel weak. Finn is back on his bed sleeping peacefully. Some of his calm would be nice.

I quickly scoop up all the papers and photos on the floor from last night's overnighter, shove them into my work bag, and sit on the staircase next to the front door and wait. What's taking so long? Feels like hours since his texts. I check my phone again.

They're...gone?

They were right here. I swipe through all my messages, up and down and back again. He did text me, didn't he? But I'm too distracted by the sound outside to pursue it further.

Tires crunch gravel on the driveway. A car door opens and closes.

God, how are we going to do this? We—I haven't said that in a long time. Are *we* going to be a *we* again? Is it too late?

Don't tell anyone I've seen him? What happened all those years ago? Did he pull the trigger, or only witness it? Was he held at gunpoint, forced to participate? I've never believed he acted intentionally, ever. What if he's about to tell me I've been wrong all this time? What if he *is* a murderer? And blames me for sending him spiraling down that road?

What if he wants revenge?

Through the frosted glass windows surrounding the front door, a figure is coming up the walkway. My chest burns. Blood pumps way too fast through my body. Is the frosting of the window making him look taller and larger than I remember, or has time changed my memory? What if it's not him at all? His stride and gait seem the same. But what if this letter writer is a master manipulator, and this is not Cole at all?

But you saw him. Didn't you?

As he approaches, I see his dark hair, but the features of his face are distorted by the glass.

He knocks.

Breathe, Faith...

Chapter Forty-Eight

The whole chain of events
Faith 2026

I don't remember taking the two steps needed to get from the stairs to the front door. Don't remember opening it either, but I must have because I'm standing face-to-face with him, nothing between us but the warm air and the last twelve years. His face is still boyish but mature, now with a few creases on his forehead. And he *is* bigger, supersized with more muscle than I remember, larger than life in a black T-shirt squeezing his biceps, dark jeans hugging his lean hips.

His face is cautious, the side of his lip curling in that familiar way, looking like he's expecting to get hit over the head with a frying pan for coming home so late. All the relentless questioning in my head is silenced. I involuntarily rush toward him as if he's pulling me in with his own hands. Our bodies come crashing together in an embrace tighter than any other. I'm instantly transported to our first kiss in the car where everything else fell away. It's the same now. The feel of his scruffy cheek against mine, his arms around me and slowing, deep breaths make it obvious nothing has changed. He feels solid, concrete. Life after death is real.

"Where have you been?" I ask into his ear.

He loosens his embrace, looking down at me. "I can explain all of this."

"Come inside." I close the door and lead him into the living room where I'd been sitting hours earlier, tormented with confusion, agonizing over the truth of this moment I didn't know was coming.

I motion him to sit on the couch. He does. There's so much to say, so much to ask, but I'm sensing we both know we'll need to pace ourselves. "Can I get you something to drink?" I walk to the refrigerator.

"Water's fine." He's leaning forward, arms resting on his knees.

I fill two glasses in a silence that's pregnant and kicking, feeling his eyes on me. Turning toward him I notice they *are* on me, eager and bright.

"Faith…" His expression changes quickly, as if the weight of the world is on him and he can't wait until I sit down to start talking. "I'm sorry for what you must have gone through back then, what I put you through, all the questions you must have had." His voice catches. "But please believe me when I say I would never kill anyone. You must know that." The last part is almost in the form of a question.

I hand the glass to Cole and sit next to him, staring back, taking in the totality of him. He's *so* much larger, from his thick neck to his broad V-shaped upper body, the veins pulsating down his arms into his hands and the muscles bulging through those jeans. It's disconcerting. He could snap me in two if he wanted.

I glance at Finn, still sleeping on his bed. He didn't even bark when Cole knocked. In fact, he hasn't moved. Odd, for a dog that gets involved with everything. Must mean he likes Cole. Dogs always know.

Cole fills the silence. "At least, I hope you've known I'd never kill anyone."

I'm not ready to jump right in like this.

"Sorry." He takes a sip of water. "Maybe I shouldn't have opened with that?"

"No, it's…" I walk to the window to buy myself some time. It dawns on me, this moment is not the same for him as it is for me. It's clear he's seen me before today, knew where I lived, was behind me in the car earlier. How many times has he seen my face over the years? He seems prepared to sit for as long as it takes for me to process all this. Always the one waiting for me.

"This is a lot." I return to the couch and sit, raising my hand to his face, running my fingers lightly down the side of his cheek. Need to look at him a little longer, feel the softness of his skin, make sure this is real and not an illusion. "I believe you, Cole." At least I *want* to believe him.

He lets out a long stream of air, as if he's been holding his breath. "I need to tell you what happened."

To my surprise, I feel a complete reversal. The shock and excitement are already wearing off and replaced with…irritation? "You've been alive all this time?" I think out loud. "Well, duh, of course you have." I roll my eyes. "But what the fuck, Cole? Do you have any idea what I've been through? What it was like for me?"

"I don't. That's why the first words out of my mouth were an apology. But I can explain all of it."

"You already said that. Maybe you should." I'm shocked by my sudden ability to disconnect from him.

This is not how I imagined it.

"Okay," he starts, readjusting to face me. "The night at the bleachers when you ended it and drove away as I stood there watching…" He opens his mouth to continue but stops. He downs almost the entire glass of water and clears his throat. I guess he's been through some shit too.

My irritation recedes. "Say it, Cole. Whatever it is."

"After that, it all went downhill. Couldn't handle it. I'd lost you again, even though I didn't fully have you. I lost what little was left of us. I know why you did it. You were right after everything I put you through. I was young and stupid and desperate, but all I could see was I'd lost you."

I shrivel, like a stretchable garden hose retracting as the water drains. I knew it. I told everyone the whole chain of events that unraveled him started with me. No one would listen. Of all the well-meaning family and friends, over-confident therapists and gazillion self-help books sitting on my shelves, none of them would acknowledge the truth of it or validate me. How could they? *He* was the only one who could have understood. And that understanding died with him.

"I was in a fog of self-pity," Cole continues. "The last few years had been you and me. Granted that version of you and me was not the best, but it was still us, and it was over. I know it was wrong, Faith." He shakes his head. "I should have never made you feel like you were my whole world in such a dysfunctional way, like I would die without you. Had no right to manipulate you like that. I was desperate, obsessed, and selfish."

"You don't have to be so hard on yourself, Cole. I was no prize then either. We were both immature in our own ways."

"The only thing stopping me from ending it all was maybe I could change your mind again. And why not? I always managed to work my way back into your life."

"Shit, Cole, even I didn't think it was over."

"You didn't? You were pretty convincing."

"Wasn't I always?" I shrug.

"So I went home with the idea of giving you a few months to yourself. I could live with that. Got up every day, went to class, to work, and out with the guys. Just tried to keep going."

"Was that when you started working for Greybridge Global?" He told the guys something was going on there but wouldn't say what. Something he needed to get out of.

"That's when it all went to shit." He stands up with his empty glass, goes to the sink, and refills it.

I wait patiently because this must be difficult for him, but the silence is becoming awkward. I sense Cole's deciding what to tell me and what to leave out and I don't like it.

"Remember when Greybridge was under investigation for child pornography?" He's still at the sink leaning on the counter like it's holding him up.

"Yeah, it was all over the news. But they were exonerated."

His head moves from side to side.

"It was true?" I ask.

"And I was at the center of it."

"Are you telling me you're into child—"

"No! God, no! I was high, made a mistake at work,

saw things I shouldn't have and got sucked in. That's when I found out my boss Jordan was the head of one of the most elusive drug and porn rings on the dark web. And I had put myself right into the middle of it. Finally understood why he had so much security around him all the time."

Cole walks to the large window and looks at the mountain. The same window I stood in front of minutes ago, trying to buy myself some time. "If I hadn't been high, I wouldn't have fucked up. Hated myself every day since."

"The dark web? The place where every illegal, despicable thing goes on?"

From behind, I watch his head drop. This can't be easy for him.

"So what happened?"

He exhales hard and turns toward me. "I played along looking for ways to get out, but only got in deeper with all the wrong people. If you're on their radar for any reason, you're most likely dead, along with everyone around you. I kept it away from the guys and you especially. Months went by. I couldn't get you back in the condition I was in. I would never under any circumstances bring this kind of mess into your life."

I bob my head up and down, trying to digest what he's saying.

"I saw a lot of shit I wish I hadn't. Did things I'm not proud of. Wish I could go back and redo every minute of it."

I'm questioning him, myself, and our entire relationship, cross-referencing what's in his eyes now to what was in them then. He knows it and lets me, patiently waiting as my investigation extends from his eyes to the features of his face. He's studying me right back. "Go on." A hairball of disgust clogs the back of my throat.

"I was bringing in tons of money for Jordan and the company." He sits down next to me. "He was paying me huge sums and providing an endless supply of drugs."

"And obviously something else went wrong," I lead.

"Eventually Homeland Security approached me. Jordan's dark web business wasn't only porn and drugs, it was a smuggling operation crossing our borders with guns, human trafficking, and terrorist activity. Jordan was the head of it all. They wanted me to testify against him. I told them it'd be suicide, they'd find me and kill me. The task force talked about putting me in witness protection, but it wouldn't be enough. There was still a chance the ring could have someone on the inside find out where I'd been placed. Not only would I be separated from everyone I cared about, I'd still be looking over my shoulder the rest of my life." He stops, like he doesn't want to say the rest.

"And?"

"They offered me a different option. They'd 'arrest' me, secretly take my statement and video testimony under oath, then 'release' me saying I refused to talk. Jordan would never buy it, but if I went home and killed myself…it would look like I snitched and felt guilty for the murder. But Faith, it was *never* supposed to happen on your birthday. They told me that morning it had to happen. I tried to get them to move it to a different day, but they said it was now or never. A suicide would fit my history. I'd be home free. No one would ever question it or come looking for me. But in exchange I'd work for them."

"Who's them?"

He doesn't answer the question. "They knew everything about me, childhood, grades, sports, how I'd been such a quick study and managed to stay alive as long as I had at Greybridge. Said I knew the inner workings of the underground world, had the raw abilities they needed and the potential to be very useful to them. They'd put me in rehab, train me, and give me a new career. But I'd be a ghost. No one would know of my existence. If anything went wrong with our operations, I'd be on my own."

Did he really just say ghost? Am I conflating fantasy with reality? "I wish I could have been there for you," I decide to say while retrieving memories of myself, a carefree college student, partying as all this was going on for him. But I'm not stupid. When the government approaches someone, it's usually because they have their balls in a vice. "Why you?"

"Hmm?"

He wasn't expecting that. I can tell.

"Why you? I'm sure there were other more experienced criminals at Jordan's side longer than you."

His face crinkles. "Jordan paid so well everyone was loyal, or afraid, and Homeland had an undercover in there, couldn't pull him out yet."

In full investigator mode, I push further. "Who was on the door camera with you?"

"You saw that?" His brows rise, almost like he's been caught, despite the fact he's coming clean.

"Heard about it. You were the one holding a gun," I challenge.

"God, I'm sorry, Faith." Cole puts his head in his hands, scratching his scalp. He looks up and continues. "Jordan brought an extra gun and told me to take it. So I did. What choice did I have? I didn't shoot that guy, but there's no honor among thieves. Within minutes of walking through the door, it all went bad. Jordan shot him. I was literally sick, puking, desperate to get myself out of there."

I say nothing and home in on his eyes, searching them, looking for something, anything I can recognize from before it all happened. Do I want to believe him, or is there cause to question everything I thought I knew about him? About us? Is he still the guy I thought he was, or did he turn into a cold-blooded killer after our split? And what about now? Which is he?

"By that point, I was relieved Homeland targeted me. At the same time, there was so much wrong with this, I wanted to say no. Everyone would think I was a murderer. I would never see anyone again. I would never see you. And I knew you would blame yourself for all of it, but what other option did I have? I'd ruined my life. You and everyone else would have been better off without me." He takes a sip of water like he can't continue without it. "They laid it all out, said I would have a fresh start, could be a new person, a better person. I'd be doing something worthwhile, saving people and helping the country. Seemed like a noble thing to do, and it would give me purpose. Maybe I could even make up for what I'd done."

What you've done? "So this is where you've been? Are you telling me you were rebooted as some kind of real-life Jason Bourne?"

"I said yes to them, but in the back of my mind

hoping it would somehow lead me back to you. We'd have to be apart for a while—a long while—but eventually I'd find my way back."

"You're taking a risk seeing me then?"

"I knew I could cover my tracks. It's part of the training, and I've proven myself enough over the years. They're not watching anymore."

"Was this the reason for your letters? All the cloak and dagger shit? Why not just show yourself to me?"

He stands up and walks to the fireplace and leans one hand on it, eyeing the framed photos of Jeremy and me. "I wasn't sure if you really wanted to see me. I was trying to figure that out." He pivots toward me. "You were still grieving. I was trying to ease you into the idea I was still alive. It was going to be a shock, and I know how your brain works. If I sent the right info, you'd figure it out, but you saw me before I was ready. I panicked. Then I had to trust you'd keep quiet about me until I could get to you and explain."

"So…" I scrunch my face, rolling my eyes around the ceiling as my brain catches up to all this new information. "If Cole's dead, who are you? They gave you a new name?"

He flashes a grin while trying not to.

"Ha, what is it?"

"Derek."

"Derek?" I can't control my expression. It's almost comical. "Derek what?"

"Gray."

"Derek Gray?" I repeat.

I'm getting a cautious nod from him, like he's waiting for approval.

"Derek Gray," I announce, trying it on for him. "I

like it. But you don't expect me to call you that, do you?"

"I'd prefer it if you didn't."

"Good," I say. "You know, you're still in the system. My source found a trace of you."

"I'll take care of that." As if I've asked him to do something as mundane as take out the trash.

Mr. X was right. This is some seriously high-level shit. What else is he capable of now? And who the hell is he really?

Chapter Forty-Nine

Yesterday and every day
Faith 2026

"Cole…" I pause, struggling to wrap my brain around all he just said. "You know I was at your house that day on the lawn, don't you?"

"Yes." He sits down next to me on the couch, squeezing his brows together as if it's too painful to think about. "I found out later. I *never* expected you to be there, outside, almost witnessing what you thought was my death." He places his hand on my leg and every part of me reacts. "I'm so sorry, Faith."

I hate this. All of it. The entire story. How could he have let this happen? How could he have been so stupid?

Maybe that's not fair. I remember how we were back then. He's right, young and reckless, thinking we were invincible. And I know now exactly what I knew then. Cole has always been a good person with a pure heart. It's what drew me to him and kept me coming back. If he got sucked into something, I can forgive him. But the murders? My jury is still out on that.

I look down at his hand on my thigh and sigh. "And I need you to know how sorry *I* am. There's so much I wish I could take back. Made so many mistakes with you."

"You don't need to say it, Faith. It was me, not you."

"You never knew I used to lie awake at night trying to figure out what was wrong with me. In my eyes, you were as close to perfect as possible and I…wasn't. I hated myself for what I was doing to you. To us. That's why I finally ended it. Not because I didn't love you, but because I did. I just wasn't very good at it. You deserved so much better from me. I thought putting a few years between us would give us a chance to mature. We'd find each other again. Maybe you'd still love me. All those months went by not talking to you…"

"Faith, you don't need to do this."

"…there wasn't a day I didn't think about picking up the phone. And then your voicemails on my birthday, Jesus, even when I knew with every fiber of my being, something was going wrong for you, I still didn't reach out. Still held back, stayed detached, avoiding my real feelings, like I always did with you. And then it was too late. I was there, right outside. I heard it, the shot that ended you, and it was over for me, Cole. From that moment on, the person I had been was gone. I'd made the biggest mistake of my life and it was going to be permanent. And the worst part? You died thinking I didn't care."

"But it was me too…"

"I wasn't there for you," I continue, cutting him off. "I should have been. It was torture. I wanted to go with you. In fact, I almost did…" My voice trails off.

"Forgive me," he pleads. I see, in his face, he's feeling the brunt of it now like never before, blaming himself for all my mental torment the same way I'd been blaming myself for his.

"We're quite a pair, aren't we?" I say. He moves closer, brushing the tears from my cheek.

"We can find a way to move forward from this, can't we?" he asks.

"I want to," I whisper. "I never thought I'd see you again. Just looking at you hurts."

"I thought…" He falters. "I worried, my death and your marriage would erase everything between us."

I kiss him, barely brushing my lips against his, tasting his rainy berry scent. "There was no chance of that. I never stopped loving you."

His arms are around me in an instant pulling me into him, his mouth fully on mine, as the years of separation melt away. All the time lost, only to recall these moments in my imagination, and now it feels so real. It must be. But he's a ghost. With no paper trail. No one can know he's returned. Even I recognize the irony, or insanity of it.

I straddle him, pulling his shirt over his head. Our lips separate but connect right back together the second the shirt is out of the way.

"I've waited so long for this, for you." He takes my shirt and bra off in what feels like one motion. His lips on my neck give way to the feel of teeth gently sinking into my skin, but they're also everywhere at once. It is almost a blur. I'm lost in him again. Nothing has changed.

Standing us both up, he returns me to the couch on my back, hovering over me, kissing my neck and breasts. Cole unbuttons my pants, and I unsnap his. We help each other pull them off, and our bodies come crashing together again, naked for the first time in what feels like the beginning of a second lifetime. His body is warm and hard against mine, but I need more.

"I can't get close enough to you, Cole."

He slides his hand underneath and onto my lower back. Our eyes lock as he seamlessly slides into me, closing the gap of the last twelve years.

"Is that better?" he whispers.

This time I will hold nothing back. We move together in what feels like a dream, except for the very real sensations of his warm breath in my ear, baby soft skin, toned arms, and the feeling of him growing larger inside me. As if we'd done this yesterday and every day before, the familiar waves of pleasure rise, as they do only with him. He tilts me into the position he knows I need. He's forgotten nothing.

"I've loved you every hour of every day since the last time I saw you," he breathes.

The intensity of his words and the sound of his voice trigger a final orgasm. We come to rest after rolling to our sides, facing each other on the couch. My throat tightens and eyes swell.

Cole holds me tighter. "Are those happy tears or something else, babe?" he asks, stroking my hair.

"I don't know. They're for all the things we shouldn't have done to each other back then, the things we should have said, the apologies we owed each other, and for this moment where it's all colliding. It's overwhelming. There's so much regret. The only thing I can do now is love you the way I should have then. Believe me, Cole, I've changed, would never do those things to you now. And I'll spend the rest of my life proving it to you if that's what you need."

"You? You want to prove it to me? I let you suffer

the guilt of thinking I was dead all this time. You have nothing to prove. If anyone has making up to do, it's me, to you."

"Maybe, but if I hadn't been the way I was, none of this would have happened in the first place. I shouldn't have stayed away as long as I did." I hear his voicemails in my head and see flashes of Jeremy.

"You *have to*. This feels like the day you came to see me in the hospital all over again. You can't blame yourself for the things I chose to do. Those are my bad decisions and mine alone. I won't let you torture yourself. It's been long enough for both of us. And who's to say if we'd never met, I wouldn't have gone down the same exact road?"

"Wait, what?" I pause, needing a minute to process this complete paradigm shift. "Wow, Cole, I never thought about it like that. Maybe you're right. This all may still have happened."

"Yep," he says. "With or without you."

"I'm impressed. How'd you get so…self-aware?"

"You always wanted me to keep going to therapy. I did. Able to see the bigger picture now. We were hyper-focused on us and our little world, but there were so many more factors involved. There always are. We were dysfunctional, separately and together. Not our fault, look what we were coming from. We both knew it but were too young to know how to fix it."

"And I was always pushing you away, needing to stay detached. I guess it would have been the same with anyone I dated because it wasn't about you. It was about me. I can see that now. But it's all changed, Cole. I've had a lot of time to work on myself too."

"Were you like that with Jeremy?" he asks without

hesitation.

I knew this was coming. It's the elephant in the room, like Cole was the elephant when Jeremy and I reconnected. I run my hand through my hair and sigh.

"We don't have to go there." He rescinds the question.

"Yeah, we do. The plan in my head was *always* to be with you, Cole. Then you were gone. Jeremy came back to Devenport, we started talking, he was different. It was easy and simple and…uncomplicated."

With his arms still wrapped tight around me, he kisses my neck, but then he speaks, sending a shock wave straight through my chest into my stomach. "I'm gonna have to leave in a few days."

Chapter Fifty

This feels like an interrogation
Faith 2026

"Leave?" I pop up on my elbow. "You can't. You just got here."

"It won't be long. I'll come right back to you." He wraps his leg around mine trying to pull me into him, but I wiggle out and stand up.

"Why? What exactly do you do now?"

"After rehab, training, and some undercover work, they felt I was best suited to working on a private security team."

"And…"

"Aaaand, I'll be back."

"Nope, not gonna work." I don't know why, but I'm pulling on my clothes.

"What are you doing? Lie back down with me," he says.

"No, I need more info." My shirt and undies are back on, and I'm standing over him, arms crossed.

"I'm under contract," he says, looking up at me. "They call, I go."

I can't hold back the snort of derision and walk to the fridge. Grabbing two bottled beers, I pop them open and place them on the island. It's an invitation.

"Okay, okay." He sits up, pulling on his jeans. I

notice several jagged scars scattered on his back and arms. He comes to the counter and leans against it sideways on his hip facing me. We lift our beers, clink them together, and both take a swig.

"Listen," he starts. "I know I just got here and this sucks, but what I do is highly classified. I can't tell you about it. After everything we've been through, please don't let this be the thing that pulls us apart."

"I know what private military contractors do." If in fact, he actually works for one. "It's dangerous. And after everything we've been through, you have an obligation to tell me *something*."

"Your job isn't the safest either." He takes another sip.

"But I can tell you where I'm gonna be. You've got to give me more. I need to know why I should think you and your *team* will be safe, outside of the normal concerns."

"Are you interviewing me? This feels like an interrogation."

"I am." I take a drink.

"I'm not used to answering to anyone. It's nice." He looks across the room at Finn, still asleep on his bed. "Good-looking dog. What's his name?"

Finn is on his bed in the same position he was in when Cole walked in.

"Finn, and you're stalling."

"All right, look, I have all the same training anyone in the military would have and then some. We've been out on hundreds of jobs over the years. We're experienced, skilled, and I trust these guys with my life. They trust me with theirs. Hell, I would trust these guys with your life."

That *does* make me feel better. A little. "It sounds like I have to worry. I don't like this. Where are you gonna be?" I ask.

He steps closer and kisses me. "You know I can't tell you. I'm not even supposed to be here."

"What if you don't come back? What if you're killed? Are you saying no one will be able to tell me?"

He pulls my shirt collar to one side, kissing my neck and shoulder. "That's a lot of questions."

"Cole, wait." I take a step back, but he moves with me. "I need to know."

"You can't know." His hands travel up my legs and around my waist under the shirt. He continues to maneuver us, until my back is against the wall. "It's for your own protection."

"You're expecting me to accept this? No questions asked?" I want to protest further, but his unrelenting lips are making it difficult.

"For now." He takes my wrists and pins them over my head against the wall, gliding his mouth across my chest to the other side of my neck.

"You have to make sure someone can tell me if anything happens to you."

"I'll work it out, Faith. Don't worry. All that matters is we're together again." He lifts my shirt over my head.

"And when you say you're not supposed to be here, where *are* you supposed to be?" His hands and mouth are so warm on my skin, it's getting hard to continue this line of questioning, but so many concerns are popping into my head at once, I can't stop. "Where have you been living?"

"Lots of places. Never too far from you." He's

moved to his knees, tongue on my belly, fingers pulling my panties down.

"No." I tilt his head toward my face. "That's not gonna work either. Tell me where in the *fucking world* you've been. Give me one place, just one."

"This sudden aggression is a turn on," he says.

"Jesus, Cole. Tell me."

"Pine Valley. That's been my home base."

"Pine Valley? The Pine Valley that's forty minutes from here!"

"Yeah," he confirms, in a manner that's way too casual.

"Are you kidding?"

"Never too far from you…"

"You've been practically down the road from me?" Unbelievable. Feeling a little lied to and wondering if some of those times I thought I saw him, I actually did.

"I don't spend a lot of time there, but yes, close."

"Then move in with me. Can you?"

"Yes."

"Yes?" I lift each leg as he removes my panties. "Just like that? Don't you need to think about the logistics?"

"Already have." His mouth is on my inner thigh. "It's secluded, the mountains provide excellent ability to observe approaching targets, you have few neighbors…" I run my hands through his hair as he moves toward the right spot. "…decent escape routes, good proximity to transportation by foot if needed…"

But I'm not really listening anymore.

Chapter Fifty-One

Those who turn one into the other
Faith 2026

Time has stopped for both of us. The last forty-eight hours have been a dream, turning my world upside down in the best way possible. But I've entered another reality, one I can't verify as true because I'm not supposed to know it even exists. I've been introduced to the shadow world only heard about in dark corners of the web. A world that's full of unanswerable questions according to Mr. X. Despite this, Cole and I have gone back to our own little bubble, excavated the ghosts of the past, and exorcized the demons with truth, clarity, and forgiveness. But we can't stay here forever. We'll have to re-enter the world in this new paradigm. I'm just not sure how.

It's almost too good to be true. He's alive, and here and now we can spend the rest of our lives together—but in secret. If Cole is a figment of my imagination, wouldn't the circumstances be the same? No one would be able to see him but me. Is this serendipity or psychiatric coincidence?

Cole's leaving tomorrow on his assignment, for how long, I don't know. He was awake and out early this morning, going for a run while I stayed in bed, warm and tangled in the comforter. He came back at the crack of dawn, showered, and headed to his place to bring some of his things back. Before bed, I mentioned installing cameras, like Steve and Leanne suggested, and Cole was all for it. Said he would install them himself. On his way back, he's picking them up.

I shower, throw on some clothes, and head to the kitchen for my routine caffeine rush when Cole returns carrying a large brown box.

"You're up." He walks to me, massaging my shoulders as I stir creamy liquid into the mug. "There's about seven boxes from my place. Where should I put them?"

"Hallway's fine for now. Coffee?" It's still hard to believe he's here.

"Na, the cold mountain air did the job." He brushes my morning hair away and kisses my neck. "There really are no words for this, are there? I mean, we went to bed, woke up together, I'm running errands and you're having coffee, like we've been doing this for the last ten years, living a mundane yet very happy life."

"Surreal, isn't it?"

"I'm gonna bring in the rest of the boxes and cameras."

"Want some help?"

"I got it. Enjoy your coffee." He heads out the front door.

I walk to the cabinet, scoop some dog food, and splash it into Finn's metal bowl. The jarring clang usually gets him going, but this morning he's still asleep on his bed. Only went out once last night. I might need to be concerned.

I call Brooke and let her know all is well but a few more days are needed. She doesn't question it, says to take all the time I need as long as it's only three more days because she'll lose her shit after that. She took over my caseload, and we won the Englehoffer case. Our client is still getting half the marital assets, but due to my investigation, the amount of those assets is now tenfold. I'm thrilled.

Cole returns to the kitchen. His phone rings as he takes the cameras out of their boxes. He looks at the screen. "I'm gonna take this outside." He walks through the sliding glass door to the deck, not fully closing it.

I inspect the new cameras while keeping an eye on him. These aren't what I expected, not your basic security cameras. They're more elaborate, the kind I'd have access to with more options for range and focus, motion sensors, heat sensors, night vision, and automatic features. The kind that can transmit great distances with crystal clarity. Did he have these on hand?

He's on the deck with his back to me, phone to his ear, free hand on his hip. Facing out toward the mountain, he's looking exceptionally hot in a blue T-shirt and black shorts. Because the door is partially open, I hear the conversation.

"Uh-huh. Yep." At first it sounds like he's confirming a take-out order, but his tone changes. "I told you when we debriefed last time, I'm not fucking around with this guy for a third time." His voice is commanding, yet in control. "This time, he's done. I don't wanna get called out on this again, do you?" He pauses, listening. "It's too high risk. We're gonna end it now. It's what we're paid to do."

He unexpectedly spins toward me. I'm startled but continue unboxing the cameras and start reviewing the instructions. He's looking at me but not really, more like through me, still engrossed in the conversation. Eyes cold, his expression and posture are belligerent, combative.

Not sure I was supposed to hear any of that and don't want it to appear like I was listening, but I can't turn off the investigator in me, even now. Especially now.

This time he's done? Done how? What does that even mean? Is their mission to take someone out? As in kill? As in assassinate?

Cole steps back into the kitchen, slipping the phone into his pocket.

"Got those cameras all figured out?" He's back to his smiling, charming, seductive self.

"Seems simple enough," I say. "You want breakfast?"

"I'm good." He looks inside one of the boxes.

"Are you putting these up now? I'll help," I offer.

"Sure."

We pick up the cameras, head to the garage for some tools and a ladder and go outside. A couple of quick zit-zits and he's done installing the first one on the front of the house before I know it.

"It's nice having someone here looking out for me," I say, as he climbs down the ladder.

We move to the backyard. Cole places the ladder and climbs up to install the second camera, pulling at a spool of wiring. "Hand me the wire cutter."

"Not sure where it is," I say, looking around the ground and feeling my pockets for it. "I must have left it out front."

"It's fine. What else do you have to cut these?"

"A boxcutter."

"That'll do," he says.

I reach down and grab the handle at an awkward angle, not realizing the blade is extended and feel it slice into the inside of my wrist. "Shit!" At once, there's blood all over.

"Faith! What happened?" He jumps off the ladder. "Oh, that's a bad one. You're gonna need a few stitches." He holds my arm above my heart wrapping a rag around it.

"Damn it!" I cringe looking at it. "I have a first-aid kit under the bathroom sink."

"Here, sit down, you're turning white. I'm gonna run to my car. I'd rather use mine."

Cole takes off around the side of the house while I sit, trying not to look too close at the now very bloody rag. He returns with a camouflage backpack, helps me to my feet and takes me inside to the bathroom.

"Shouldn't we be getting in the car to go to the hospital?"

"Nope, I can take care of this."

"Ummm, excuse me?"

He puts the toilet lid down, gently guides me onto it, and washes his hands. I watch in disbelief as he takes out a needle and vial, drawing liquid into it. His movements are swift and deliberate.

"Are you serious right now?" I'm not a fan of needles in any way, shape, or form.

He unwraps the towel from my wrist, lays my hand and arm face up on the counter, but feels my hesitation as my muscles resist. He looks directly at me. "Faith, trust me."

I inhale deeply and let out a shaky exhale.

"It's okay." His voice is gentle and reassuring. "I've done this many times, on myself even. Look away. It'll be quick."

And he's right, except for the pinch I'm numb instantly. By the time I have the nerve to turn back, he's about done stitching the gaping slit closed.

"Should I even ask when you learned to do this?"

"Just part of the training. You know what this reminds me of?" He's cleaning up the bathroom and my bloody arm.

"Yeah, me, cleaning *your* arm. Boy, things have changed."

Our eyes meet, recognizing how far we've come.

"All good?" he asks.

"Yep," I say.

"I'm going to finish the cameras. Why don't you sit this out and rest for a bit?" He sits me on the couch, kisses my forehead, and goes outside.

I watch him as he leaves the room and can't help but think back to our early days. How different he is now, yet the same. Still sweet, kind, loving, loyal, but now confident, assured, decisive, and apparently unflappable. The irony is not lost on me—the fact that we've chosen professions requiring similar traits. But it's one thing to be tracking people down, gathering intelligence, and providing protection details and quite another to be part of a kill team, if that is in fact, what he's doing. And who is he doing it for? Has my imagination run wild? Or is this why he's being intentionally vague?

Is there any circumstance where this is acceptable? Morally or ethically justified? From where I sit, there are very few absolutes in this world. Most of the time, truth is relative, based on time and circumstance. Back then, triggerman or not, he would have been a murderer, clearly wrong and on his way to jail. But now, killing a dangerous target to save others, possibly hundreds if not thousands of innocents, is more than okay in my book. He's risking his life for the greater good.

Is Cole doing this for redemptive purposes, making up for the past like he said? Or is there a darker side that's always been there, needing to be fed? Maybe I've watched too many episodes of *Dexter*. How will I be able to tell the difference?

He's just become my own personal living, breathing paradox.

Chapter Fifty-Two

I'm your concerned neighbor
Faith 2026

"All done," he announces, walking into the kitchen.

"Wow, you're fast." I'm standing at the counter looking through the new mail. "No more letters coming from you, I suppose?"

He slides across the room moving right behind me. The length of his body presses directly against mine, smelling of the outdoors. "Nope." His arms stretch around me, one coming to rest on my stomach underneath the shirt, the other around my neck gently nudging my head to the right. I feel his lips on my neck and rest my head back onto his chest. How easy this is, after all the years of wishing this to be real and struggling to accept it never would be again.

Being able to share this with someone would lend to its credibility. This seems true, he feels corporeal, tangible, but I've questioned my perception over the last few weeks and didn't someone once say perception is reality? That we live in a fantasy, a world of illusions, and the great task in life is to find the reality. Which reality am I in?

"You can keep sending them if you want. They were romantic," I say.

"Maybe I will then." His warm breath is in my ear. "You feel like home."

"You *are* home, Cole."

Wrapped in his arms, I hear nails clicking on the wood floor. Finn's finally up. He meanders his way over to us, then drops down onto the floor, legs splayed.

"Shit, Cole, this is definitely not normal." I get onto the floor to examine Finn, running my hands over his back and sides. His breathing is short and choppy. He lifts his head and vomits.

"That's it, he needs to go to the vet right now." I look up at Cole.

"Poor guy." Cole grabs some paper towels. "Let me drive."

"You can't come." Finn lies there panting. "We can't be seen together. You can't be seen at all."

"You shouldn't take him by yourself while he's in this condition." Cole's wiping up the vomit, and if I didn't already love him, this may have sealed the deal.

"I'm not some damsel in distress. I manage quite well on my own." That came out harsher than intended. "I only mean we shouldn't risk it."

"I'm coming." He lifts Finn from the floor and heads to the garage.

"Then you're waiting in the car." I follow without bothering to grab the leash.

Cole places Finn into the back seat with me, and I call the vet on the way. As soon as Cole drives into the parking lot, Mary, the tech I spoke to minutes earlier, comes out to help. Shit. I flash Cole a panicked look.

"I'm your concerned neighbor." He winks.

Mary rushes over.

"Thanks for seeing him on such short notice," I

say.

"Of course, Faith. We love Finn. We've had an outbreak of parvovirus. It's urgent. He needs to be seen right now." She practically lunges into the back seat.

"Parvovirus?" My anxiety about Cole being seen disappears.

Mary quickly places her hands under Finn. "When did the symptoms start?"

"Yesterday, I think."

"When did he eat and drink last?" For a petite woman, she lifts him out of the car with ease.

"Yesterday also." I look at Cole, surprised she didn't acknowledge or even look at him. He shrugs as I slam the door and follow her inside.

Mary helps Dr. Gardner examine Finn. "Well, he's got something. I don't want to take any chances, Faith. This virus is highly contagious and possibly life-threatening. I'd like to get him on antibiotics and fluids right now. I'll run the test and call you in a few hours."

"My boy may die?" The words choke out of me.

"You caught it fast." Dr. Gardner takes Finn in his arms and heads toward the back treatment area. "I think he'll be fine. Don't worry, Faith. We'll take good care of him."

Back at the car, I ask Cole to take the passenger seat. We head home while I berate myself for not paying closer attention to Finn. But with Cole's reappearance, can anyone blame me?

"I really think he'll be okay, Faith." Cole reaches for my hand and squeezes it. "And you see? Nothing to worry about. She didn't even notice me."

Returning home, the house phone rings. I'm startled and not sure if my nerves are on edge from the scare with Finn, the worry that everything could have gone to shit if Cole was seen, or the gnawing suspicion I've lost my grip on reality and he's not actually here at all. I hesitate.

"It's okay," he encourages. "Answer it as if it were the morning before you went to court."

"It's not that easy," I say.

"You'll get used to it, go ahead."

My eyes are glued to the phone, as if it's going to jump up and bite me. The caller ID doesn't reveal who it is. Maybe I should let it go to voicemail, but that might look suspicious to Cole. Or is that in my head?

"You'll do fine," he reassures. "And put it on speaker."

Speaker? Why? Doesn't he trust me? The more it rings, the more urgently it seems to need answering. I press the speaker button.

"Faith, it's Steve. I wanted to check in on you. Everything okay?"

"Steve, yes, I'm fine. Everything's fine." I look at Cole who immediately sits down on the couch, head in his hands. Hearing his old friend's voice for the first time in years must not be easy for him.

"The more I think about it, the more I don't like it," Steve continues. "The person writing these letters could be a psychopath. With your address. You're alone on that mountain. Anything can happen. Have you considered installing the cameras we talked about?"

"I really appreciate your concern, but I have Finn. And you'll be happy to know I already installed those cameras."

"Really? That's great news."

"And you know what else? You don't have to

worry. I found out who's been writing the letters."

Cole's head pops up, eyes bulging, looking at me with an expression I have not yet seen from him until right now. Surprise and seething rage at once, maybe.

"You did? Who is it?" Steve asks.

"A friend from college I dated. You wouldn't know him. He's harmless. Called me the next day after you were here. I'm sorry, I should've told you right away." I flash a grin at Cole.

"Is he a good guy? I mean, you have to admit the way he went about reaching out to you is kinda creepy, don't you think?"

"We took a class together, Mystery and Suspense Writing. It's how we met. Both loved the class. Used to try to out-write each other. He thought it might be a cute way to get in touch."

Cole's eyebrows lift in agreement, seemingly surprised by my sudden ability to create what I think is a pretty convincing lie. Doesn't he know this is what I do for a living? I'm a professional liar of sorts. He's nodding, and his protruding lower lip tells me I've done well, not bad, not bad at all.

"Are you gonna see him?" Steve asks.

"Not sure. I'm considering it. Maybe for coffee."

"Well, okay, but I want to be there somewhere in the background if you do so I can check this guy out. You know, just in case."

"I won't make a move without you." I laugh. "How's the relocation going?"

"Great! Found a nice place in the Glen Allen area. I'll have you over once I'm settled."

"Perfect."

As I end the call, Cole walks to the wall of

windows overlooking the backyard and mountain. He sighs a loaded heaviness into the room. I see the reflection of his face in the window. He seems to be looking past everything.

"Are you all right, Cole?"

"I like that he's still looking out for you." His back remains toward me.

I walk to him. "It's nice to know someone like that is around."

"Did anything ever happen between you two?"

"Seriously?" My tone goes up an octave.

"Yeah." He still isn't looking at me.

"No," I say.

"No?"

A swirl of anger winds up inside me desperate to come out my mouth. Is he doubting my feelings for him? After everything? Some things never change. "Cole…"

He turns toward me. "I'm sorry, but hearing his voice, listening to the two of you talk…makes me realize how much I've missed. How it could have been for us if I hadn't completely fucked things up."

"And *I* think the reason you completely fucked up falls *completely* on me. So there's that."

He pulls me closer, trying to shield me from my own regret. What's done is done, but neither of us has shaken off the mistakes of the past. There's some lingering mistrust and remorse, still blaming ourselves for the pain of the other.

And why not? Time heals nothing. Not a conversation, an event, a feeling, not a damn thing. Time only carries things further away, like those moving walkways at the airport. Sometimes if you get off and look back, you'll see it there, whatever *it* is, still perfectly intact, only smaller.

Being together again is just like that. We are both seeing our mistakes close up. Every detail is back in focus and larger than life. He's leaving tomorrow, and I'm starting to wonder if there's anything we can do now to ever change that.

Chapter Fifty-Three

A different kind of darkness
Faith 2026

My eyes open to the faintest glimmer of orange
glow outside my bedroom window, enough to cast light
on his sleeping face. He looks peaceful. *We* are
peaceful, lying face-to-face in each other's arms,
perfectly still, breathing as one. I'm more in love with
him than ever. As my eyes come into focus, I study his
face. It's the same, but different. *He's* the same, but
different.

One minute it feels like no time has passed—the
birthmark on his hand, the expression in his eyes
making me feel like I'm the only woman on the planet.
His half smile when I say something half funny, the
softness of his lips. It's exactly the same. But then, it's
not, at all. The way his eyes can change from kind to
cold on a dime, his rock-hard body and the various
scars I'm still finding on him, none of which he wants
to talk about. In some ways, he's almost a complete
stranger. There's something dangerous about him now.
What might he be capable of doing? I'm seeing a
different kind of darkness there. I sense he has the
ability to be brutal if necessary.

As if able to detect my thoughts in his sleep, the
hand he'd been resting on my waist comes to life,

tightening into my skin. He glides his fingertips up my back wrapping his vein-streaked, powerful hand around the nape of my neck, pulling my face to him. I know how much he loves me right back. He doesn't need to say it, I can feel it. Always could. That crazy intensity he always had for me is still there. But what else is there? I bring my lips to his, barely touching. "Please don't go."

He opens his eyes, meeting mine. "I'll always come back to you."

"What if you don't? What if you can't?"

He kisses me, rolling on top and into me simultaneously. It takes my breath away every time.

"Cole, I need to know what to do. You're leaving in a few hours."

But that answer never came.

****

And just like that, he's gone. As quickly as he came back into my life, he left it.

Again.

The ache this time is almost worse than when I thought he was dead. To have him back, only to possibly lose him again forever. It's cruel. Is this going to be my life now? Our life? Constant emotional ups and downs every time he comes and goes?

My conclusion? Still better than not having him at all.

Dr. Gardner calls and tells me Finn's parvovirus test came back negative. Thank God. He's got some other infection and while not life-threatening, they'll keep him for a few more days. I'll stop by and visit him later with his favorite blanket.

With Cole back, I'm more determined than ever to

bring my questions about Jeremy's accident to an end. I need closure, some peace and happiness. I think I've earned it.

As I drive to the gates of the police impound, the attendant recognizes me, opens the gate, and points me in the direction of Jeremy's car. It's easy to find, being one of the most mutilated cars on the lot. I park, approach his car, and notice all the snow has melted off. Good, this should make things quick and easy.

My eyes scan my dead husband's car, assessing its condition. The front right side is a mangled mess from the rollover and impact with the tree, but the left side of the car is in almost pristine condition. I walk down the left side, and there it is, clear as day, a dent and scratch on the quarter panel over the left rear wheel. Kneeling down to get a closer look, I run my hand over the cold jagged depression in the metal. My eyes fill.

It's clear seeing it in person, this car did not completely roll over. It must have rolled up on its right side against the tree before bouncing off. What's more, there's red paint transfer on Jeremy's white car in and around that jagged dent.

Was he hit and pushed into that tree?

The report must be wrong is my thought as I study the deep scratches. He *must* have been hit. There's no other conclusion. I've handled my share of accident investigations and this is not roll-over damage. How could they have missed it? Who would leave the scene of an accident? What kind of person would leave someone to die? Unless it was intentional. Planned. Deliberate.

I'm contemplating going to the station to discuss this with the detective. Or not? Maybe I should let it go.

It's not gonna bring him back.

But who would want Jeremy dead?

He didn't have any enemies. I barely knew anyone who didn't like him, certainly not enough to kill him. But at this moment, whether I like it or not, Cole's face pops into my head. I try to dismiss it, but flashes of our past rush into my brain. It all becomes clear—the three of us—me, Jeremy, and Cole, since we were teenagers. I've known the two of them half my life. The rivalry between them started in high school. And for Cole to have found out after all these years I married *him*? Shared a life with *him*? The same *him* who would always have a piece of me Cole thought he couldn't?

It can't be. The Cole I used to know would never…but the Cole I know now, might. And more importantly, *can.* He has all the capabilities needed to carry this out. But would he?

A new scenario bursts into my brain. One involving Cole, in some kind of red vehicle, following behind Jeremy, wipers fluttering on high in the billowing snow, waiting for the perfect moment to strike. I imagine Cole tailgating Jeremy, forcing him to drive faster than he would have, and Cole, having already calculated which curve had a tree that would cause the most damage, picking the perfect time to drive his car left of center and forward just enough to hit Jeremy's car and…

Am I being dramatic? Hypervigilant? Conflating and confusing this into something it's not? This is what goes on inside an investigator's head—*all* the possibilities. Should I go to the impound office on the way out and release the car, releasing all these wild thoughts with it? Or pursue this? Do I even want to?

My head's spinning. I return to my car in a daze and drive straight out of the lot without stopping.

****

An hour later, I'm down on Long Island walking through the doors of the café for our regular lunch and find Leanne sitting at a table. I'm uneasy. Not only due to the state of Jeremy's car, but because for the first time in our twenty-year friendship, speaking freely with Leanne is not an option. The person I can say anything to, the person who knows every event, thought, and feeling inside me since 2005 and now, I'm gonna have to hold back. It feels wrong, dishonest, and downright deceitful. I don't even recognize myself.

"I haven't heard from you in days, Faith! And now you're late for our lunch? Have you taken a secret lover?"

It's uncanny, like a truth grenade flying through the air at top speed, landing on me, and exploding. I freeze in my tracks.

"I'm sorry, the damn Expressway and…I got really busy with work prepping to testify on a case." This is not a lie, only a stretching of the truth.

"No, that's not it. You were supposed to call me after I left you and Steve alone at your house. You didn't." She reaches for a slice of the spinach quiche she already ordered for us. "Then you didn't return any of my calls. It's not like you."

"I know! Sorry! But there wasn't anything to tell." I use my left hand instead of my right to pour myself coffee from the carafe, hoping my bandaged inner wrist will stay hidden. "We had another round of drinks, he told me about the woman he married and is now divorcing, and he left."

311

"And did anything else happen before he left? Is *he* your secret lover?"

"No!" This feels so wrong. "But we sort of left the door open," I say, thinking this might hold her off for a while.

"Not buying it. Something's going on." She's matter-of-fact.

"Okay, there is. I know who the letter writer is." I place quiche on my plate.

"I knew there was something! Do tell."

God, I want to tell her the truth. It almost starts coming out of my mouth before I can stop it: *It's Cole, Leanne! He's alive. Alive and well and back! I knew he wasn't dead...* But that's not what I say.

"It's Aiden." And there it is, the first lie. Right out in the open. I shovel quiche into my mouth.

"Who?" She drops her fork and stops chewing.

"Aiden Waters, from college. Remember him?" And there's the second lie. There is no Aiden Waters from college.

"No." Leanne's brow crinkles.

"We had that mystery writing class together? Spent hours talking and trying to out-write each other?" Lie number three.

"Nope, but I'll grant you immunity on this one. So, he's your new toy?"

She won't let up. "No! We've only spoken on the phone. Not sure I'll even see him." The coffee goes down hard, like it doesn't want to be swallowed.

"How did you find out it was him?" She resumes eating.

"He called. We talked."

"Couldn't he have done that in the first place,

without all the drama?"

"Yes, but the writing class. He was trying to be cute."

"Ah, got it. But something's different." She pauses, studying my face. "You've had sex."

Unbelievable! "Fine. I met Aiden for coffee one evening, and we ended up back at my house." Lie number four. It's excruciating and clear I'm going to have to give up some parts of my relationship with Leanne to have one with Cole.

"I knew it!" Leanne's satisfied face is beaming.

This is torture. And what about Jeremy's accident? Should I even bother to mention the red paint transfer to Leanne? The idea that this is no accident at all? That Jeremy could have been murdered? How can I, when one of the possibilities rolling around my frazzled brain is the murderer could be Cole, who's also dead?

It *is* the perfect crime, a dead person killing someone. They'll never solve it. Now that I know this shadow world of ghost people exists, how often does this actually happen? The more I think about it, the more talking to someone seems necessary. Maybe Mr. X. What I consider to be objective workable theories in my professional life, don't necessarily translate in one's personal life. The sanity is draining out of me. And by Cole's estimate, he'll be back in four days.

What then?

Chapter Fifty-Four

Layers of deniability
Faith 2026

It's a ridiculous thought, is what I'm thinking as I
drive home from the vet with Finn in the back seat.
Cole *did not* kill Jeremy. Except five minutes ago, I
decided Cole *did* kill Jeremy. There's plenty of reasons
to pin this on Cole. I've been toggling between the two,
about as easily as my fingers alternate between criminal
histories on my computer. One screen says, "No way.
This is not who Cole is," while the other yells, "It's so
obvious! Radio silence for twelve years, Jeremy dies,
and the letters start, are you blind?"

Finn seems good as new, and after almost a week
cooped up, I'm sure he'd love a walk. Maybe it'll clear
my head.

Cool spring mornings are giving way to the slow
heat of an approaching summer. Ten minutes into the
walk, my head is not clear.

Every time I think about the day Jeremy died, I get
stuck. We woke up, there was a snowstorm, we
watched the news and learned of the Paris terror
attacks. Unbelievably, he got dressed for the gym. We
had some words about it, but then my brain gets stuck.
The next thing I remember is opening my door to a
state trooper asking if I'm Mrs. Ansley. Trauma can do

that, create gaps in time. Like when Cole died and I couldn't remember how I got from his front lawn to Steve's house. Leanne says it's the brain's way of shielding itself from too much pain. Maybe it's better this way.

Cole should be back tomorrow.

Finn and I reach the top of the hill, and I dial Mr. X knowing I should tread carefully, but she's the only source who could shed some possible light. Cole's not only working for a private military company, he's a *ghost* working for a private military company. If there's some record of where he was on the day Jeremy died, it would put an end to this. I'd even accept hearsay regarding his whereabouts.

"Is this related to the partial hair match I found?" Mr. X asks.

"Yep."

There's a long sigh on the other end and a squeaking and a thumping, like she's leaned back in her chair and propped her feet up on the desk.

"Listen, you're not gonna find what you're looking for. First, these companies are shrouded in layers of deniability. They operate behind thick walls of secrecy and shell companies. They're obligated under the law to keep records, but even those are sketchy. After the Blackwater mess, they were all in the spotlight, legislation was passed, laws were altered, but the powers that be often choose not to enforce them. And these companies know it. So there's no reason to put anything on paper or a drive somewhere. Even if they did, we'd never access it. Second, your person doesn't exist on paper. I'm sure he's got a new name and dossier, but I have no doubt it's severely limited in scope as in, he was born in 1995 and hired yesterday. Do you have a name?"

"Yeah."

"You can give it to me. I'll put out some feelers, but even asking could put me at risk."

"No, don't, appreciate your insight." I don't want to put her on dangerous ground.

The conversation is rolling around my head as I return home with Finn. For one thing, Cole's vehicle is not red. Then again, he probably has access to many vehicles. For another thing, there's…there isn't another thing. Nothing to rule him out completely.

I also don't *want* this to be true.

And what about that big red target on Finn? Forgot about it with all the commotion. Could Cole have been trying to tell me that I was over the target?

He just didn't. Cole did not murder Jeremy to be with me. He didn't murder anyone all those years ago either. My spidey-senses are telling me so. I can feel it in my bones. It isn't true.

I reach my front door and unleash Finn. He runs into the house like he always does, rounding the corner from the hallway to the kitchen. It's his ritual, nails frantically click-clacking on the hardwood floor, sliding sideways into the wall before making it to his water bowl in the kitchen. But today, Cole's boxes are there. Finn slides right into them, knocking several over.

"Oh, Finn!" The overturned boxes are surrounded by a variety of items now strewn across the floor. Finn's happily lapping up his water as I bend down and place items back into the boxes as best I can. What went where? Replacing everything as he had it is impossible, and I hope Cole won't think I've been snooping while he's gone.

He didn't bring everything to my house, has to maintain the appearance of a home elsewhere. I pick up the clothes and place them back into a box with other clothes, but there are more items I'm not sure about. Things that fell out of much smaller boxes and look like they could be job related: maps, floor plans, currency from different countries. And a small key. I immediately think of a similar key for my lock box at the office. Don't know why, it could be for anything. But I would expect someone in his profession to have a need for a secure, transportable safe box, like I do.

I *could* put it back with everything else and walk away or…I mean, he shouldn't be expecting one hundred percent trust from me in only a few days. Should he? We're still getting reacquainted. There's a lot more we have to learn, which will come out eventually, and I'm looking forward to it, but in the meantime, this'll just speed up the process. Besides, whatever this key goes to may not be in any of these boxes.

I pick up three boxes. None are heavy enough to contain a safe or lock box. There's four more. Lifting each, I decide to open the heaviest one. I move some clothes and find something hard and heavy wrapped in sweatpants. A black metal box about the size of an 8.5 x 11 sheet of paper. It's locked. I bring it and the key to the kitchen counter and stare at them. But not for long. Why waste time thinking about it when I know I'm gonna open it? I jam the key into the lock and lift the lid.

What I find is an assortment of passports, each with his picture bearing different names, along with birth certificates, more money, several sets of keys, and a bunch of flash drives. But the most intriguing items are a collection of DVDs. I'm more interested in them than the flash drives because it's almost a certainty he has password protected the drives. Or they may blow up my computer. The DVDs are more likely unprotected and hence, accessible to me.

Each has a white label and is coded with a letter-numbering system I don't understand. Except for one nondescript DVD sitting in its unmarked case. It could be blank, waiting for future use. Or it could be so important, labeling it would be a mistake. I could easily pop one of these into my laptop, or several of them. There's plenty of time. He's not coming back until tomorrow. If I were to pop one in, I'd start with the unlabeled one.

So much about who Cole is now feels nebulous. I want to know more about all the experiences he's had during our years apart but also don't want to push. He hasn't wanted to talk about the scars on his body. I'm hoping he'll share the details of his life in time, but I also know they may never come out. The need for passports and birth certificates makes sense, shady, but expected. The maps and floor plans can tell me where. But if I can get a quick look at what's on these DVDs, I bet they'll reveal plenty more. Real-time live video, whatever it's of, will give me the best sense of what he's all about now. And maybe there's something on here that will put an end to my suspicions about him coming back into my life right after Jeremy died.

Before I know it I'm sitting in front of my laptop at the counter, heart racing, DVD already in the slot, waiting for the black screen to flicker into images. Even after all the rationalizing, it still feels wrong, but I don't dare blink.

It starts with a bright image and looks like the beginning of a nature video, forest, mountains, green rolling hills. But I sense the person filming isn't trying to capture the beauty. Whoever is making this recording is walking silently. A trail comes into view. I hear the wind flowing past the microphone. I've done a lot of hiking and it looks and sounds like high altitude, possibly close to the top of a mountain.

Panning around the landscape, the camera eventually stops on a cluster of tightly spaced homes in the valley below. It's extremely quiet, like this is some kind of reconnaissance mission. It's amazing how mountain towns look so similar, even mirroring my own. Still zoomed out and turning to another view from the top, there's a second grouping of homes. These are more spread out and private.

The camera slowly focuses a bit closer, moving from home to home, as if it's searching. The images become clearer with each press of the zoom button. *Wait...isn't that...the Mitchells' house?*

Fresh adrenaline burns my veins. This is *my* neighborhood. My eyes widen. I feel my hand over my gaping mouth.

The images blur and jump as the viewfinder moves too quickly before steadying in on my own home. Once focused there, the view gets closer and closer, moving in and in and in, until it's directly on my backyard and stops, like he's found it. The landscaping is different, everything's smaller. I thought the camera had reached its maximum zoom capacity at my backyard. It hadn't. It continues moving closer in like an invisible person, walking itself right through the wall of windows and into my house as if it opened the back door and invited itself in. Moving from the stove to the cookie jar on the counter, to the sink, I see Finn's puppy bowls upside down on the drain board. It pans over to the living room floor where the first few toys we bought him lie on the rug, chewed up and disposed of long ago.

My God. I'm pretty sure I've stopped breathing. The camera continues to pan around the room until it hits activity. Jeremy walks into the kitchen, followed by me holding a tiny Finn in my arms. He must have been a few months old, wrapped in that soft green blanket we brought him home in. Friends follow us into the house. Finn jumps out of my arms and clumsily runs over to them falling all the way. It's like watching my own home videos, except it isn't. It isn't at all. This is something entirely different.

The image goes black, cutting away to a new scene, from a different angle, one where I'm kicking a ball around the back lawn with Finn, who's slightly bigger now. And then to a night scene where Jeremy and I are sitting outside on the deck having drinks and talking. The screen goes black before the images show up again, this time depicting Jeremy on a jog, then me barbecuing in the backyard with friends, my hair longer.

My eyes start to fill, partly with nostalgia, partly with a mix of anger and despair as I realize the truth of what I'm seeing. The flashing images appear in chronological order, a dinner party with friends, Jeremy helping his niece with homework at the kitchen table, me walking into the food store. Jeremy pulling his car out of the driveway. Me sitting on surveillance eating a sandwich. Jeremy walking out of his office, getting into his car in the parking garage, driving on the mountain going toward town, at the gym. Me sitting at his grave. Me meeting Leanne for lunch…

On and on it goes.

The screen goes black again. I'm frozen but rewind to the final image. It's me, not long after Jeremy's accident, sitting on the couch in the living room, nighttime, in the dimly lit room. That telephoto lens of his is extremely powerful and slightly unsteady, focusing on my face, then to the papers I'm reading. They're Cole's old letters, and I'm crying.

I get up and walk to the window, staring up the mountain. Finn gets off his bed and follows me. My eyes home onto the spots where he must have been perched to video these scenes. The earlier ones were further away, the landscaping younger and smaller. But as the trees grew, he moved in closer. The hairs on my arms stand up as I realize he must have been at the exact spots where Finn's been barking, right up until a few days ago.

"How many times were you barking at him, boy?" I rub his ear as he sits at my side.

"All of them, Mom," is what I'm sure he'd say if he could.

I exhale a long, tired breath, twelve years' worth.

What does this mean? If this is the old Cole, these videos are simply the result of the sad truth of our situation. We're separated, he desperately wants me back, longs to see me, so he does, and records it to keep it with him when he needs it. Nothing more.

But with this new Cole, the answer might not be so simple. In this scenario, we're separated, he desperately wants me back, longs to see me, so he does. He begins visiting me when he can, videoing and keeping tabs on Jeremy, on his habits, his routines, his routes so when the opportunity presents itself he can take matters into his own hands and insert himself back into my life…

Which is it?

Chapter Fifty-Five

You know me
Faith 2026

"You've been watching me for years!" I slam the laptop closed.

"Faith, I can explain."

"You've been saying that a lot lately."

Cole walked into the kitchen three minutes ago, back from his assignment, to find his lock box open on the counter and me sitting in front of my laptop, video cued up, arms crossed. Since first viewing this video yesterday, I'm done. Done with the guesswork and the suspicions and giving the benefit of the doubt. I've done the work, grown, become a better person and I'm all-in, one hundred percent, but I won't be in a relationship where there's so much mistrust and ambiguity. We both deserve better.

"Some of these videos are from when Finn was a puppy." Finn, lying on the floor near me, hears his name and pops his head up. "*Years*, Cole."

"I was watching you. I admit it. I had the ability to do it. I wanted to see you, to make sure you were okay, to know if he was treating you well. And I watched you more recently only to gauge whether or not I should come back into your life." He looks at Finn. "How's the little guy doing?"

"Better." But I'm shaking my head at him in disbelief. "Don't change the subject."

"That's the *only* reason, Faith. I didn't know if I should disrupt your world by throwing myself back into it. Me, from twelve years ago. Did you want to leave the past in the past? Did you miss me? Did you ever think about me? I didn't know. I was trying to figure it out. That's *all*."

"That's all?" My face should be making it clear I don't believe him. "You've been lying to me."

"You know me. Don't doubt it now. I'm not some psychotic stalking maniac. I just love you." His eyes are pleading. "And I was trying to protect you."

"From what?" I have no control over the sharpness of my tone.

"Anything...*everything*. It was the least I could do." He pauses. "And from me, from bringing up all that pain for you again. You *have* to believe me."

I *want* to believe him.

"It's clear you haven't told me everything, Cole. And I'm not talking about your work. I'm bound by confidentiality too. About *you*. How much do you know about me and Jeremy? I need the truth. It's now or never."

"All right." He draws a long breath and exhales in a puff. "After I *died*, you were failing some of your classes, but the professors took pity on you and gave you passing grades. You graduated with a 3.2 GPA, which would have been much higher had it not been for me. You needed therapy, and the records indicate PTSD and complicated grief for everything I did to you. It took years for you to go back to a normal life. Your work helped because you love it so much. You'll stop at nothing on a case until you've resolved it to your satisfaction. Your tenacity is what makes you so good at what you do."

He pauses studying my face but continues. "You prefer to go to bed early because you like getting up while it's still dark to see the sunrise. You love having coffee out on the deck, and you don't like to miss a workout."

I'm listening, frozen in my seat.

"You and Jeremy seem to have had a good relationship. Over the years, it fizzled, but you still respected each other. And because he was as loyal to you as I knew he would be, he appears to have never cheated on you and you, surprisingly, never cheated on him either."

I roll my eyes and snort.

"You've kept yourself fit, eat healthy, but display guarding behavior on your left side from that old college injury. Your shoulder bothers you a lot, but you hide it."

I say nothing. Don't need to. After that disclosure, I'm sure he can read the shock and distrust oozing off me. In my mind, we were finally back together, we could fall back into each other without any drama for the rest of our lives and now this. *This* changes everything. It's creepy. Not sure how to feel. There's no precedent for it.

I turn my head toward the mountain and the spots where he must have been perched.

"Why did you do that to Finn?"

"I didn't make him sick if that's what you're thinking."

I look at him sideways. "No, on the mountain."

"I didn't do anything to Finn. You know I love dogs. What happened to him?"

My eyes drop and focus on the manila envelope on the counter containing the final accident report, and then to him. He instantly knows what I'm thinking.

"Fucking Christ, you think I killed him?" His eyes widen. Finn lets out a low whine and sits at attention.

"It would make sense, Cole. You always hated him. Saw him as your competition, someone who would always have a piece of me you couldn't. How many times did you say that to me? And then I married him, and you knew it because you were watching. It must have killed you, pun intended. Is that why you were watching us? To find out what our lifestyle was like, to learn our patterns? So you could figure out a way to make it look like an accident?"

"No, Faith…" He moves toward me, but I put up a warning hand as Finn moans a low growl.

"Clearly you have the skill set to do it." I'm wondering why I chose to have this conversation without my gun holstered to me. "Did you let me stay married to him all these years because you had to wait, had to put off revealing yourself to me until it was safe? Finally you were ready, so you did more surveillance, planned it, executed it, and now, here you are. Even your letters were perfectly timed and strategic."

"Faith, you've got this all wrong. I didn't do *any* of that. I was only watching you because I was desperate to see you and make sure you were okay. The police report said it was an accident. I've already seen it."

"I bet you have." I glare at him.

"I didn't kill Jeremy." He leans on the counter placing his head in his hands, thick silence hanging in the air between us. Rubbing his temples in defeat, he says, "I'm the one who brought him back into your life."

"What?" My blood is boiling. "How?"

He lifts his head and looks at me. "You have your network. I have mine."

I blink.

"Mine's more…connected, more…far reaching." He hesitates.

"And…" I lead.

"It was no coincidence Jeremy's dream job brought him right back here to you. And yeah, I hated him in high school, his fucking ego got in the way of everything he did, but I had to admit, barring that, he was a *good guy*. He'd always do the right thing. It was only a matter of time before somebody was gonna pursue you, Faith. If I could get you two in the same room, he'd still love you and be loyal to you. If I couldn't have you, at least I could be sure you'd be with someone who'd truly love and take care of you."

Jesus, how far does his influence reach?

"If I wanted him dead, Faith, he would have been dead *long ago.* I could have killed him with you sitting right next to him if I chose to, without you ever knowing what happened…or how."

"How dare you! You know, Cole, I was so happy thinking nothing had changed between us, but now I see that, yeah, nothing *has* changed between us. You're still manipulating me, every part of my life. None of it has been my own."

"This conversation has gone far enough in the wrong direction, Faith. It's still me. I'm the same person you knew."

"No, you're not." Adrenaline forces me out of my chair. "You need to go."

"I'm not going anywhere." He again moves closer.

I take a step back. Finn is now at a stand, a few feet from us, tail straight up, head and shoulders slightly down.

"Faith, I won't let you think this of me. You *know* me."

"Stop saying that."

"But you do." His tone is even and relaxed. "You know I love you and always have." Finn sits, twisting his head at Cole. "I finally have you back. I'm not gonna let you walk away like I did back then."

"Because you'd have to kill me?" I'm fully aware of how many steps it'll take to get to the knives sitting in the block on the counter.

"My God." He lets out an exasperated laugh. "Put yourself in my shoes. What would you have done in this impossible situation? Wouldn't you have wanted to know where I was? If I was okay? Wouldn't you have tried to make the rest of my life as peaceful and happy as possible, if you could have?"

He's right. Of course I would have done the same for him. I'm teetering between stabbing him for deceiving me and wanting to drag him to bed at the thought of making sure I was safe and loved by someone else while he suffered all those years of separation. It's twisted, but in a romantic kind of way. This *is* an impossible situation.

I can't go searching for records to see where he might have been that day. Those records don't officially exist. And neither does he. Maybe he's a natural born killer, and this is the perfect niche job for him—the murders, his work, Jeremy. Could he someday kill me too if the situation required? Or have I got this all wrong?

I just. Need. Something.

"I hate you right now," I say, but do I? If I'm being honest, somewhere in the back of my mind a little voice is whispering, *It doesn't even matter. Jeremy's gone.* Over the years, there were moments I'd look at him and feel a seething rage. Who doesn't feel that way about their partner every now and then, right? And on some level, I'm sure I'm never gonna let Cole go again, no matter what he may have done. Is that twisted too or are we the perfect pair?

"So hate me, I'll wait," he says, "for as long as it takes."

He'll never give up. He wouldn't back then, and he won't now either. I can't even look at him.

"What do you need me to do to prove it to you?" There's sincerity in his eyes. "Just tell me."

Both versions are spinning my brain around. Mine and his.

"Look at me," he says.

I shake my head.

"Faith…" He moves around the counter closer to me. Finn stands between us, head up, eyeing Cole.

I'm inspecting him too, studying him. Again. It's so hard to tease out the emotions and connectedness I feel for him, but I do have all the objective tools needed, skill in evaluating truthfulness and detecting deception. Been trained to identify behavioral abnormalities, distinguish between valid and invalid indicators in rates of speech, micro facial expressions, blink rate, gestures, and body language.

And regardless of who he's become, I *do* know him, better than anyone.

His face is as solemn as I've ever seen it. Body language indicates openness, posture is at ease. Rate of speech has been genuine, authentic, and sincere. And his eyes, those eyes that could never hide a thing, are filled with honesty, undying love, and fear. Not fear that he's been found out, but fear that I may never believe him. Even Finn acquiesces, as evidenced by the fact that he has switched sides, now sitting next to Cole panting a smile, leaning into a forehead massage.

What more *do* I need? The truth is right in front of me. Isn't it?

"Cole." I look down. "I'm sorry, this has all been quite the coincidence, and you, looking like this and being so vague about what you do…"

He reaches for my hand and wraps his around mine, flipping on all kinds of switches inside me, reconnecting us. "Tell me what happened the day Jeremy died." His tone is warm, filled with genuine curiosity.

I narrow my eyes at him in confusion.

"Humor me."

"Why do you want to know?"

"Walk me through it. You woke up and…"

"There was a snowstorm. I woke up and turned on the news like usual. It was the day after the terrorist attack in Paris. Every news station carried it. I'm sure you remember."

"I do." He nods.

"As I watched, Jeremy came out of the bedroom dressed for the gym. I couldn't believe he was going in the storm. We had a few words about it, but his mind was set." Actually I think it was more than a few words, but that's not relevant right now. "We watched together while rescue workers raised flags from all over the world on top of the pile of rubble where the Eiffel Tower had stood. For those few days, the world stopped. Everyone was united. The photo of the flags being raised went viral, a symbol that good always triumphs over evil."

"You mean that photo?" He points to it on the wall.

"Yeah."

He takes a few steps into the hall. Finn follows as he rummages through his boxes, coming back with a handful of photos. "And this photo? And this one?" He lays several glossy three-by-fives on the counter in front of me. They're all of that day, of rescue workers raising those flags from angles I've never seen.

I'm confused. "Why do you have these?"

"Take a closer look," he says.

"I've seen this hundreds of times. What am I looking for?"

"The men raising the American flag."

I lean in. One of the reasons this photograph has become so iconic is because of the massive amount of debris and destruction behind the men raising the flags. Never really paid attention to the men themselves. I squint on their faces. Wait...and pull it closer. I wish it was on a phone so I could use my fingers to zoom in. Instead, I walk to the drawer and get a magnifying glass. The man in the middle, the one placing the flag on the cord...I look up at Cole. The side of his lip curls, eyebrows raised, looking vindicated.

"This is you?" My eyes go wide.

"And part of my team."

I move the magnifier back further, making the image even larger. It hurts my eyes, but I'm focusing on the man's hand and I find it. Cole's birthmark. It's him, a rescue worker halfway around the world the day Jeremy died.

"You can give these photos to your forensic people," he says. "Enlarge them and prove they haven't been manipulated. There's lots of them from different angles and other sources taken on that day. You'll find the same thing. This is real. I was there."

I *want* to feel relief and do, but not completely. How do I know he didn't have someone else kill Jeremy? I really wish my analytical, fact-finding brain would stop doing this. It's both a blessing and a curse.

"But Jeremy's car *was* hit," I hear myself say.

"It was an accident." Cole is emphatic.

"No, it wasn't, Cole. I went to the impound yard and looked at the car myself. There were scratches that were not part of the rollover."

"Jeremy's car was completely mangled, Faith. It would be impossible to separate out all the damage."

"It's not. That's what accident reconstructions are for. I've done hundreds of them. Jeremy was hit," I say again.

"I know how hard it can be to let go." He takes my hand like I'm a patient at a mental hospital. "But you need to."

"Coming from the guy who recently finished stalking me for the last dozen years?"

"That's fair. What I mean is, you *should* let it go."

"Should?" I rub my brow. "That's an odd thing to say. Especially when you claim to know me and my tenacity so well. Just because *you* weren't there, doesn't mean one of your *connections* wasn't."

"Please don't go down this road any further."

I scan his face, and I don't like what I see because that's exactly what someone who's guilty would say. "In that case, I'm barreling right down the center of it."

He looks at the ceiling, shaking his head, biting his lower lip. I can tell he's losing patience with me. "He's gone. I'm here. Why can't we just move forward?"

"Okay, let's, by you proving to me you didn't have someone else kill Jeremy."

"You know I can't do that."

"Because you did it," I say.

"Are you gonna let this stand between us? After everything?"

No, of course not, but I don't say that out loud. Now that he's back, I'm sure I can find a way to forgive him for anything. But I need to know what I'm dealing with.

"I thought about it so many times. I'll give you that. It would have been so damn easy too. But I didn't kill Jeremy or have him killed or whatever else you're thinking. So tell me right now, if I can't prove to your satisfaction I didn't kill him, are we over?"

I say nothing, which should very clearly indicate a yes, playing chicken, waiting for him to make the next move.

"I didn't want it to come to this, Faith." He blows out a long slow breath. "You're just so damn persistent. You want everything wrapped up in a nice neat little bow, all tight and clean."

"See, you do know me," I taunt.

"Real life doesn't work that way. Things are not always black and white. In fact, they rarely are. They're a shiny, solid gray. But you keep pushing. So it's gonna be over between us?"

I remain silent.

"Really? I thought we had a stronger bond than that." He runs his fingers through his hair. "What if I told you, it's the other way around?"

"Like what? He killed you? You're dead again? Are we playing a game now?"

"No." His face softens. "You can't wrap your brain around it, can you? And it's okay," he says again, like I'm a mental patient.

"You're talking in riddles," I say.

"I'm not." His eyes are gentle. "I didn't kill Jeremy. You did."

Chapter Fifty-Six

The backup system
Faith 2026

Cole's in front of me, hands on my shoulders. "I know this is hard, Faith. But no matter what you did, I'm on your side."

I back away. "On my side? What are you saying?" Didn't he write that in one of his letters?

"The minute I found out Jeremy was dead and could get a break from my rescue detail, I came back here and looked into it. I saw the red paint on the quarter panel and was concerned someone may have meant to hurt you, not him. You do tend to piss people off with your work."

"I killed Jeremy?" I barely hear my voice, as I back myself down onto the couch. Has he lost his mind? Is he gaslighting me? It's ridiculous. Isn't it? But as he speaks the gears in my brain come to a screeching halt while another, separate cognition system is set into motion, like a backup generator that only kicks on in emergencies. I didn't even know it was there until right now.

"It was you," Cole continues in his most empathetic voice, "on the mountain with Jeremy. You were driving the red car."

"No." But even as the words come out I'm not

entirely sure he's wrong. That backup system unveils images of wipers waving frantically across a smeared windshield, unable to keep up with the heavy snowfall. I see my own hand on the shifter, gears labeled one through five with a capital R and N—a manual transmission. I don't even know how to drive one of those.

"Yes. It was you, Faith."

"Me?" Finn instinctively leans against me, placing his head in my lap. His version of a hug.

"I did everything I could to rule you out. There were no traffic cams over there, and the police had already canvassed the area for private ones."

I stare straight ahead but feel a depression in the cushions as he sits next to me.

"All the residents said no cameras. I managed to find a farmer in this country illegally, wanting nothing to do with the police, who installed some of his own to watch his cattle. He took the cameras down after the accident, but I used an IED detector to locate the current in the wire that was still running to the road. He confirmed the camera was there and let me see the footage."

I visualize driving past the farm.

"It shows Jeremy's car going by and a few minutes later a red car passing the camera moving much faster than his. It was blurry from the speed and snow, but I got a partial plate and ran it."

As if a teenager was driving a stick for the first time, the car lurched forward and back as I shifted gears, feeling the curve and the car sliding as it tried to grip the road under tires moving too fast for conditions. I regained control, caught up to the car in front of me before the next curve, the only other car on the road that day and…

"I narrowed it down to a Stacy Waters who bought the car three weeks earlier, all cash at the Mountain Cliffs Dealership fifty miles away. Took a visit there and looked at the security camera on the day of purchase."

Cole's voice becomes echoey, as I recall receiving credentials in that name and flash forward to writing it on a form, handing over cash. I look at him.

His expression is solemn, like a police officer making a death notification. "It was you at the dealership."

My God, the dreams! Of me and Jeremy and Cole in the car on the mountain. I was there in the dream because…I *was* there…But why? Why would *I* kill Jeremy?

"Faith, I know you, and I'm sure you had a good reason. Was something happening I didn't pick up on? Was he beating you? Did you find out he was a pedophile or cheating on you? Even if he didn't do anything, I'm on your side."

"No," I say, defeated. "He wasn't beating me, wasn't a closet criminal. He didn't do any of those things."

Still questioning whether Cole is even truly here, my backup system is now fully booted up and running smoothly, allowing the full memory to flood through. It was the day before my birthday. I was cooking and listening to the radio on full blast. Jeremy was cleaning the windows. Finn was outside and cut his paw on something. He yelped and cried and ran inside leaving a blood trail all over the house. I found him and tried to help, cleaning up the blood dripping from his paw.

At the same time I heard it in the background, the song that had disappeared into music history where one-hit wonders go on vacation, rarely if ever played on the radio. *The* song. *Our* song.

All the compartmentalizing I had done about the day Cole died, wiped out with one chorus. The song and Cole intermingled freely again in my head and heart along with visions of blood dripping from Cole's arm when he cut it in front of me, calling the ambulance, visiting him in the hospital, his calls on my birthday, Jeremy saying *I knew you'd come back to me, he was never good enough for you…*the sound of the gunshot…and anger. A rage toward Jeremy welled up inside from a place so deep, Satan himself would've had to ask for directions.

I should never have been with you on that day, Jeremy. Should never have let you talk me into it. If I had been with Cole, where I belonged, none of this would have happened. YOU are the reason he's gone.

Jeremy was dead by the end of the week.

"You don't have to explain if you're not ready, Faith. But I'd like to know. Why did you kill him?"

"Because he wasn't you."

Chapter Fifty-Seven

A fine line
Cole 2026

Eleven years, nine months, and five days. That's how long Faith and I were separated. She was right all those years ago when she broke it off and tried to maintain the distance. We did need time apart, space to mature, to learn to stop dumping our shit onto each other. I just never thought it would last this long. Everything went to hell so fast. If I could go back and change it all, would I? From where I'm sitting, no. I wouldn't be the person I am today. But for Faith? I'd change it all in a heartbeat. I put her through an emotional meat grinder and wasn't sure there was anything I could ever do to make it up to her.

Until now.

Watching her all these years gave me a feel for what her life was like, how she was faring, if she was okay. I know firsthand what trauma can do to a person. I lived it as a child. And as much as I never wanted her to experience it, she did. At my own hand. As inadvertent as it was, I still passed it on to her. They say people who are damaged are capable of doing great damage.

"This hike feels much longer than I remember." I'm breathy, lagging behind her as we climb the steepest part of Prescott Peak.

"It's not," she calls over her shoulder.

"Damn, Faith, exactly how much coffee did you drink this morning?"

"Enough to make me faster than you today." She laughs.

I love it when she laughs.

"Almost there," she yells.

She really did seem okay at first, in a relatively happy marriage, with friends and family around, running a successful business. Which, by the way, is no easy feat in her chosen profession, a male-dominated field that required her to be more than on top of her game. Despite living with PTSD and complicated grief, when it came to work she was her usual overachieving, spot-on, consummate professional. Intelligence, resourcefulness, and the ability to work through large amounts of data with a logical, clear analytical mind that knows what to keep and what to discard without bias was her superpower.

But there's a fine line between brilliance and psychosis. I eventually realized these skills did not translate to her personal life or anything having to do with me because with trauma, you detach, bury shit. Her undercover work demanded the ability to live truthfully in imaginary circumstances, to basically be comfortable living a lie. I realize now, that's exactly what she was doing.

Even though I was happy for her, keeping my distance was torture. I wished it was me with her. From afar she seemed to be thriving despite it all, but I know her. The connection we've always had was still there. Underneath the happy, accomplished veneer was immense sorrow. I could feel it. And something else too. I wasn't sure what was simmering below the surface.

The minute I heard about Jeremy I came back. His accident was just days after her birthday and the anniversary of my death. Coincidence? I was hoping so. I had to get involved. My intent was to protect Faith. When each piece of information pointed to her as Jeremy's killer, I used every bit of impartial detached reasoning I could muster to stay objective and let the investigation lead me to the truth. It wasn't easy. I learned what I had suspected all along, what I was afraid might happen.

You can't put a lid on a volcano. Memories and beliefs collect way down deep. Ignored and unprocessed, they build up and force their way out. There's no way to prevent an eruption. You can only put safety strategies in place for when the inevitable happens. *I* planned on being her safety strategy. Ultimately it was always going to be my job to come in and clean up the mess, since I'm the one who created it. She had pulled me off the ledge more than once, and it was time to return the favor. She needed me now more than ever, but in her delicate state, I had to proceed with caution. The letters were my way of easing her into the truth that I was still alive.

She didn't even know she'd killed Jeremy, buried that too. I had no intention of ever excavating it for her. I was happy to let it be and move forward with a watchful eye so if the recollection did manage to burst to the surface, I could help. Then she confronted me and even though she only had circumstantial evidence I killed Jeremy, her stubbornness would never have let her believe otherwise. I would have gladly taken the blame, but she said it would be the end of us. I couldn't have that, not after everything we've been through. I *had* to tell her. And now I will be here for her, help her understand the truth of what she did. And who knows, maybe someday I can share my truth with her too. I bet it would bring us even closer.

Twenty grueling minutes later, we're at the top of Prescott Peak, catching our breath and unloading the food we prepared. I sit with my knees bent in front of me, holding an open water bottle. Faith plops down by my side, leaning into me, looking over the peak and across the valley. The way the sunlight hits her face…she's still as beautiful and perfect as ever.

"Remember after the prom I said I could imagine us living up here?" She lets out a long-satisfied breath, as if releasing years of stale hope from her lungs.

"Yep. You want a water?"

"I got it." She reaches across me for the backpack.

"I could have handed it to you." She's always been independent, headstrong, and free-spirited. You could never really tell her what to do. When she was younger, it made her fun and carefree, but it's quite a dangerous combination for someone living with unresolved feelings of guilt and shame. It doesn't matter how intelligent and put together she appeared, she could never be therapied out of the belief she was to blame for my death. Instead, she buried it, compartmentalized, and threw it all into a locked box on a shelf way in the back of her mind. I don't know what the trigger was, the key that unlocked her box. She hasn't shared it yet. I hope she does in time.

What I do know is the ugliness that can come out

of the box when it does finally open. A self-loathing so strong, so unbearable, it must be shifted. Guilt and shame transform into denial and anger and need to be assigned somewhere else. It makes perfect sense to me. Her brain twisted things just enough to blame Jeremy for my death. It's a survival mechanism, a form of self-preservation.

I know it's possible because it happened to me too, when I attacked my mother's boyfriend. And Jeremy after the party. And my asshole neighbor. And Faith's "study partner." And when I shot that guy I confessed to murdering. And now, channeling it for good every time I go on a mission to protect this country. We are never stuck being who we are. Alter one circumstance, and the potential for change *always* exists.

Faith runs a finger along my skin, tracing the veins of my hand to my arm and inner wrist where you can still see the faintest trace of those scars. The ones that bound us together in sickness then and hopefully health now. She turns toward me and once again, all these years later, flips my wrist upward to look at them.

"I thought we weren't gonna replay it anymore, babe," I say.

"I'm not." She continues running her finger on the raised lines. "It feels like a lifetime ago. It's part of who we are. Like these mountains—traumatic forces pushed them together and broke them apart over and over, until they were finally driven upward creating all this beauty. It's built into this landscape just as much as our past is built into the landscape of us."

"I love that image, Faith. Leanne used to say behavior is simply adaptations, protections to keep us safe from pain. Who am I kidding? She said it so many times I should've printed it on shirts and sold them."

She nods. "Everything that happened helped me to look at myself in ways I may never have. So much of who I am is because you died. Now you're here. It can be confusing. I still don't understand how I could have…and I'm still losing time and…"

"Faith, it's okay." She's been out of sorts, forgetful, and in a deep state of remorse since I told her. "You're getting a little better every day. It's not easy facing your demons."

Fingers crossed she doesn't direct whatever is left in that box at me one day.

"But Cole, I'm scared."

"I know you are. The police closed the investigation; you'll be fine. And if anyone ever does come asking, you can disappear with me."

She squeezes my arm tighter. "Do you think we'll ever be able to see our friends together, as a couple?"

"I can't imagine any scenario where it happens, but we can hope. What'd you decide about Andy?"

"I'm making him the lead on the new account. Brooke and I both agree, he'll be great."

After some time off, Faith went back to work and landed a contract with a huge law firm in the city. It means expansion, more cases, more agents and staff, and bigger offices. She's slowly getting herself back up to speed.

"And how long will you be gone this time?" she asks.

"Could be a few weeks. Are you set with the plan or should we go over it again?"

Faith and I have realized we're being watched. She finally told me what happened on the mountain with

Finn. And before I showed myself to her, someone nearly knocked her off the road. I would never do either of those things. It could have to do with her work, but it's far more likely to be mine. And that is bad. Very bad. I have put security measures in place.

"God, Cole…" She sighs. "You don't have to baby me. I got it, I'm good."

"You *are* good." I rearrange us so she's sitting between my legs, back to me, my arms around her. "I'm proud of how you're handling everything. And I like the new you. You know, if you think about it, we only had one good year together. After that, we went in circles trying to get it back. There was always something in your way, blocking you from me, keeping you distant. Feels like that's gone."

"It is." She turns her head and kisses my cheek.

"Faith and Cole two point oh?" I say.

"Yep," she agrees.

We watch a few cotton ball clouds in the sky blanket the great expanse of hills and valleys with slow-moving shadowy figures, interspersed by streams of hazy sunlight. Running my hands up and down her shoulders, I'm transported back to the high school gym where I stood in the doorway, locking my eyes onto hers like the active guidance system of a missile. Back to *before us*, the pre-Cole and Faith days when the air between us was filled with sparks of innocent expectation and unlimited possibilities. Who knew? Whoever can?

"Remember after the prom I said I could picture us living up here?" she asks. Again.

"Yeah, babe. It really is something." I squeeze her tighter into me, dotting the side of her neck with soft kisses, creating a shiver down her spine. It's just going to take time. She'll be okay. I'll make sure of it.

There's nothing left to do, nothing about us left to question. We've solidified our love into a united, solid alliance. We'll face whatever's coming together. Our future, while unconventional, matches the promise of our commitment to each other, certain, bright, and absolute.

She turns her head, looking at me with smiling eyes like only she can. All is as it should be. I sweep the hair away from her ear and nibble on the fleshy part, letting my lips linger there before whispering, "And even if those damn mountains crumble to the ground again, we'll still be safe, still be sound."

Resources

If you or someone you know is struggling, you are not alone. Help is available.

For immediate support in a mental health crisis, call or text 988—the Suicide & Crisis Lifeline.

For mental health information, education and support, visit NAMI.org—the National Alliance on Mental Illness.

If you are grieving the loss of a loved one to suicide, visit Allianceofhope.org—a community for survivors of suicide loss.

Please take care of yourself. Help is always within reach.

Acknowledgments

If this—my first book—was ever published, I planned to thank everyone who taught and encouraged me along the way (I have a list). Turns out, there's not enough room.

To my husband, who absolutely did *not* wait patiently to read it "when it was done" and has been my loudest cheerleader. To my daughter and son, who never fully understood what I was writing but, thankfully, never felt neglected. To my Wednesday writing group—for the mechanics, the momentum, and the belief. To every alpha and beta reader who gave time and thoughtful feedback, especially Darrin Reed and one of my dearest friends since seventh-grade home ec, who read every draft, psychoanalyzed every scene and told me it was good—sometimes even when it wasn't. To everyone at The Wild Rose Press for giving this story a home and polishing it.

And finally, to the mountain of rejection letters—like seriously, there were a lot—each one a tiny papercut to the soul and a nudge to keep going and get better.

Thank you for purchasing
this publication of The Wild Rose Press, Inc.

For questions or more information
contact us at
info@thewildrosepress.com.

The Wild Rose Press, Inc.
www.thewildrosepress.com